MOURNING
IN MINIATURE

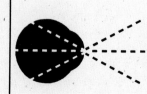

MOURNING IN MINIATURE

MARGARET GRACE

WHEELER PUBLISHING
A part of Gale, Cengage Learning

GALE
CENGAGE Learning

Detroit • New York • San Francisco • New Haven, Conn • Waterville, Maine • London

GALE
CENGAGE Learning™

Wheeler Publishing Large Print Cozy Mystery.
The text of this Large Print edition is unabridged.
Other aspects of the book may vary from the original edition.
Set in 16 pt. Plantin.
Printed on permanent paper.

LIBRARY OF CONGRESS CATALOGING-IN-PUBLICATION DATA

Grace, Margaret, 1937–
    Mourning in miniature / by Margaret Grace.
        p. cm. — (Wheeler Publishing large print cozy mystery)
    ISBN-13: 978-1-4104-2310-8 (softcover : alk. paper)
    ISBN-10: 1-4104-2310-7 (softcover : alk. paper)
    1. Porter, Geraldine (Fictitious character)—Fiction. 2. Class reunions—Fiction. 3. Miniature craft—Fiction. 4. Large type books. I. Title.
    PS3563.I4663M68 2010
    813'.54—dc22   2009047317

Published in 2010 by arrangement with The Berkley Publishing Group, a member of Penguin Group (USA) Inc.

Printed in the United States of America
1 2 3 4 5 6 7 14 13 12 11 10

ACKNOWLEDGMENTS

Thanks as always to my dream critique team: mystery authors Jonnie Jacobs, Rita Lakin, and Margaret Lucke.

Thanks to my friend Brian Callahan, one of Boston's finest chief engineers, who was an immense help in shaping the fictional Duns Scotus Hotel and its staff; and to the wonderful Inspector Chris Lux for advice on police procedure. My interpretation of their counsel should not be held against them.

Thanks to my sister, Arlene Polvinen; my cousin, Jean Stokowski; and the many writers and friends who offered critique, information, and inspiration; in particular: Judy Barnett, Sara Bly, Margaret Hamilton, Anna Lipjhart, Ellen Schnur, Mary Schnur, Sue Stephenson, and Karen Streich.

Thanks to my brother-in-law, Skip Polvinen, for insight into the construction business (it's not his fault that I twisted his words to create a crime); to Jerry and Mil, who were generous with information on their Eichler home; to Mike Kaplan, who helped Maddie with her avatars; to Mark Streich, who introduced me to Maloof; and to mystery author Juliet Blackwell (aka Hailey Lind), who inspired me with her Alasita stories.

My deepest gratitude goes to my husband, Dick Rufer, the best there is. I can't imagine working without his 24/7 support. He's my dedicated Webmaster (www.dollhouse mysteries.com), layout specialist, and IT department.

Finally, how lucky can I be? I'm working with a special and dedicated editor, Michelle Vega, and an extraordinary agent, Elaine Koster.

ELEVATORS

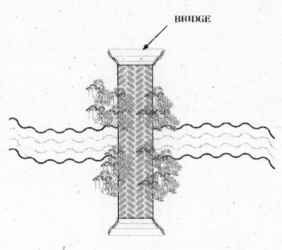

BRIDGE

FRONT
DESK

COUCH

PHONES
&
RESTROOMS

GIFT
SHOP

DUNS SCOTUS HOTEL LOBBY

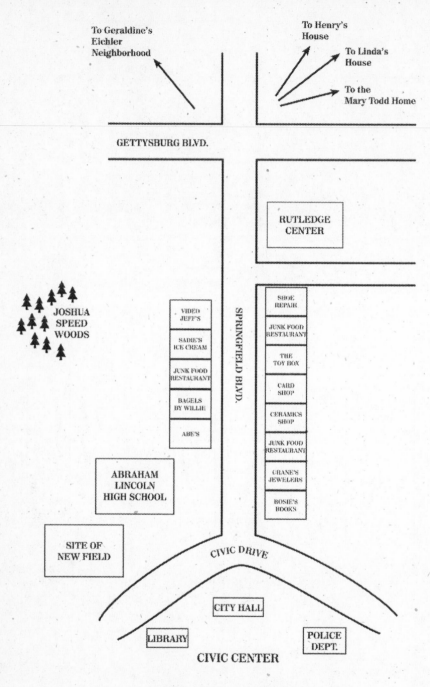

LINCOLN POINT, CA

PROLOGUE

David Bridges checked the minibar in the suite for the third time. He'd made a couple of special requests for the evening and wanted to be sure they'd been carried out. He assured himself once again that his staff had come through, right down to stocking a bottle of the best white wine the Napa Valley vineyards could offer.

He thought of the elegant Duns Scotus as his hotel. His position as chief engineer at one of the best-known hotels in San Francisco brought him high-level responsibilities and a great deal of respect. He oversaw the entire maintenance staff and was a member of the management executive committee, with a say in all the important contract negotiations for facility and equipment upgrades.

He'd cashed in on his status at the hotel and assigned himself this royal suite on the eleventh floor.

David tugged on his dark suit jacket, a little too snug around his waist these days, but on the whole he thought he kept pretty fit for a middle-aged man.

He congratulated himself on all his successes.

This weekend his high school classmates, his cheering fans, were coming to the city for their thirtieth reunion. David had arranged for everyone to get a good deal on rooms at the Duns Scotus, much lower than the rack rate. How many of the smart kids who made the honor roll and played chess could do that for their friends?

Three decades, he thought, like the snap of his fingers. He ran his hand along the silky floral comforter, a match to the drapes, and looked ahead a couple of hours. He had big plans for tonight, both business and pleasure.

He walked to the window, an entire wall of glass, and took in the sweeping view of the San Francisco Bay — a commanding view, the Duns Scotus brochure said — from his spot on a hill higher than any building in his hometown of Lincoln Point, California, an hour to the south.

This suite and every other room would be even more spectacular once he made sure the right contractor got the approval for the remodel.

David pulled his heavy trophy out of his luggage and held it up so the stone base was waist high. The cold eyes of the bronze drop-back quarterback met his, transporting him to his years at Abraham Lincoln High School three decades ago. The trophy and his jersey, number thirty-six, had been on display in an ALHS hallway all these years, but this weekend it would have center stage at the hotel as his whole class gathered to reminisce. He relished the idea of reliving his glory days.

Too bad his personal life was in shambles. But it wasn't all his fault, and by Monday things might be better along those lines, too.

On the whole, the outlook for the weekend was good. Promises had been made and it was time to call them in, one way or another.

The phone rang. He picked up the unit in the living room and listened to the insistent voice on the other end.

"We're clear," David responded. "It's do or die."

He hung up and sat on the sofa, facing his trophy where he'd placed it on the credenza, his name visible, of course. He thought back to his starring role in the big games on Thanksgiving and Homecoming Weekend, the hallway of lockers where he'd had his share of quick embraces, classrooms where he'd done as much note-passing as note-taking.

He sat back and linked his hands behind his neck. A small shiver of doubt crept up his spine. He shook it off. This was his weekend.

What could go wrong?

CHAPTER 1

I maneuvered through the store's narrow, crowded aisle carrying a loaded plastic basket on my arm. When the metal handles dug too painfully into one arm, I shifted the basket to the other. For a break, I set the ugly green container in the only clear space, a corner of the back counter, and reviewed the items I'd collected. I matched them against my shopping list.

Three bathtubs. *Check.* Fourteen lamps. *Check.* One outdoor swing set. *Check.* One baby carriage. *Check.* One life preserver. *Check.* I still needed six counter stools and two refrigerators, one modern and one 1930s style with the motor on top.

The minute I'd told my crafters group I was headed for a dollhouse and miniatures store in Benicia, sixty miles away from our town of Lincoln Point, they clamored to capture my attention and give me their wish lists. There weren't that many independent miniatures stores in northern California anymore, so when one of us was able to make the trek to a shop, we all submitted our needs.

Another half hour of browsing and I was weighed down with all the desired items, plus unplanned "must-haves." I gathered up a few tools — a mini drill, a miter box, and needle-nose pliers that were on sale — and lugged the basket toward the cash register.

I'd been successful with everyone's list but my own. I couldn't find the perfect six-inch Christmas tree. That may have had something to do with the fact that it was August and nearly ninety-five degrees, although crafts stores generally carried at least some inventory for each holiday year-round. I checked the Christmas bins again and found eighth-inch mistletoe and a set of one-inch stockings, all of which I added to my basket, but no "tall" spruces to my liking.

On this weekday morning, the store was nearly empty. While I paid for my purchases (the grand total was anything but miniature), I chatted with Cindy and Jim Cooper, the store's owners, reminiscing about the time when there were shops like this in every town.

I could have stopped for lunch at one of

Benicia's many cafes. A charming small town on a strait of San Francisco Bay, Benicia offered a variety of cuisines, including Thai, my current favorite. I chose instead to head home to Lincoln Point, more than an hour away, to arrive in time for leftovers with my eleven-year-old granddaughter, Madison Porter.

As I walked to my car, passing vintage Victorian houses, antique shops, and clothing boutiques, tempting smells and interesting music wafted from doorways. But cafes were ubiquitous and would be around for a long time — who knew how much longer Maddie, approaching the years of teen angst, would want to eat with her grandmother?

Maddie was staying with me for three weeks while she attended a high-tech summer camp program at Lincoln Point's Rutledge Center, the town's educational and all-purpose facility. I considered it surprising, and amazing good luck, that our tiny town offered a computer program not available in Maddie's new, more sophisticated residence city of Palo Alto, home to Stanford University, among other grand institutions. Her parents were using the time for a little camping of their own, at a cabin at Lake Tahoe.

I was thrilled to have Maddie to myself.

I drove home with a smile, wondering what her latest computer joke would be.

"Why are computers skinny?" Maddie asked.

This was easy, a rerun from the first day of her class. "Because they eat only bits," I said.

Maddie frowned and kicked her legs under my kitchen table. "I already told you that one, didn't I?"

I admitted as much as I scooped ice cream into cone-shaped, cone-colored dessert dishes.

"Is that all you're learning at computer camp? Jokes and puns?" Once in a while I assumed the role of strict grandmother, but it never lasted long.

"It's not computer camp, it's technology camp," Maddie said, pulling a bowl of ice cream toward her. "We're learning how to do two- and three-D video, flash animation, and modding for games. Some kids are on the robotics track, which I'd like to do next year. They're attaching a Bluetooth interface to a robot so they can control it from any location connected to the Internet. Cool, huh?"

Like most children her age, Maddie grew

up with computers and had surpassed me in the language a long time ago. My only contribution now was, "Yes, very cool."

"Does that sound like we're just telling jokes all morning?" Maddie asked. Then, much to my relief, she broke into laughter and came over for a hug that she knew would turn into a tickle and a messing up of her red Porter curls.

Bzzz, bzzz, bzzz.

Maddie ran to the door. We both knew it was probably my nephew, homicide detective Eino Gowen, whom she called Uncle Skip. First cousin once-removed had been too much for her as a toddler and no one in the family thought there was a reason to revisit the uncle title.

"Looks like I'm just in time for dessert," Skip said, helping himself to a handful of my just-made ginger snaps. "I could smell these half a block away."

I scooped a generous portion of caramel cashew ice cream, Skip's favorite, into a bowl for the second redhead at the table. A Porter by marriage only, I didn't share in the redhead gene and had to make do with ordinary dark brown hair, now tinged with gray.

"What timing," I said. "I think you have a GPS on my oven and freezer door."

"That's not how —" Skip started until he caught my look.

I liked to keep my family guessing about just how much of a Luddite I was.

"Uncle Skip, what did the computer's fortune cookie say?" Maddie asked. She'd finished smashing her chocolate ice cream with her spoon, to a mushy consistency, just as she did when she was three years old. Aspiring robot maker or not, she was still a little girl.

Skip put on his best thinking expression. "Hmm. Not a clue. What did the computer's fortune cookie say?"

"Take one data at a time," Maddie said, triumphant.

Skip slammed his palm against his forehead. "Good one." Unlike inconsiderate Grandma/Aunt Gerry, Skip not only let Maddie have the punch line, he also laughed harder than I did. No wonder she adored him.

"Are you busy down at the station, Uncle Skip?" Maddie asked.

"There's not too much going on right now."

"No big cases or piles of folders on your desk like you have sometimes?"

"Nope. I guess all the criminals are too hot to work."

"And August is the only month when we don't celebrate an Abraham Lincoln event, so there are no big crowds to worry about," Maddie added.

"Exactly. Next month we're back on track with the big Emancipation Proclamation Convention."

"But August is pretty clear, right?"

Uh-oh. I knew where she was going with this.

"You're doomed, Skip," I said.

Maddie swooped in. "Remember you said when you weren't busy you'd teach me some police things, like how to do fingerprints and how to investigate? And tour the building" — here she shook her spoon in his direction — "including the jail."

Skip hung his head. He'd been had. I saw it on his face. Twenty-eight years old and a preteen had bested him.

The good news was that our little town of Lincoln Point was homicide-free for the summer, a comforting statistic.

Skip cleared his throat. "Let me look at my calendar when I get back from my meeting, okay?"

"Promise?"

"Hey, any cute boys in your computer class?"

Nice try, I thought. But Maddie had

something to say about that.

"Are you kidding? The boys are all dorks. We had a class photo taken for the newspaper and the boys all made funny faces." Maddie splayed her fingers, held a hand to each ear, and wiggled her fingers. "Like this."

Skip mimicked her hand gesture and stuck out his tongue. "It's no good without the tongue," he said, once he could talk.

Maddie and I rolled our eyes. "Boys never grow up," I warned her.

It was a dream come true for me when Maddie had decided she'd like to be part of my Wednesday-night crafts group. During the school year she stayed overnight with me and I drove her back to her home in Palo Alto early on Thursday mornings in time for classes. We'd all agreed that we'd keep this schedule as long as her schoolwork didn't suffer.

"Not likely," I'd told my son, Richard, Maddie's father. "She's a genius."

"So you say," said the orthopedic surgeon, a man of few words who knew better than to argue with his mother.

For our group project this summer, we crafters borrowed from a Bolivian tradition, Alasita. We'd learned about it from Beatriz,

20

a woman who joined us briefly while visiting her mother in Lincoln Point. We were fascinated by the concept: during the Alasita festival, people made or bought miniature versions of what they hoped for in the coming year.

"In the markets you find everything," Beatriz told us. "Tiny cars, houses, and food, and even little bitty marriage certificates, passports, and money. Men buy hens and women buy roosters in the hope of finding a partner before the year's end. If you buy these things or make them, it's supposed to bring them into your life in the next year, as long as it is blessed by a shaman."

"Do you think there's a shaman in Lincoln Point?" Karen Striker asked now, as we sat around a large table in my primary crafts room. (According to my late husband, and everyone who was familiar with my house, the whole rest of our four-bedroom home was a secondary crafts area.)

Karen, five months pregnant, was building a lovely nursery, augmented by the one-inch-scale baby carriage I'd picked up for her this morning in Benicia. "I want to send good vibes into the air on every possible wavelength," she told us.

"I know a priest," Mabel, our oldest member, offered.

Her husband, Jim, the only male in our group, grunted, conveying doubt that a Catholic blessing would work as well. Mabel and Jim were working on a ship's cabin, a model of the luxury version they hoped to occupy on their fall cruise to the Mediterranean.

Maddie enjoyed playing hostess on these evenings and tonight she seemed to have fun refilling glasses of ice tea and plates of cookies, running back and forth between the kitchen and the atrium of my Eichler home. It took the record-breaking heat we were experiencing to get us to move all our supplies from my crafts room to the cooler atrium, and this week had qualified.

For her own project Maddie had chosen to build a miniature soda fountain. She'd worked diligently on a sign that named flavors after her own friends and relatives. In her red-striped shop, one could "buy" Ginger Grandma, Pistachio Porter, Strawberry Skip, Tutti-Frutti Tracey, and so on.

"Does this mean your goal for the year is to eat all the ice cream you can?" Karen asked.

"For now," Maddie said.

I was happy that my granddaughter considered her life so good that all it needed was more ice cream. I also loved that she worked the spectrum of creativity, from computer programming in the morning to crafting tiny ice cream sodas in the evening.

Of all the projects, Rosie Norman's was the most interesting and packed with meaning — she was building a half-scale room box replica, one-half inch to one foot, of the hallway of lockers at Abraham Lincoln High School.

"It's where David Bridges, the star quarterback, kissed me," was her only explanation the first week.

Rosie, who owned the bookstore in town, was a student of mine during my first years teaching English at ALHS, right after Ken, our three-year-old son, Richard (Maddie's father), and I moved to California from the Bronx. Rosie had also become a good friend who sometimes watched Maddie when I had undisclosed errands at the police station across the street from her shop.

Rosie's class was holding its thirtieth reunion at the end of the week. At first I questioned the math, but finally grasped the reality — it had been three decades since I helped distribute diplomas to my first graduating class. Faculty, current and retired, like me, were also invited to the gala weekend, most of which would be spent at the beautiful, old Duns Scotus Hotel in San

Francisco. (Apparently, no one wanted to party at Abe's Beard and Breakfast, the only motel in Lincoln Point.) Rosie had talked me into going so she wouldn't have to walk into the opening cocktail party alone on Friday night.

"Why are y'all bothering to go?" Susan Giles asked, her heavily accented "y'all" referring only to Rosie. "You always say how you weren't very popular in high school."

"You wouldn't get it," Rosie told her.

Rosie was probably right. Susan's voice betrayed a lack of understanding, and I pictured her as a class officer and prom queen of her Tennessee high school. Rosie, on the other hand, had had a reserved personality and an almost matronly body even as a teenager. Thick glasses and a slight lisp hadn't helped.

"Well, I just think you have to be realistic," Susan said. "People don't change, and if you think you didn't fit in then, you probably won't now."

Harsh words from someone whose "realistic" hope was to win a trip around the world. Susan was working on a set of miniature luggage, using tweezers to manipulate in place tiny pieces of floral brocade and minutely thin strips of leather. I hoped the trip would be all expenses paid; otherwise the life-size version of this seven-piece luggage set would cost a fortune to check at the airport.

Over the summer weeks, as Rosie had added scuffed sneakers and spiral binders to the three-inch-tall (six feet in real life) lockers, and posters, photos, and mirrors to the insides of their doors, she'd revealed more and more about her history with David Bridges.

"I had a huge crush on him," she'd told us. "And one date, almost, which had a sorry end, but it wasn't his fault." She promised us all more details on that later. The important thing was that now, out of the blue, after thirty years, David was sending her presents and notes about how eager he was to meet her again during the reunion weekend. He'd sent flowers, candy, and jewelry. "I don't want to wear the bracelet he sent until the reunion weekend, but I'll tell you it's really, really beautiful. Tiny emerald and diamond stones. David did not spare any expense."

Sooner or later in their four years at ALHS, every student, some more memorable than others, passed through one of my English classes. My memory of David Bridges was of a good-looking and popular young man. A star athlete, but not a very engaged student. He was immature for his age, as were the boys in his crowd, if I remembered correctly. For Rosie's sake, I hoped that the responsibilities of adulthood had brought him more wisdom and perspective.

The chatter during this last crafts meeting before the big weekend seemed to be completely devoted to what Rosie would wear to the opening cocktail party on Friday night. Something classic, but not dowdy. Flattering, but not trashy. Bright, but not gaudy. We talked as much about Rosie's dress as we did when one of us needed help designing a canopy for a miniature Victorian bed or a yarn rug for a log cabin kitchen.

Rosie had been invited to David's room for a private party on Friday night after the cocktail party. I, of course, would be her guest. That gave me only two days to come up with an excuse for getting out of it.

"What's David doing with his life now?" Karen said.

That question, intended or not, sparked a very long response from Rosie. "David has the title of chief engineer at the Duns Scotus, which you all know is the premier hotel in San Francisco."

This was a very responsible job, Rosie explained, often meaning he was the only manager on duty for days at a time. How else did we think her class was getting such a good rate on rooms? He'd been married briefly but was now divorced, with one son, Kevin, whom he hadn't seen in a long time. He lived in South San Francisco.

"I thought you lost track of each other a long time ago. How do you know all this?" I asked.

Rosie blushed. She lowered her head to apply a sealant to the floor of her room box. She'd achieved a decent semblance of the ALHS first-floor hallway, with ugly linoleum on the floor and steel gray lockers lining one wall. "I haven't talked to him in all this time, but I volunteered to put together the booklet that has information on everyone's life at the present time. It's like a yearbook, but updated."

"And you got that input from him? Even the part about his being estranged from his son?" I asked.

"Uh-huh. He filled out the form I sent to everyone in the class and he just drew a line next to the question about children's occupations. So, I'm assuming they're estranged."

"Maybe the kid's just unemployed," Susan offered.

Rosie waved her hand as if to say, "So

what?" She smiled broadly. "I want you to know he didn't just fill in the blanks; he added a personal note that said, 'Thanks, Rosie.' "

One thing crafters were good at — talking and working at the same time. Fingers were busy gluing, cutting, trimming, painting, and sewing while questions and answers continued to fly. There was also a fair amount of snacking from the potluck bowls that had arrived with my guests.

"And these presents — do they come with a note, or a phone call, or anything?" Karen asked.

"How do y'all know these presents are from David?" Susan jumped in.

"You both sound like my dad. He's the only other one who knows about this. I'll tell you what I tell him. I know it's David, that's all there is to it. And besides, there's a card with each present, signed *Love, D. B.* That's for David Bridges." Rosie rolled her eyes. "Who else?"

I saw that we were all tiptoeing around a warning to Rosie that there was something not quite right about this reunion within a reunion. Mabel gave it the best try.

"Have you called him, to thank him for the presents?" our polite, most senior citizen asked.

"Of course not," Rosie said with a tense laugh. "Our meeting is supposed to be romantic and dramatic. And besides, girls don't call boys, remember?"

"What if it doesn't turn out the way you think, Rosie? What if he's toying with your feelings?" Karen asked. "You said your first and only date didn't go well. Maybe he's setting you up for another fall."

Rosie lifted her eyes from the tiny brush dripping with red paint from the last application of trim on the wall of the school hallway.

She gave us all a deathly serious look.

"Then I'll kill him," she said.

Silence washed over the room.

I forgot that Maddie was with us until I heard her small voice.

"What do you get when you drop a computer on your toes?" she asked. She waited a beat, then answered her own question. "Megahertz," she said.

We all took a breath, followed by loud laughter. I didn't dare look over to see if Rosie was amused.

CHAPTER 2

The plan was that Maddie would stay with
Beverly, my sister-in-law and best friend,
for the weekend. For once, Maddie didn't
complain about being left behind. The arrangement would put her at the center of
attention in yet another Lincoln Point
household, with a surrogate grandmother
whom she loved and ready access to her
Uncle Skip. The better to nag him about
giving her junior detective status with the
LPPD.

Nick Marcus, Beverly's companion for the
last several months, had learned the rules
early on: "Love me, love Maddie." Not that
that was hard to do, he told us, and he was
welcomed immediately into our extended
family.

On Thursday evening, Maddie and I were
packing her new grown-up (non-pink) luggage for her trip across town when the
phone rang.

"I can't believe this, Gerry." Beverly's voice carried both sadness and disappointment. "Nick's grandfather passed away up in Seattle and the services are this weekend. I've never met him, but I think I should be there for Nick."

"How sad, Beverly. Of course you should go. Please give Nick my condolences," I said, at the same time running down my list of usual alternatives to watch Maddie.

"Skip and June are coming up, too, so the families can all meet. Even though it won't be under the best of circumstances."

"I'm glad you'll all be together," I said, meaning it, but also mentally crossing two more people off my list.

Rosie Norman, another loyal backup, was de facto out of the picture. My friend Linda Reed was on call at the Mary Todd retirement home where she worked as a nurse, meaning she'd be sleeping in their nurses' lounge over the weekend.

I could try to get Maddie to Tahoe where her parents were, four hours away even with no traffic, but that seemed like a lot of trouble for everyone.

"Gerry?" I wondered if Beverly had been talking the whole time. "I'll bet you're going through your list. I feel awful about this. I suppose we could take Maddie with

31

us, but —"

"No, no. Don't give it another thought. I'll just take her along. You get ready and I'll see you next week. And, again, please tell Nick I'm sorry for his loss."

Why did I think I'd have trouble breaking the news to Maddie? She was always at least a step ahead of me. She'd figured it all out from my side of the conversation and was ready for me.

"Is it as hot in San Francisco as it is here?" she asked.

How quickly my granddaughter adjusted. I thought of the quote often attributed to Mark Twain: "The coldest winter I ever spent was a summer in San Francisco."

"It'll probably be freezing," I said.

Rosie was a little less enthusiastic about the change of plans. "I thought we'd have some time together," she said on the phone, her tone carrying an edge of disappointment.

Instead of sticking with our initial plan to ride and room together, I now preferred to drive myself with Maddie to have more flexibility. I had to admit that the idea of the hour's drive to San Francisco talking to my granddaughter was much more appealing than having the love-struck Rosie by my side. I wasn't sorry about missing excruciating details of a thirty-year-old high school crush. I'd had enough of that during my twenty-seven years of teaching.

"We can do something special another time," I said. "Thanks for understanding."

"You know, I'll probably be busy with David, anyway," she said.

I wondered if she believed that any more than I did. It wasn't as though David had to fly across the country for the reunion; he lived in South San Francisco and could have taken her to dinner any night of the week. If he were really sincere about picking up their relationship (if there ever was one), why would he be going about it in such a dramatic way? Unless he was as immature now as he was then.

It occurred to me also that Rosie's behavior was not her usual responsible, mature way of dealing with life. She had a degree in English literature, owned and operated a good-size bookstore, and had been on her own most of her adult life. But she seemed to have become a different person, acting starry-eyed and unrealistic, now that a potential boyfriend was in the picture.

I'd seen a lot of that also during my years with adolescents.

I picked up Maddie at Rutledge Center

after her technology camp on Friday and drove straight up U.S. Route 101 to San Francisco. The weekend schedule called for shuttling back and forth to San Francisco for the cocktail party on Friday night, then back to Lincoln Point on Saturday afternoon for a groundbreaking event for the new ALHS sports stadium, then to San Francisco again for a banquet on Saturday night and a brunch on Sunday morning.

I got tired thinking about it.

The inconvenience of managing the disparate locations had been trumped by the desire of the powers that be to break ground for the new athletic field the same weekend as the reunion. I hoped thirty-year alums and their faculty would hold up. What had been a forty-minute drive between Lincoln Point and San Francisco thirty years ago now could take double that time in heavy traffic. When it wasn't commute time holding us up, it was construction that closed a lane or two.

I hoped the payoff for all the driving stress would be worth it, especially for Rosie.

My old Saturn was loaded with Maddie's laptop, videos, and enough snacks to make it easy to avoid the expensive refrigerated M&M's in the hotel minibar.

"No computer jokes today?" I asked her.

"Nah. I have to stop that. When I get back to my regular school, no one will like me."

"You mean you have to give up something you enjoy to fit in there?"

"No, no. Don't get all worried. Forget I said it. My mom is already on me not to sell myself out. Or short. Or whatever."

I'll bet she was. Mary Lou Porter had softened a bit from her activist days at UC Berkeley, but she was still on the watch for signs of inequality wherever it might be. She'd won the battle to get Maddie admitted to this summer's program even though she was younger than the minimum age of thirteen. All she'd needed to hear was that a ten-year-old boy with less computer experience than Maddie had been allowed to register.

"Knock, knock," I said.

Maddie gave in to a little-girl giggle. "You're not supposed to start the joke, Grandma. You don't know any punch lines."

"I tried."

"We're totally booked," said the young woman in an unattractive navy power suit. Pinstripes in polyester seemed an oxymoron to me. I heard *click, click, click* as she worked the keyboard, conflicting with the *clang, clang, clang* of a cable car on Powell

Street, right outside the door. "We've got a wedding and a reunion and a trade show and . . ." She threw up her hands. "It's an old hotel, you know, with mostly single beds."

Above the woman's head was a large painting of John Duns Scotus himself, in his Franciscan robes. I wondered what the symbolism was. Did he or any other Catholic theologian care about the sleeping arrangements of tourists from the suburbs?

I all but pointed to the little girl beside me, and Maddie obliged by looking forlorn and temporarily homeless. Never mind that she had a new cell phone, an iPod Touch, and a state-of-the-art computer in her designer backpack.

"Can you add a cot to the room Rose Norman and I already have?"

"We're not supposed to . . ." She looked down to see Maddie struggling with her suitcase. She smiled at Maddie and took a deep breath. "Well, let's see . . ." *Click, click, click.* "It will be a little tight, but . . ." *Click, click, click.* "There, I moved you to a slightly bigger room with space enough for a cot. I think you'll be comfortable enough and I don't think anyone will mind."

I hoped her boss was among those who

wouldn't mind her giving us special consideration.

"Thank you very much," Maddie said, in a sweet voice that she didn't use for normal conversation or for computer jokes.

I made a note to get her a special treat. As if I wouldn't have otherwise.

Rosie had so much luggage, I doubted there would have been room for me in her car if we'd gone with the original carpooling arrangement.

"I brought a few wardrobe choices," she said, out of breath from unpacking her suitcases on the bed nearer to the door. "I need your help with what to wear, Gerry." She looked at Maddie, busy hooking her computer equipment together. (Since her birthday she'd acquired many more items that began with *i.*) "And yours, too, Maddie."

"You'd do better sticking with Maddie's advice," I told her, though it was no secret that my own palette ran from white to creams to beiges to the occasional pale blue. I'd brought one of my fancier beige outfits for the cocktail party, which meant that the slacks and tunic were silk, nicely complemented with long pearls from Ken. It was my standard outfit for weddings and anniversary parties.

"You're lucky you're so tall and thin, Gerry. You can wear anything."

I heard the same thing often from other friends, all of whom seemed to have a hidden agenda — to brighten my wardrobe. Occasionally I broke loose and bought a flowery jacket or a blouse in bright green or glittery blue. My shopping bags with donations to charity were full of these purchases.

I was surprised to see that Rosie had brought her unfinished locker room box with her. She set it on a corner of the long dresser that held the television set and took up most of one wall.

"This is my favorite project in the group," Maddie said, running her finger along the slatted vents in one closed locker door. She turned to me. "I love yours, too, Grandma."

I gave her a forgiving smile. "It's okay. I know a cottage Christmas scene is no match for this." It was neither the time nor the place to share my own dismay that apparently I had no Alasita-type goals for the year other than a Merry Christmas. "Do you think you'll have time this weekend to work on the scene?" I asked Rosie.

She shook her head. "I . . . I thought David might like to see it."

"I like the little toothbrush on the top

shelf of the locker on the end," Maddie said, saving me from having to make an optimistic comment.

It took an hour before Rosie considered herself ready to meet David at the cocktail party. "I'm sure we'll bump into him before the private party in his suite," she said, justifying the fuss.

From six to seven o'clock, she tried on several combinations of dresses, shoes, and jewelry, asking for our votes each time. In the end she went with a simple black dress with a low V neckline and a ruffled hem. She carried the smallest of the three black evening purses she'd brought, this one with a large silver buckle that took up most of one side of the purse, and a silver chain strap.

"Are you sure I look okay?" she asked, moving her hammered silver pendant to the exact center of her cleavage.

"You look cool," Maddie said, then returned to scouting out the amenities in the room.

"You look wonderful," I told Rosie, meaning it.

Maddie called out from the bathroom, ticking off the contents of the counter. "We've got shampoo and conditioner, a shoe shine cloth, mouthwash, a shower cap, and body lotion," she announced. Back in the room, she came upon a book in the table between the twin beds. "This is a funny Bible," she said.

I took a look and was surprised to find the collected works of Duns Scotus. "It's not a Bible," I said. "These are writings by the monk this hotel is named after."

"That's weird, naming a hotel after a monk."

I scanned the chronology at the front of the book, to get my dates straight. "He was a Franciscan who lived in the thirteenth century," I said, as if that made everything clear.

"Oh, I get it. San Francisco. Franciscan."

Apparently, clear enough.

A few minutes later, I sent Maddie off with a group who came to the door. I felt sure she'd enjoy the special kids' program, which started with an evening of swimming in the hotel pool, more than a cocktail party with middle-aged men and women and their teachers.

"Here it is," Rosie said, still concentrating on her outfit. "The final touch."

She'd added the pièce de résistance — the sparkling (allegedly) emerald and diamond bracelet that (also allegedly) David had sent. Why was I being such a skeptic? I wondered, and chided myself at my lack of romantic spirit. I needed to bolster my friend.

"You look lovely, Rosie," I said, reinforcing my earlier compliment. "And the bracelet is gorgeous."

That wasn't so hard.

One last tug on her dress, a puff up of her chestnut bob, and Rosie and I left the room. I felt as nervous as she did, hoping the evening wouldn't end in disaster for my friend.

We might have been in an elegant San Francisco hotel, but the decorations at the cocktail party were 100 percent Lincoln Point. We could have been entering the Abraham Lincoln High School gym — the official maroon-and-gold school banner was draped above the portable bar of the converted meeting room; small gold napkins with a maroon silhouette of Honest Abe lay on the high tables.

We picked up our name badges, entered the room, and walked along the edges, where several large easels held poster-size collages of photos of the reunion class. The snapshots were interspersed with ALHS pennants, ticket stubs, and graduation tassels. Here and there on narrow pedestals were large sports trophies that on every other day resided in cases in the halls of ALHS.

Rosie quickly found the one with David Bridges's name on it. I could barely distinguish the football statuettes from those with hockey or bowling stances, let alone determine which position the figures represented, but Rosie knew exactly what was depicted in bronze on David's trophy.

"It's a well-known quarterback pose," she said.

I knew for a fact that Rosie hadn't been to or watched a football game of any kind since she cheered for David on the ALHS field.

As a miniaturist and former teacher, I suffered from two occupational hazards: giving close scrutiny to even the most casual crafts project, and forgetting that I was no longer responsible for giving grades. This evening, though no one asked, I assigned no more than a C-plus to the decorations. The posters especially were crudely done, with evidence of a bad glue job congealed around the sides of the objects, which in their turn were affixed to the cheapest cardboard sold at a crafts store.

My judgmental attitude came to a halt when I found myself in front of a memorial board with yearbook photographs of the nine class members who had died in the intervening years. I looked at each face and saw a lively teenager cut short in life's journey. Just as parents didn't expect to outlive their children, teachers assumed their students would carry what they learned long into the future.

I took a breath and focused on the center of the room, alive with blaring seventies music and loud chatter.

I was getting used to having all the professionals in my life, like doctors and repairmen, being younger than me. But seeing a large group of my former students with wrinkles around their eyes and gray at the temples was almost overwhelming. It had been many years since I'd been to one of my own school reunions. I decided to skip all such gatherings in the future.

I took my cue from Rosie and crept along the walls of the room while she surveyed the crowd without reserve. She frowned and screwed up her nose the way Maddie did when she was concentrating on her homework. Finally, we'd made a full circle, back to the entrance. I made a move to go to a table a few feet in when I spied a student I recognized, but Rosie pulled me along with her.

"Stay with me, okay? I'm nervous."

Surely we weren't going to circle the room again. "Why don't you just try to find someone you know and —"

"I know lots of people here, Gerry. But I don't need to visit with the ones who still live in Lincoln Point. They're my customers. I see them all the time."

I saw her point. Sort of.

Unfortunately for Rosie, one of my students found me before Rosie found David.

Frank Thayer, newly appointed principal of ALHS, and one of the brightest lights in my special Steinbeck seminar, introduced me to his wife, Paula. "This is the best English teacher I ever had," he told her, making it well worth the trip for me already. The fact that the loud chatter and earsplitting music ("Margaritaville" at the moment) caused him to shout out the compliment made it even better.

Rosie was itchy while we reminisced about the miniature project we'd worked on for the Steinbeck class — a replica of Steinbeck's home in Salinas, California. Frank was a wonderful woodworker and had contributed his skills to the enterprise. He told us he and his family had recently celebrated a birthday lunch at the old Victorian home, which now included a restaurant and gift shop.

If I didn't like her so much as a friend, I'd have said Rosie was rude as she paid little attention to the conversation, though she'd also been involved in the Steinbeck seminar. She'd written an outstanding report on *East of Eden,* if I remembered correctly. And when it came to English term papers, I usually did.

"Didn't you make a set of miniature books for that project?" Frank asked Rosie. "Sort of presaging your future career as a bookshop owner."

"Uh-huh," she said, her eyes roaming the room for David. "There he is," she whispered to me, her breath catching. "Two tables over, near the doorway. In the beautiful navy suit and yellow tie. His hair is still thick and dark."

I thought I heard her sigh, and hoped I was wrong. Was it a coincidence that "I Just Want to Be Your Everything" was now playing?

I turned to see an older David Bridges, still looking quite fit, arguing with a man in a gray jumpsuit. A maintenance person, I thought.

"They don't look happy," I told her, noticing somewhat antagonistic gestures on the part of the stocky man in the hotel uniform.

45

"Remember I told you David's in charge of the maintenance crew here at the hotel. That must be a whiny employee. You'd think the guy would leave poor David alone to celebrate for one night."

"We have empty seats at our table," Frank said, commanding our attention again. I wasn't surprised that the new principal didn't isolate himself at a head table, in spite of his position. He pointed to a set of six bar stools and a high table not far from where we stood. "Henry Baker and his granddaughter are there. Remember him? He taught shop."

"Of course, he was a great help with a lot of our miniature building projects."

"Come and sit with us," Paula said.

Rosie shook her head, but too late. Frank took our drink orders and insisted on treating us.

I felt more than saw Rosie's glare as we made our way to the table to the tune of "Muskrat Love." But I was more intrigued by a little girl of Maddie's age sitting next to Henry. Either Henry didn't know about the special kids' program or he wanted his granddaughter by his side. I couldn't imagine the other alternative — that a nine- or ten-year-old might insist on attending a function like this.

I felt a bump on my right hip. "Oops, sorry," said a booming voice behind me. "Oh, hi, Mrs. Porter," the man added. "I didn't mean to run into you like that."

"Don't worry about it. It's rather tight in here, isn't it?" I said, not knowing exactly to whom in the crowded space.

Rosie drew in her breath. I turned to see what had caused the reaction. It had been David Bridges, now free of his unhappy employee, who had bumped into me. No spills or dire consequences, except for Rosie, who stuttered, "D-David!"

"Hey," David said, steadying his drink. "Rosie Esterman, right?"

Rosie's face reddened, visible even in the dim light. I could have sworn she lowered her eyelids, coy and flirty. "Yes, David."

I took a seat on one of the stools at the table, to give Rosie clear access to David.

The employee in the jumpsuit wasn't through with his boss, however. He'd followed David through the spaces between the high tables, looking out of place among the dress suits and fancy (except for mine) outfits in the ballroom. "This isn't over, Bridges," he said. "I can burn you."

"Look, Ben, you're out of line, here. Let's take it up next week."

The irascible Ben locked eyes with David.

"It might be too late by then," he said and rushed out, knocking into my stool as he passed.

This repartee was in low voices and thus caused only the slightest stir among the closest revelers.

David turned to Rosie and me and transitioned to the broad smile that made him Most Popular Boy thirty years ago. "Don't mind Ben. He didn't get the raise he hoped for and he's a little out of sorts right now. I'll take care of him on Monday."

David gave each of us a perfunctory hug — still very muscular, I noted — while an attractive, slight brunette approached. She looped her arm around David's and pulled on him. I recognized the head cheerleader, Cheryl (nee Carroll) Mellace. C-minus on her *As You Like It* paper, I remembered. She'd changed less than any of us, looking like she could still pull off her youthful acrobatics and climb onto the shoulders of the girls in her squad.

"I'll see you all later," David said, seeming to enjoy the tension on his arm from the lovely Cheryl.

"Around ten thirty, right?" Rosie said.

"Uh, I guess?" David seemed to be asking a question, perhaps because he was in transit from Cheryl's pull and her high-pitched, "C'mon, Davi-i-id."

"What room . . . ?" Rosie's question trailed off as David and Cheryl strolled out of earshot. Rosie looked at me. I was happy no one else seemed to notice what I'd have called a brush-off. "Well, I think the room number is on one of his gift cards," she said. "I'm sure he expects me to know it."

I looked at her hands, clutching the silver chain of her purse. She'd twisted it into a tangled mess.

Trying to make up for a distracted Rosie, I talked more than I usually do at such events. My task was made easier by Taylor, ten years old, who told us about the new dollhouse her grandfather, Henry Baker, ALHS's former shop teacher, was building for her. My kind of family.

"Oh? What scale is it?" I asked, feeling more and more at home at the table. Leave it to a child to provide the only cocktail (ginger ale in my case) party conversation I'd ever enjoyed. "Rosie and I are miniaturists, too," I offered. I doubted Rosie heard me.

"It's regular one-twelfth scale, but it's really an apartment complex," Taylor explained. Using hand gestures generously, she described the three floors, the winding outside stairway, and how each apartment had a balcony. "It's so cool," she added, but I was already convinced.

I heard myself gasping at this new take on dollhouses. "What a wonderful idea," I said.

"One balcony has a small barbeque with a really cute set of tools, and another one has a little garden, and —"

Henry put his hand on Taylor's arm to interrupt her.

"They're only one-bedroom apartments, with one bath and small kitchens." Henry seemed apologetic about his creation.

"I have to see it," I said, before I realized the implication.

"That can be arranged," Henry said. "If you'll show me yours."

It was my turn to blush. And was Henry's face red, too?

CHAPTER 3

As cocktail parties went, this one wasn't too bad. Class President Barry Cannon kept his remarks short, thanking the committee who put the weekend together. I noted that gratitude for the decorations went to Cheryl Mellace. If I were the kind of teacher who let personal feelings influence grades, I might have changed the C-plus I'd given the decorations to a D, based on her rudeness toward Rosie.

Taylor's presence added to the fun as she told us tales of school and her Girl Scout adventures. I hoped she and Maddie (and, yes, the grandparents) would be able to sit together at tomorrow night's banquet. One problem with venues like this was that you could hardly hear anyone other than the people on your immediate right and left, and it was nice to know ahead of time who would occupy those slots.

At one point, Barry Cannon visited our

table and directed most of his conversation to Rosie. I thought back to the young Barry — front row seat and a solid B-plus on his Dickens paper. The math- and chess-club type rather than a sports hero. I couldn't hear them, but Rosie seemed at times pleased and at times confused, and all of the time distracted. I guessed Barry wasn't measuring up to David, or at least not to her fantasy of him.

The party at our table broke up at about quarter to ten. The Thayers invited us all to join them for a late dinner at a San Francisco restaurant with a long Italian name.

"I'm pretty full myself, but this finger food doesn't do it for Frank," his wife said. "We've scouted out a place in North Beach that stays open very late."

"Thank you, but I have another engagement," Rosie said and left. To re-primp for David's gathering, I assumed.

I was never one for late dinners, not even in San Francisco's highly regarded Italian neighborhood, and also declined the invitation. "I have to pick up my granddaughter at the pool," I said. "The lifeguard goes off duty at ten."

"The pool's open? We thought it closed early," Taylor said, screwing up her nose much the same way Maddie did.

"There's a special kids' program this weekend," I said. "They've matched the pool schedule to the events of our reunion."

I saw a little frown, as if Taylor regretted having spent an evening with us when she could have been frolicking with her peers, but she was too polite to let it show much.

"Let's go check it out now." Henry turned to me. "Do you mind if we go with you, Gerry?"

"Not at all." Why was I blushing again?

I learned a lot about Henry Baker in the short trip to the swimming pool, two floors down from the reunion room. We'd been on the same faculty for many years, but other than two or three sessions together with students for the Steinbeck project, Henry and I saw each other rarely, in the cafeteria or at the occasional faculty meeting. Now it seemed we had so much in common, I thought Henry was making it up. He retired the year after I did, and for the same reason: to take care of a terminally ill spouse. He lived only a few streets north of me in Lincoln Point and now spent his time with his granddaughter and doing woodworking projects for various crafts fairs and charities. It was a wonder I hadn't remet him before tonight.

"I was still teaching, so I heard about Ken," he told me. "I'm sorry I didn't send my condolences, but it was all I could do at the time to keep things going with my classes and taking Virginia back and forth to the hospital until I was able to retire."

I knew exactly what he meant.

Maddie had charmed the lifeguard into opening the diving section so she could practice her cannonball. We watched two performances before she reluctantly left the pool, her red curls plastered to her head.

After introductions all around we headed for our rooms. Maddie and Taylor seemed to connect immediately with a discussion of a certain diving maneuver that was particularly difficult.

"We'll be at the high school tomorrow. Grandpa says it's a groundbreaking, whatever that is. Will you be there?" Taylor asked us.

"Yeah, it's a date," Maddie said.

Enough said.

Rosie opened the door to our room for us, her other hand holding an assortment of makeup tools. "I was sipping and noshing all evening, so I had to reapply here and there," she explained.

Maddie dug out her pajamas and tooth-brush. I moved a few totes off the easy chair and plopped into it. Cocktail parties take a lot out of me. For one thing, I was hoarse from trying to carry on a conversation at full volume. For another, considering David Bridges's lukewarm attitude toward Rosie and Cheryl Mellace's appropriation of his arm, I was tense about Rosie's social pros-pects this evening.

"Can you get my nightgown from the top drawer, sweetheart?" I asked Maddie. "And the sandwiches from the cooler?"

"Cool," Maddie said. "Supper in bed."

"What do you mean?" Rosie asked, flus-tered. "We have to go to David's room, Gerry. It's almost ten thirty."

"I thought you might have changed your mind and preferred to go alone, Rosie."

"No, no. It's not like that. It's supposed to be for a few special people." She took a note from her everyday purse, perched on her luggage, and unfolded it. "See? It says, *Join me as a few special people come back to my room.* We can bring a guest, like the person we're rooming with, I'm sure."

I couldn't believe Rosie had carried the note from Lincoln Point. But then, she'd carried the entire ALHS hallway of lockers.

"You seemed to hit it off with Barry Cannon tonight. He and David were good friends in school and I'll bet he'll be there."

Rosie waved her hand. "Barry. He and David went to grade school together, too, otherwise do you think they'd have been hanging around in the same crowd in high school?"

"Didn't David like smart guys?"

"That's not what I meant, but you know how it always was at ALHS. The jocks hung out on one side of the quad and the nerds on the other. Anyway, that was a strange conversation Barry and I had tonight. He kept asking me about my father."

"Do they know each other?"

Another wave. "Apparently. They've had some business dealings."

"Your father is retired, isn't he? I forget exactly what kind of business —"

Rosie huffed a long breath. "Gerry, we have to go," she said.

I looked at the narrow but inviting bed with its three plumped pillows plus a matching blue-and-mauve bolster and the soft, lightweight comforter. Maddie was arranging sandwiches and chips on paper plates left over from the last birthday party at my house.

"Truthfully, I'd rather —"

"Gerry, I need you," Rosie said in a near wail.

"I'll be fine here, Grandma," said Maddie, more grown up at eleven than Rosie in her late forties. Maddie had already bit into a tuna sandwich and downed a handful of potato chips. "I have homework for class."

Although we were long past the time I could help Maddie with much of her homework, I would have given anything to stay, even for an hour or two, listening to programming language.

My late husband often called me a patsy. The term had probably gone out of style by now, but I was still a patsy. "Just for a little while," I said to Rosie.

"How did you find out David's room number?" I asked Rosie as we stepped off the elevator on the eleventh floor.

"I asked old Coach Robbins, figuring he'd be going to the party, too. He didn't seem to know anything about it, but he didn't have a problem telling me David's room number. His whole team is up here on eleven. It's almost like high school, with everyone sticking together in the old groups."

I thought back to Susan's remark at our last crafts meeting, that if you didn't fit in then, you won't fit in now.

We walked down the hall toward eleven forty-three, Rosie alternately speeding up and slowing down. I was sure some of her pacing problem had to do with her stilettos, a far cry from the tennis shoes she wore in her own milieu, Rosie's Bookshop. At one point I thought (hoped?) she was going to turn around and forget about the party.

When we got to David's door, Rosie adjusted her dress and fingered each stone in her bracelet, a gesture she'd made repeatedly since she'd put it on her wrist. She gave me a look that said I should be the one to knock.

I did, gently.

No answer. Except for the giggling we heard through the door.

I knocked again, a little louder.

David opened the door, revealing expansive, handsome quarters. Looking down the opening he'd given us, I caught a glimpse of a panoramic view at the end of the suite. He'd shed his jacket and tie and swirled a drink in a short, stubby glass.

Cheryl, in a peach chiffon spaghetti-strap number meant for a younger woman, was on his arm, as she was at the cocktail party. Had she ever let go?

There was no sign of anyone else in the rooms.

"Hi," Rosie said in a bright, nervous voice. "Are we too early?"

Cheryl swung her long brown hair back and laughed. "Too early for what?"

David looked confused. "Can I help you, Rosie? Mrs. Porter?"

I let Rosie handle this one.

"I . . . uh . . . I thought there was a little get-together tonight. In your room. Your note . . ." she said.

"We're already getting together," Cheryl said, her hair still swinging, her tone disparaging.

"I'm sorry," David said to Rosie. "I don't know anything about a get-together. I think everyone went out to dinner or something."

I understood the "everyone" to mean David's inner circle.

"Maybe she means the party tomorrow night, David," Cheryl said.

Another confused look from the football star. "That's just for —"

"Right," Cheryl said. "I didn't see her name on the list." Cheryl laughed, emphasizing *her,* and apparently enjoying the third-person references. "Maybe she's on the list that has Math Bird on it."

Rosie put her hand on my arm to steady

59

herself. I thought she was going to faint.

David grinned, then seemed to have an attack of conscience. "Do you want to come in for a drink?" he asked.

Too little, too late, I thought, as Rosie recovered her balance, turned, and walked away.

"I think there's been a misunderstanding," I said to David.

"I guess so. Sorry, Mrs. Porter," David said, closing the door. I figured he apologized to me, forgetting I wasn't responsible for grading him anymore.

I went after Rosie, the sound of Cheryl's laugh following me down the hallway. I recognized the reference to Math Bird, a nickname for one of the smarter boys in the class, but I had no idea why his name would be invoked tonight.

Apparently some of the thirty-year alums of ALHS weren't just reuniting, they were sticking to the cliques of their high school days.

Even in her stilettos, Rosie managed to get to the elevator and ride away before I got to the doors. I took the next car and rode down to our room on five, feeling a heavy sadness for my friend. I was sure she didn't expect to be humiliated. Who ever does?

With all the misgivings I'd had from the beginning of Rosie's journey to the past, I was still caught off guard. Warnings and forebodings were one thing; the full manifestation of all our fears was another.

I entered our room, where Maddie was already asleep on her cot in front of the television, a mostly eaten sandwich on her lap. All that swimming had taken its toll.

There was no sign that Rosie had returned to the room. I thought about checking the bar to see if she'd gone there, or the all-night business center where she could be doing bookshop work on a hotel computer. I decided not to interfere beyond putting a note on the cooler that she should help herself to sandwiches and snacks.

I covered Maddie, turned off the television, and settled down for a sandwich myself. As for David and the nonparty, I couldn't guess what had happened. Did Rosie misread the note? She'd held the note out to me, but I hadn't read it myself. Was this a cruel game David was playing with her? All the gifts were now called into question. Had the whole drama been Cheryl's idea all along? I couldn't fathom.

I waited up for Rosie, reading until well after midnight, but she didn't come back. I eased my fretting by assuming, and hoping, that she'd found a quiet place to reflect, or cry, or do whatever she needed to in private.

When I woke up on Saturday morning I expected to see the sun streaming through our east-facing windows, but this was San Francisco, where the summer days usually started with a serious fog bank.

I looked over at the second twin bed and breathed a sigh of relief that Rosie was there, also just waking up. She might have been a battered woman, for all the black and blue and puffiness on her face. I realized it was simply eye makeup running into cheek makeup.

She caught my eye, inadvertently I thought. It was hard to think of an appropriate greeting. "What time did you get in?" I whispered, not wanting to wake Maddie, curled up in a corner of the cot.

"Around two, I think. I just had to clear my head. I went to the fitness center."

"Rosie, I'm so sorry about —"

She waved away my concern. "No problem. I just needed a little workout." From a supine position, she lifted imaginary barbells in the air. "I'm really fine now."

Why didn't I believe her? Maybe one reason was because as long as I'd known her, Rosie had never been to a health club or lifted a barbell.

Maddie and I left the hotel about eight o'clock, while Rosie was still packing, her mood swinging from angry to moping. I wanted to get an early start on the drive back to Lincoln Point for the groundbreaking ceremony. Rosie had told us she doubted she'd return to San Francisco for the banquet tonight, and I couldn't blame her. I'd wondered about keeping the commitment myself, but Maddie and I decided we would go back. After all, the room was paid for, and if nothing else, we could enjoy some of the tourist attractions.

"And be much cooler than in Lincoln Point," Maddie added.

"Do you mean the temperature or what we can do there?" I asked.

"Both."

When we reached the garage, I saw Cheryl Mellace coming down the entrance ramp in a black convertible. If she'd kept on a straight path, she would have passed in front of us, but she veered off and drove up another row and parked. My guess was that she had no interest in greeting me. The feeling was mutual.

We had nasty traffic the whole way home,

but Maddie always made a car trip more pleasant than it otherwise would be. We never lacked for topics of conversation, knock-knock jokes, and plans for more time together.

One question, like "What are you working on in class?" could be good for many miles. Today she tried to explain video game design using something called fusion software. To me, fusion was a style of cuisine, and probably always would be.

"It's version two," she said, as if that meant anything to me.

"As long as you're having a good time and learning a lot," I said, resorting to generalities.

"You'll see when we have our big demonstration at the end," Maddie said, with a grin. "It will be like a crafts show."

"Smarty," I said. Too bad tickling was an unsafe driving practice.

We'd agreed it would be a good idea to stop at home as soon as we got to Lincoln Point, to replenish the food supplies in the picnic cooler. This habit had a little to do with economizing but more to do with being sure Maddie had food she would eat. I was afraid the gourmet restaurants of San Francisco would be lost on her and leave her hungry.

64

Except for the "food" at the Ghirardelli chocolate factory, where we'd taken her when she was about two years old, but not since. At the time, the whole family shared one serving of Ghirardelli's famous earthquake sundae, in which "cracks" in scoops of ice cream are filled with whipped cream, nuts, and cherries.

The more I thought about it, the more eager I was to return to San Francisco this afternoon. We'd have time for a Ghirardelli stop before the banquet. I wanted to see Maddie's face this time when the enormous sundae arrived at our table. And I wanted to dig into it myself.

But an exciting groundbreaking ceremony in Lincoln Point had to come first.

CHAPTER 4

The noontime groundbreaking ceremony in our hometown was to launch the construction of the new athletic field and stadium for ALHS. Personally, I'd been pulling for a remodel of the old wing of the library instead, but the majority on the city council had ruled otherwise. "Alumni don't show up for National Library Week in the numbers that they do for a high school football game," went the argument.

I'd seen the plans for the facility in the *Lincolnite.* At the entrance would be an archway that was trying to be much too grand for Lincoln Point. My architect husband would have agreed with me that such structures belonged only in Rome, Paris, or New York City's West Village, where they already were. I was also less than thrilled about the ornamentation on the arch, which was of a frowning cartoon feline. I knew the idea was to tie the school mascot to Abraham Lincoln, like everything else in the town, but Abe was said to have loved stray kittens, not angry cats. Besides, everyone knew that his favorite pet was Fido, the family dog.

I supposed I should have been grateful that the artist hadn't given the growling, fanged cat a beard and a stovepipe hat.

Maddie and I joined the crowd on the field, entering from the edge of the parking lot closest to our civic center. A large sign that I'd passed many times, but never paid much attention to, announced that the project would be carried out by Mellace Construction Co., of Lincoln Point. I was glad the business would stay in town.

The sun beat down, the only breezes created by tri-fold programs waving in front of individual faces. At this distance we couldn't see the ceremonial shovel, but the image on the program showed a gold-plated shovel with a large maroon-and-gold bow to match the school colors. Balloons of the same colors dotted the area. At the entrance to the grounds were baskets of yellow-frosted cookies in the shape of hard hats. A sign in front of them read, *Compliments of the Football Mothers.*

I'd often contributed to school baking projects, but not one of this magnitude.

If the *Lincolnite* predictions were correct, there would be more than a thousand people attending the ceremony today. That was a lot of oven time, and in very hot weather.

I hadn't paid attention to all the details of the project, so this was my first clue as to exactly where the new field and stadium would be located — across Civic Drive from the complex of city buildings. I wondered about the wisdom of situating a noise-generating stadium, with most likely a state-of-the-art PA system, across from the library, but unless I was willing to serve on political committees, I had no right to complain.

We expected a presentation shortly by principal Frank Thayer, our cocktail companion of last night, and probably a few words from Lincoln Point's mayor and council members, as well as past and present faculty and student leaders. (Read: the coaches and student athletes.)

Cliques aside, I'd enjoyed my years on the ALHS faculty and I was proud of the students I taught. As with the party at the Duns Scotus, today I derived great pleasure from all the greetings of "Hi, Mrs. Porter, nice to see you." The short visits peppered the half hour while we waited on folding chairs for the official first turning over of dirt.

"Poor Mrs. Norman," Maddie said at one point. "I hope she'll be okay."

As usual when there were tough grown-up issues in play, I wondered how much Maddie knew and how she was handling it.

"She had a serious disappointment," I told her. "I'm sure she'll be fine in a few days."

"My dad would say, 'As long as it's not life-threatening, you should get over it.' "

It seemed like a good rule to me.

A John Philip Sousa march rang out from my purse. My ring tone of choice for the summer. It was one of many cell phones that rang intermittently around the great lawn, so I wasn't as embarrassed as I might have been otherwise. I was proud that I'd learned how to program my cell phone ring tone and was no longer at the mercy of my tech-savvy granddaughter. I even took the trouble to change it according to the season.

I clicked the phone on.

"Aunt Gerry? Are you at the high school ceremony?" Skip asked me, with no prelude.

"Yes."

"Is your friend Rosie Norman with you?"

"No. Are you calling from Seattle?"

"Do you know where she is right now?"

"No, I don't. I suppose she might be in this crowd." I stretched my neck and scanned the crowd. Being tall has its advantages at times like this, but given Rosie's small stature, it didn't help me much in this gathering. "I don't see her. We left the Duns Scotus before she did this morning. Why are you looking for her?"

"I thought I'd give you a heads-up. One of the BMOCs in your reunion group was found dead this morning."

"BM—"

"You know, Big Man On Campus. David Bridges."

My throat went dry. I thought everyone in my vicinity would notice how my knees had become weak. I cupped my hand over my mouth, conscious of Maddie at my side. Happily, Henry Baker and Taylor were approaching and were a distraction for her. Maddie had made sure to save seats for them, and had been on the lookout for her new friend.

"David Bridges is dead?" I whispered the question to Skip.

"Okay, well, I guess that's it," he said. "I knew you were traveling with Rosie to the reunion so I thought you might know her whereabouts."

"Whereabouts" sounded much too official

70

to suit me. "Where are you, Skip?"

"I flew in early this morning. Glad to be back in the sun. It rains even in August in Seattle."

"Why are you asking about Rosie's whereabouts?"

As if I didn't know. Nephew or not, when a homicide detective tells you about a death, probably the next person he mentions has either been murdered or is a key suspect.

"You'll hear an announcement about Bridges's death pretty soon," Skip said, avoiding my question. "We've alerted Frank Thayer."

How? Where? Who? Why? came rushing to my lips.

"You have to tell me something, Skip. You called me, after all."

Skip answered, albeit only the simple questions. "Bridges was bludgeoned to death with his trophy, but even though the body turned up in Lincoln Point, we're not sure yet where it happened. Do me a favor, Aunt Gerry, and just forget everything for now, okay?"

He clicked off before I could agree or not.

In too few years, David Bridges had gone from BMOC to "the body."

What reason could the LPPD possibly have to suspect Rosie? Surely she hadn't

71

broadcast her severe disappointment last night — who else could have known besides me, Cheryl, and David? Skip wouldn't have zeroed in on her without some evidence, however.

There I went, leaping ahead unjustifiably. Skip had simply asked where Rosie was, hadn't he?

I thought back to Maddie's observation, quoting her father. Had Rosie's disappointment been life-threatening after all?

ALHS principal Frank Thayer stepped up to the podium in the nick of time, before I had to make polite conversation with Henry and Taylor, who'd just taken their seats next to Maddie. I gave them each a wave and as friendly a smile as I could manage in my state of distress over David and over Rosie.

Frank tapped the microphone on the makeshift stage. "Testing, testing" came out, along with static.

Among the dignitaries on folding chairs behind him were his wife, Paula, and key people in Lincoln Point administration. At this distance I could still recognize members of the Faculty Senate, some of whom were first-year teachers during the end of my career, and others of whom I'd known for many years. They all seemed unaffected by the extreme noontime heat, not even waving their programs in front of their faces as Maddie and I were.

I pretended to be listening with rapt attention to Frank's uttering of the fascinating, "One, two, three. One, two, three."

Frank's voice carried all the way back to those of us at the edge of the high school property, where the parking lot ended at Civic Drive. Skip's office was in the building complex in front of us; Rosie's Books stood across Springfield Boulevard to our left. Understanding the connection between the two locations at the moment made me dizzy. Given the urgency in Skip's tone, I couldn't shake the conclusion that my friend Rosie was suspected of killing David Bridges.

Rosie was high on my list of babysitters for Maddie, and one of the first people I called when I finished a book and wanted to discuss it.

She couldn't have done it. That was that.

Rosie's behavior so far this weekend seemed uncharacteristically immature and dramatic, to be sure, but that was a long way from having murderous intentions. Just for drill, I indulged in a worst-case scenario — if Rosie Norman were going to kill anyone, the victim would have been Cheryl

Mellace. Poor David had been much more civil to Rosie in the doorway of his hotel room, even inviting her in for a drink. It was the petite, popular Cheryl who'd mocked her so mercilessly.

Frank called us to order, his voice booming over the PA system. The crowd quieted, and I knew it would grow even quieter in a moment.

"Welcome to the future site of our new athletic field and modern stadium. It's great to see so many Lincoln Point residents and friends. I want to extend a special welcome and thank-you to the alumni of the thirty-year reunion class. Your fund-raising drive gave us the largest single contribution to the project."

Loud applause, whistling, and the cheering appropriate to a stadium erupted. I tried to imagine my tutoring sessions in the library with an even better PA system at full volume like this at game time.

When the noise died down, Frank began what must have been one of the most difficult addresses of his career — announcing the death of a classmate. "And now I have a very sad duty. I've just learned that one of our most illustrious alumni and a friend to all of us, David Bridges, who was to address us today, has passed away unexpectedly."

Frank stepped away from the mike. I imagined how shaken he must be. "That's all we know at the moment," he continued, with a shaky voice.

A mixture of gasps and groans rippled through the crowd. I hadn't looked at the program carefully, finding it more useful as a fan, so this was the first I'd realized that David was to speak. I wasn't surprised, however. I knew that more than just his own classmates had appreciated David's fame as a football star. I thought of the large number of glassed-in cases in the ALHS hallways that were dedicated to displays of sports trophies and photographs of teams in action. Even all these years later, top athletes like David were embedded in the school's memory and credited with giving the school status in the county.

How would his fans and friends react if they knew that David didn't just pass quietly away, but died at the hands of a murderer?

Maddie tugged my arm. "Grandma? Do you know that man? Isn't that the one Mrs. Norman talks about on crafts night?"

"Yes, sweetheart, but it's nothing for you to worry about."

Maddie looked up at me, squinting into the sunny sky. "I heard you say Uncle Skip's name, you know, on that phone call. Was it about the man's death? Did he call you for help investigating? You know how helpful I can be," she said.

Maddie had adopted the perfect combination of techniques used by her father and his cousin at that age. My son, Richard, used intimidation, drilling us with questions that demanded straight answers. Ken and I were sure he was going to be a prosecuting attorney some day, not the orthopedic surgeon he became. His cousin, Skip, took the calm road to getting what he wanted. He remained soft-spoken, teasing, and charming, your best friend — who ended up a cop. Go figure.

I had to remain strong in the face of a young opponent who'd mastered both approaches.

"There's nothing for us to do, Maddie. All we know is that the man passed away."

She sank back in her chair and picked up her fanning, appeased for now.

I caught Henry's eye. He seemed to be aware of my conversation with Maddie. We shared looks of sadness and confusion. He stroked Taylor's head, his fingers reaching to her ears, as if to protect her from any further unpleasant news.

But there was no more information coming from the stage. Frank closed by asking us all to take a moment of silence to think of David and to pray for his family and loved ones. While we reflected, the high school band played a few somber notes, sounding like a modified "Taps."

Barry Cannon, class president and Rosie's current best friend among her classmates, it seemed, stepped to the mike. "We're all stunned and very sad. Frank — Principal Thayer — gave us the word only a couple of minutes ago." Murmurings continued to ripple through the crowd as Barry's voice cracked, then recovered. "The officers of the thirty-year reunion class have decided to hold the banquet tonight as planned, because we think David would want us to be together." Barry had a stentorian voice, for someone so small in stature. He seemed to break down, but rallied and went on for a few more minutes, his closing remarks advising us to take every opportunity to enjoy life, since "you never know."

Several other speakers stepped up to the podium, expressing gratitude to the chief donors and predicting great victories for the teams of ALHS in the new facility, but all in very moderate tones, more befitting a memorial service than a happy ground-breaking ceremony.

I tuned out most of the rhetoric, my mind on Rosie and the investigation. Usually I'd be bothered by the oppressive heat, but today that was a distant second to the discomfort I felt over David's murder and Rosie's situation.

I wondered if the LPPD was ready to arrest Rosie or if they simply wanted to question her. I was itching to know how Skip had glommed on to her in the first place? Had the police interviewed David's reunion classmates already? I tried again to think if there was something untoward about her behavior at the cocktail party, something that would have been picked up by her party-going peers. When I'd literally bumped into David, all had been cordial. The only ones who were aware of Rosie's unhealthy obsession were the members of the crafts group and Cheryl. I didn't know all of Rosie's other friends, but I doubted she'd advertised her wishful thinking far and wide.

Finally the group of dignitaries gathered around the shovel. I'd forgotten that's why we were here. Tall as I was, I still couldn't see the little ceremonial plot where the earth would be turned over. I knew the deed had been accomplished only by the smattering of applause as the crowd dispersed, its mood somber.

"Grandma?"

I realized I'd spaced out again. "Are you hungry, sweetheart?" Food to the rescue, a time-honored Porter tradition.

"Why don't we all head for bagels at Willie's," Henry said. "My idea, my treat."

Problem solved.

On the way out of the grassy area, I saw a small knot of thirty-year alums. Among them was Cheryl Mellace, wearing an eye patch. On me, the sight of a plastic cup with gauze sticking out the sides would have looked repulsive, as if I'd become a member of the Cyclopes, but it seemed to make Cheryl even more alluring. I doubted she'd chosen it as an accessory, however, and wondered what was wrong with her eye.

"I'll just be a sec," I told the other three in my own party and wandered to Cheryl's group. Henry and Taylor were more help than they could have imagined in allowing me to dodge Maddie's scrutiny.

A much subdued round of greetings came my way from the small clutch of men and women that included Cheryl Mellace. "I'm so sorry about your friend," I said. "I know David meant a lot to all of you."

The murmurings in response seemed

heartfelt. I focused on Cheryl, looking for a more intense reaction, but saw none. I looked at the patch over her eye. "I hope that's not too painful," I said.

Her one good eye glared at me. "Thanks for asking," she said. There was no doubt in my mind that she remembered my presence outside David's hotel room when she delivered her insults to my friend.

"And I hope your last evening with David was a good memory," I said.

Cheryl gave me one more angry look, then she sniffled and buried her face on the chest of the man next to her, no one I recognized.

"She and David go way back, Mrs. Porter," he explained, patting Cheryl's back. "They were very close."

"I know."

Like so many establishments in Lincoln Point, from banks to car rentals to dress shops, Bagels by Willie had an Abraham Lincoln connection: Lincoln's third son, named after his uncle William. Willie died of what was likely typhoid fever when he was Maddie's age.

That didn't explain the bagel shop's New York décor, dominated by a set of black-and-white photographs of the Empire State

Building, the Statue of Liberty, and other New York City landmarks, but not everything had to make sense.

I went through the motions of greeting patrons I knew. My GED student, Lourdes Pino, took my order for an asiago cheese bagel and tried to start up our usual bantering about the peculiarities of the English language.

"Don't put flour on a flower" was her offering today. Ordinarily I'd respond in kind, but today I had nothing to counter with. "I'll see you next Tuesday as usual, Mrs. Porter?" Lourdes asked, as if seeking assurance that I wasn't withdrawing altogether from our relationship.

I nibbled at my bagel and tried to tune in on the enjoyable chatter among Henry, Taylor, and Maddie, about the miniature apartment building and other woodworking projects that, on another day, would have fascinated me. I perked up a bit when I heard mention of a half-scale (only a half inch to every foot of life size) rocking chair and a dining room table with an inlaid wood design.

Maddie took up the slack for me, making up for my drifting attention. Except for frequent cell phone text messages, she kept the conversation going. First we had to deal with e-mailing, then ubiquitous cell phoning, and now text messages. One more high-tech way to stay connected had invaded the environment.

During one moment of halfhearted listening, I thought I heard Maddie say she'd like to buy one of Henry's rockers for her dollhouse at home in Palo Alto. I had the feeling I should step in and monitor my granddaughter's interactions, but I didn't see any harm. I trusted Henry not to take advantage of her in these dealings. In fact, in any negotiation with Maddie, I always worried about the other party.

Maddie and Taylor, who had proclaimed themselves BF, best friends, left to get ice cream for all of us. Lucky for Lincoln Point residents, Sadie at the ice cream shop two doors down and Johnny, who ran the bagel shop, were good friends who allowed each other's customers to supplement different parts of the meal.

"I'll have my usual chocolate malt," I'd told Maddie.

Henry had said, "Surprise me."

"They seem to get along so well," I said, for lack of a good transition to adult conversation.

"Did you notice that they were TMing each other while we were talking?"

"And they probably didn't miss a thing," I said.

I was proud that I recognized the abbreviation for text messaging, but not pleased that most of the interaction at the table had gone right by me. I was glad it was Henry who opened the topic that had captured my attention.

"David Bridges. I can't believe it," he said, scratching his head, full of brown hair that was barely starting to thin. "I wonder how it happened. A heart attack, do you think? We saw him just last night and he looked great. He couldn't have been more than . . . what? . . . forty-seven or -eight?"

I couldn't meet his gaze. I pushed a bagel crust around with my cream cheese knife. "Not more than that," I said.

The news would soon be the talk of the town, but I wondered how soon citizens without relatives in the Lincoln Point Police Department would know that David's was not a natural death, that he'd been bludgeoned with his own trophy. The crowd at Willie's included many people from the abbreviated groundbreaking ceremony, but with so little information released, there wasn't much to talk about. Most of the snippets of conversation I heard had more to do with the one-hundred-degree temperature than with the death of David Bridges.

I didn't feel I could share what I knew, little as it was, with Henry, but I needed someone to talk to. My head ached from the stress.

There was only one sure way to ease the tension.

I knew what I was about to do was sneaky. Maddie would never forgive me. Not until I took her to Ghirardelli's this afternoon, anyway.

I looked around at the crowd and leaned over the table. You never knew where there was a mole. "Henry, I have a big favor to ask."

"Hit me with it," he said.

Bad choice of words. I swallowed hard.

"I have an important errand to run that I can't take Maddie to. Would you mind taking her home with you and I'll pick her up later?"

Henry's eyebrows went up a tad, surprised, but he recovered nicely. "Can I have your chocolate malt?"

I liked his style.

CHAPTER 5

A little knowledge is a dangerous thing, I reminded myself, so I was on my way to get more. There was no use having a nephew, one whose hand you'd held crossing the street not that long ago, on the police force if you couldn't take advantage of it.

I walked the few blocks down Springfield Boulevard, past the high school and the now-deserted groundbreaking site, to the police department, part of the civic center complex along with the city hall and the library. On my way down the street and up to Skip's second-floor cubicle, I rehearsed.

"You got me involved," I'd say, reminding him of his phone call alerting me to David's murder and requesting my help in locating Rosie. Maybe that was too junior high, reminiscent of many such "he started it" exchanges between Skip and my son, Richard.

"I'd like to help" wouldn't work, since

Skip consistently reminded me that the Lincoln Point Police Department had enough sworn officers to take care of business.

"Excuse me?" he'd say. "Do you have a badge?"

"I'm your only aunt and you owe me" might do the trick, but I'd used it before.

I realized I needed some new material.

I always preferred dealing with female LPPD officers, not because of any sexist or feminist leanings, but because usually they were hot for (Maddie's term; I still preferred the old-fashioned "sweet on") Skip. This meant that they'd be especially accommodating and nice to me. It didn't seem to matter that Skip and June, my next-door neighbor, were practically engaged. Maybe even one step closer this weekend since Skip had taken June to Seattle to meet his mother's boyfriend's family. Never mind that the weekend was cut off at the pass. His intentions spoke of commitment.

Was every extended family this complicated to talk about?

I was in luck. Lavana Rollins, an attractive member of the almost-thirty crowd, like Skip, was on duty at the front desk. After the hot-weather talk, I got to my point.

"Too bad Skip had to cut his trip to

Seattle short," I said to Lavana.

"Yeah, we got this big case, and so many people are on vacation in faraway places. Poor Skip was close enough to be called back."

"I just heard the announcement. It's such a shame about David Bridges," I said.

"Too true. I didn't know him, but I guess he was very popular around here during the football heyday at the high school."

The days Lincoln Point expected to get back with a new stadium. "I had David as a student a long time ago. I hope you're making progress finding his killer."

"Ha. They don't tell me anything. I'm just a uniform," she said. "Don't get me wrong. I love my job. I get to carry the evidence." Lavana's laugh was hearty, befitting her substantial frame. "The strangest thing came in this morning, though. You'd have found it very interesting."

I didn't have to fake my intense curiosity. "Oh?"

"Hey, Rollins." I heard a deep voice from behind the wide front counter where Lavana stood. "How about those files?"

"Gotta go," Lavana told me. "Skip should be here any minute. You can go on back and wait."

That was my hoped-for scenario: that I'd

have a few minutes alone at Skip's desk to reflect. Or to snoop, depending on what you wanted to call it. I did wonder about the evidence Lavana mentioned, but it would have been unseemly to act nosy.

"Thanks, Lavana." I gave her a grateful smile. "I know the way."

"You didn't happen to bring any of those ginger cookies?" she whispered. Apparently if I did, she wasn't planning on sharing.

As a matter of fact, I had pulled a bag out of the cooler in my car, as an offering to Skip, but I was willing to use them to barter wherever necessary. I opened a small plastic container within the bag and invited her to help herself. It was a small price to pay for a few minutes alone in Skip's cubicle.

Food as sycophantism. Another time-honored Porter tradition.

I sat in Skip's office, in the visitors' chair, facing the cubicle opening and his bulletin board. I had a paperback of *To Kill a Mockingbird* open on my lap, for effect. I really had wanted to reread the classic, but today it served double duty as a cover.

The beige corkboard was cluttered with business and personal items, including a wonderful photo of a very young Maddie, her father, and me. I remembered the long-ago trip to Pier 39, one of San Francisco's many fun places for kids. If Skip gave me any grief today, I'd remind him of his loving family.

Maddie looked happy in the photo, next to a life-size yellow cartoon animal of no particular delineation. Unlike now, I mused, when she was probably fuming as much as an eleven-year-old could fume. Maddie was in a prolonged Nancy Drew phase and hated to be left out of any investigative tasks. She was at least in an environment she might like, this time, with someone her own age and a wonderful (I guessed) workshop to browse in.

I saw nothing useful on Skip's bulletin board. I'd been hoping for a to-do list. *Clear Rosie Norman* could have been an item. Then, *Arrest John Doe.* I started a mental list of who John Doe could be. No one had asked my opinion, but I thought the police should be looking into David's ex-wife, his estranged son, and especially the Duns Scotus employee we all saw him arguing with last night.

I moved my chair slightly, to have a better angle on the desk. Lavana had said Skip would be back "any minute" and I didn't want to be caught out-and-out snooping. I scanned the clutter for a file labeled *Aunt*

Gerry's Friend, Rosie. Or, simply, *Norman.*
Nothing.

Nothing big, that is. But there was something small. Under a few loose sheets of paper, I saw the edge of a hotel key card.

Still keeping an eye on the cubicle opening, I flung my left arm out, felt around for the card, and pulled it out. A Duns Scotus key, like the one in my purse. This one had a slightly different likeness of the Franciscan metaphysician, but it was the Subtle Doctor himself, in his brown habit.

The key cards to the hotel were imprinted with different reproductions of paintings of Duns Scotus; even keys to the same room had different images. I found the same policy at the last hotel I'd been in, in Monterey, where the cards bore a variety of pictures of the ocean. I didn't see the point, except in terms of exposure to art. The bottom line was that there was no way to tell which key went with which room these days. No more large numerals etched on circles or flat metal keys. All for better security, which was on everyone's mind.

I didn't know yet where David had been murdered, but wherever it was, all the sophisticated, increased security in the world hadn't helped him.

Whose key card was I holding? David's?

Rosie's, therefore mine?

It wasn't a good sign if the Lincoln Point police went to all the trouble to go to San Francisco and enter our room. Skip had said they didn't know where the murder had taken place. If David had been killed at the hotel, then the San Francisco police would handle it. Pangs of guilt accompanied my desire to have LPPD in charge of the case so I could keep track of it.

I was betting on the key's being for David's room, probably found on his person. I wondered if it had been reprogrammed or if it would still work. Should I take it? It would certainly help if I needed to do some investigating myself. If Skip needed to get into a hotel room, I reasoned, he could just flash his badge.

What would I do with it? I had a pretty good idea. Was it evidence? No, if it were evidence it would be in a marked bag. It was now LPPD property, however — hard to get around that. Unless it was Rosie's key card, in which case, it was also mine.

Before I could decide the level of misdemeanor I was willing to risk, I heard Skip. His tenor voice came closer and closer as he greeted his colleagues with a "Hey," or a "Dude," or a "What's up?"

I had no time to place the key card in the

exact location I'd taken it from. It made sense, therefore, to slip it into my pocket. With the jumble of papers, folders, and notes on his desk, he wouldn't miss it. Not right away at least. I could always sneak it back later.

"Hey, Aunt Gerry, you're late," Skip said when he entered his cubicle. He looked at his watch. "I expected you over an hour ago, right after we hung up."

Very funny. "I had to take Maddie to lunch," I said.

"And you brought me . . . ?"

I handed over the rest of the ginger cookies. I could have sworn he stared at the spot on his desk where the key card had been. I had to concentrate, swallowing hard, distracting myself from looking there myself. I remembered a thriller I'd seen where the suspect revealed his guilt merely by looking at a spot on the wall where the bullet had penetrated, something he couldn't have known unless he'd put it there. I held fast, but I was sure I saw out of the corner of my eye a red glow where once the key belonging to the LPPD had been.

"I thought you might want to share more with me. About why you were looking for Rosie Norman?"

He chewed slowly on a ginger cookie.

"Mmm," came out of his mouth instead of information. "Still the best, Aunt Gerry." He picked up my paperback, which had fallen to the floor. "This is your snooping cover, right? I don't see a bookmark."

My nephew was so annoying when he was right. "Skip? You called me, remember? I just want to know what in the world makes you think Rosie murdered David Bridges?"

"Did I say that?" he asked.

"Not in so many words. Do you deny that you think she might be involved?"

"Not exactly."

My heart sank, my last miniature amount of hope flitting away. I clung to his qualified answer. He hadn't given me an outright "no." "Can you at least tell me where his body was found?"

"A group of teenagers found him when they went to Joshua Speed Woods for some early morning necking. We don't know if that was the actual scene of the crime, though the last word was yes, probably he was killed right there. The kids' statement says that the trophy was next to the body. They picked it up to see whose it was. I have a feeling every one of them handled it, so we're still sorting out whose fingerprints are recoverable."

Up to now, when I'd had occasion to pass

by or talk about the wooded area to the west of the main part of town, I imagined the look on the face of one of Lincoln's closest friends, Kentuckian Joshua Speed — if he could have known that his namesake woods were used mostly as a lovers' lane. Now, for a long time, I'd remember it as a murder scene.

The worst realization at the moment, however, was that Rosie lived on Joshua Speed Lane, which bordered the woods.

I felt the strangest regret that I hadn't listened more closely to Rosie when she described her long-ago relationship to David. All the times she'd gone on and on at the crafts table, and most of us absorbed less than half of what she said, I guessed. She'd mentioned one "date gone bad" as I recalled. I didn't care at the time, but now I wished I knew precisely how badly it had gone.

Skip bent down to the floor on the side of his desk and picked up a brown paper bag. Too large for lunch. Big enough for evidence.

I was on pins and needles as he reached into the bag. What he pulled out was one of the last things I would have guessed, right before "a flock of seagulls."

Skip took his time. Rosie's locker room

scene emerged from the bag, one tiny, gray locker at a time. I couldn't blame Skip for playing out the drama.

I didn't remember so much red in the décor. I looked more closely. The scene had been trashed. *I hate David* had been written in red paint across three or four adjacent lockers. The tiny jersey with David's old number thirty-six had been torn to shreds. There was "trash" everywhere, in the form of bits of cloth and paper and a deflated football.

"Where did you get this?" I asked.

"Can you identify the item?"

I gulped. I felt as though I were in a witness box. Or on trial myself.

"It's Rosie's," I said. "I mean it looks like Rosie's. What do you think it means?"

"My question exactly." He placed the room box on his desk. "Look carefully. It's been dusted, as much as we could, considering where we found it, but you still shouldn't touch it."

The most I could ever hope for from my nephew was that he would answer half the questions I asked. I didn't push the issue, lest I inadvertently give away something that incriminated Rosie.

I squinted at the ravaged scene. I reached into my tote for the magnifier I always carry and held it close. It took a great effort not to run my finger across the red paint. I grimaced as if it were real blood.

I saw what had impressed Skip. The most striking addition to the scene was a bottle of poison. It seemed Rosie had taken a piece of white filter paper from the coffee system that every hotel room has these days and fashioned a small cylinder to resemble a bottle. She'd used the plastic packaging from a coffee pouch to shape a bottle top. Not too many people would have been able to identify this clever use of found objects, but it happened to be my specialty. The work had been done in a hurry (or in a state of torment) but was what my crafters group would have declared "cute."

Except for what was written on the bottle. Rosie — or someone else, I reminded myself — had drawn the shape of a label, with a skull and crossbones and the word *poison*.

Lavana Rollins had been right when she called it a strange piece of evidence that I'd find "very interesting."

"Well?" Skip said. "What's it supposed to be? Something other than a clue to her state of mind? And, by the way, there's more potential evidence that I can't tell you about right now."

I felt it necessary to explain the craft

group's Alasita project to Skip, hoping the context would work in Rosie's favor. "Before the vandalism, it was like a prayer for a happy meeting between Rosie and David," I said.

"I've heard of that."

"You have?"

"When June and I went to Mexico we saw a version of Alasita. They had parades and dancing and all, but the miniatures were nothing as fancy as this. They were more likely to do something rough or just buy a little key chain if they wanted a car or a house." He rummaged around the back of his desk and extracted a wooden owl. "June got me this. To bring me wisdom."

"You said there was something else. More potential evidence? Not that this is evidence."

"Yeah, well, never mind that right now."

"But David wasn't poisoned. Doesn't that count?"

"Gotta go, Aunt Gerry."

I managed a few more Q-and-As before he got serious about my leaving. The gentle pressure on my arm as he led me from his cubicle told me that it was time.

If I ever needed an owl, it was now.

I drove north on Springfield Boulevard

toward my neighborhood, and it so happened, Henry's also. Since this was the main street for markets and shops, there was medium-to-heavy traffic this Saturday afternoon. Not usually an impatient driver, right now I couldn't wait to see how Maddie was faring.

Skip had been as forthcoming as he was going to be. It was neither surprising nor unusual that he'd gotten more from me than I'd gotten from him. After all, he was highly trained in investigative and interviewing techniques. I didn't know whether to be ashamed or proud of myself for getting away with the hotel key card.

I'd given Skip a watered-down version of Rosie's behavior of late, trying to make her out to be less a stalker than she was. It couldn't hurt to act as a character witness to balance out her miniature crime scene. I told him the truth about my temporary roommate, that I'd seen her leave David's doorway about ten thirty last night and then saw her again in her bed when I woke up this morning.

"If you could tell me the time of David's death . . . ?" I'd asked, to no avail.

Skip had brushed off the fact that David had been beaten, not poisoned. That his body hadn't been left in the old locker hallway, as might be indicated by Rosie's little amended scene. That there must have been many other people from David's current life with a better motive to kill him than one who hadn't seen him in thirty years. (How about Ben, that unhappy employee in the jumpsuit, for example? Or the son he hadn't seen in years.) That Rosie was one of the last people I'd expect to have the will or the strength to beat someone to death, especially a large man like David Bridges.

I wondered where the locker scene had been found, where Rosie was now, and where she had been between ten thirty last night and seven o'clock this morning. I couldn't be at all sure how long she'd been in bed when I woke up. She might have been fully dressed under the covers, having sailed in only a moment before.

I wished I knew where and when David was killed.

I wished all I had to think about was what fun it would be to see Henry Baker's woodworking.

I barely had my car in Park when Maddie ran up to me. She and Taylor, trailing behind her, were soaking wet. I caught a glimpse of the backyard swimming pool and marveled at her hearing, or some other sense that told her I was approaching the house.

"I'm sorry I skipped out like that, sweetheart," I told Maddie, bracing myself for a wet hug and a barrage of whining.

I got both.

"I know what you were doing, Grandma."

I tickled her bare midriff, always an effective distraction, then addressed Taylor. "So, what have you two been up to?"

Henry came out of the garage as the girls gave alternating reports of their hour and a half of fun. A little television, a little computer work, and more swimming.

I allowed myself to enter the world of Henry's workshop, physically and mentally, and forget the stress of the day. Thanks to Ken, I recognized a good-quality new band saw in the corner and an old table saw next to it.

Henry showed us a rocking chair he had just finished, a beautiful cherrywood creation with the longest, most graceful rockers I'd ever seen.

"It's in the style of Sam Maloof," he said, as if I might know who that was.

"I'm afraid I don't know much about life-size furniture," I said. "Ken knew every style of architecture backward and forward and he taught me a lot, but he wasn't interested when it came to interiors. And, as for me, I've always stuck to dollhouse-size furniture."

"I didn't mean to name-drop. The Maloof style's very well known in the circle of furniture designers. His work is in museums and in the White House." Henry pointed to a photograph of Jimmy Carter in a woodworking shop. "He had a lot of fans."

I stepped back to admire the chair again. "It's like a piece of sculpture," I said.

" 'Art at the service of utility' is Maloof's trademark. But you might relate better to these chairs." He steered me to another corner of the workshop, where about a dozen tiny rocking chairs were lined up. All standard sizes for room boxes and dollhouses, all in different wood tones, all beautiful.

My breath caught. I bent over the worktable, my arms folded lest I break something.

Henry picked up a chair that was an exact replica of the life-size Maloof rocker. He handed it to me. "They're not as delicate as they look."

I ran my hand across the curved piece on the top back of the chair — as smooth a finish as I'd ever felt, fabric store visits included. "How did you do this?"

I meant the question as rhetorical, but Henry answered. "It's a technique called 'bent lamination.' I cut thin, curved layers of wood using a band saw, and then laminate them back together."

He showed me a form that he used to bind them. The assembly resembled a wood sandwich, with the forms as the bread and the rocker as the meat.

"Which one do you like best?"

I picked up a dark mahogany-stained half-inch-scale chair. "They're all amazing, but I love the color of this one."

He took the chair from my hand and wrapped it in a piece of newspaper. "Take it, please."

I felt my face flush. "I couldn't. Maybe I can buy it —"

He shook his head. "I'd be very pleased to see it in one of your dollhouses."

Taylor, who'd been giving Maddie her own tour of the wonders in the garage, came up to us. "Grandpa's always giving things away," she said. "He says then he has an excuse to make more."

I understood that theory very well, but I'd never given away anything as beautiful as the rocking chair being offered me now.

Henry's grin was lopsided, in a charming way. "See? It's nothing really. I hand them out all the time."

"I don't get things like this all the time. Thank you very much."

I turned away. Someday I'd try to figure out why I found it so hard to accept gifts.

My gaze landed on a smaller workbench, filled with scraps and broken furniture. A chair missing its rungs, a table with only three legs, a lamp with a broken shade.

The collection took on the appearance of a trashed room. Or a trashed locker hallway. I remembered Rosie's plight.

The mood was broken. The life-size world called.

CHAPTER 6

It seemed wasteful to drive a two-car convoy back to San Francisco, but like most Californians we'd built our lives around having independent transportation. Maddie and I made another stop at home and then took off for the Duns Scotus about four o'clock. We set a time to meet Henry and Taylor in the lobby so we could go into the banquet room together and be seated together.

When we got to our room, I took out the key I'd borrowed — stolen? — from Skip's desk. I slid the key in the slot and waited for the green light. None. But in my experience with hotel key cards, they often didn't work the first time. It had to do with the speed with which they were inserted, I thought. I tried again. No green light.

I pulled out the key card I'd received at registration and worked hard to pull off a switch without alerting Maddie. My own key card worked, of course. Skip's key card must be for David's room. Or for one of the other five hundred rooms in the hotel, I realized.

"I know we talked about doing something fun," I told Maddie as we got resettled in our room. "But it's already kind of late. The banquet is at six and I have a couple of things I have to do. Would you mind waiting until tomorrow for a real San Francisco experience?" Not one in a hotel where a murder victim recently worked.

She put her hands on her narrow hips. "Are you going to investigate?"

Maddie gave every syllable its due, with equal emphasis. "Investigate" and its many inflections had become one of her favorite words, once she understood how exciting it could be to help her Uncle Skip.

"I'm going to . . . uh . . . check things out in case we have our next crafts fair here."

That was enough to provoke an outburst of giggles. "Here," she said. "Instead of the Lincoln Point high school multipurpose room, like every year since I was born." There was incredulity, but no question mark in her tone.

"Once, when you were about three, we had it in the city hall auditorium," I said.

She blew out a raspberry — something I hadn't seen from her since that time we had the crafts fair in the city hall.

Maddie let me go peacefully, saying she had a lot of computer work to do.

"Tell me about the project," I said, though I was eager to go on my mission to the eleventh floor.

"Oh, it's just gaming stuff. We're learning how to make GUIs. That's graphical user interfaces." She said these words with great ease and familiarity. Was it that long ago that Maddie had a hard time pronouncing "Abraham Lincoln"?

"How interesting."

"It's okay, you can go, Grandma. I need to TM a few people in the class, too."

I'd watched her nimble fingers all month, working the tiny pad on her cell phone, using abbreviations that were as new as the technology that spawned them. Besides the easily decipherable U8? I learned LSH-MBH (laughing so hard my belly hurts), ?4U (I have a question for you), 1DR (I wonder), and GGN (gotta go now).

It took me a while to figure out why <3 represented "heart," or "love," as in "I <3 U," until I realized that, looked at from a ninety-degree angle, the sequence was heart-shaped.

"Duh," as Maddie would say.

"Thanks, sweetheart," I said since she let me off the hook. "GNG."

"It's GGN, Grandma."

I could hear laughter as I closed the door, pulling it several times to be safe.

I got off on the eleventh floor and approached room eleven forty-three. The room was quite a distance from the elevator bank, down a long hallway, the carpet of which was a swirled pattern in shades of brown (dull, but, as even laypeople knew, the hallmark color of St. Francis). I passed the alcove that held the ice machine and a drink dispenser and another smaller nook with a table and a house phone. On the walls were many renderings of Duns Scotus and of St. Francis of Assisi himself, accompanied as always by birds and small wildlife.

I heard voices from several rooms as I all but tiptoed down the corridor. Otherwise, the hallway was quiet, the only sound that of a motor or generator doing I didn't know what. The very busy Union Square with its shops and restaurants, just outside the door, might as well have been miles away.

As I rounded a corner I saw yellow-and-black tape, denoting a crime scene or construction (who was I fooling) across what had to be David's room. I wondered if that meant he'd been murdered here in the hotel, or if the police were simply being thorough and checking where David spent his last night alive.

I closed the distance and stood in front of the door. I was surprised to see that the tape said simply *Caution,* not *Crime Scene.* Was it possible that the police hadn't released the fact that David was murdered? This was the wrong place to be standing to ask Skip, so I deferred calling him until later.

If my possessing the key at all was questionable, entering the room crossed the line, so to speak. On the other hand, there was no officer guarding the room. For all the police knew, every guest who passed the room went inside for a look. I fingered the key card in my pants pocket. Probably not many other guests had the key, however. I took the key card out and oriented it for use. The face of the middle ages looked up at me. Was that disapproval I caught in Duns Scotus's expression, or just the monk's meditative state, full of gravitas?

I slipped the card in the slot.

Green light.

My heart skipped. Should I be doing this?

The green light went out.

I'd waited too long.

Another decision point. I could still turn around, pick up a San Francisco T-shirt for Maddie in the gift shop, and have committed only one transgression. I could always say that the key card must have gotten knocked off Skip's desk and fallen into my pocket or my purse.

No one had entered or exited any room in the hallway since I arrived. There was no sign of housekeeping or maintenance personnel. I wouldn't have minded running into a maid to get her scoop on Ben of jumpsuit fame, but I knew it was a long shot at this hour.

On the floor directly across from David's room was a room service tray with a limp rose and two coffee mugs. A silver dome hid the remnants of what must have been late afternoon noshing.

I heard stirrings from the room service guests, as if they were about to leave. I had no choice now. I couldn't be caught loitering.

Better to be trespassing. I inserted the key card. I'm not "breaking," I told myself, just "entering."

Green light.

I pushed down on the heavy metal handle, ducked under the loosely draped yellow tape, and entered the room.

I realized I hadn't taken a breath in a while. I let out a long one. It dawned on me that the room might not be empty. Why hadn't I thought of that a minute ago? What if someone else had the same idea I had? Someone like David's killer.

I stood still in the dark entrance. The drapes were drawn across the large picture window. I noted again, as last night, that David's accommodations were significantly more elaborate than ours. I thought of Maddie six floors below, unsuspecting of the risks her grandmother was taking. I couldn't bear it if my actions were putting Maddie in danger. There could be a killer hiding in the closet of this suite, one who might go after my family after he finished me off.

I rocked back and forth, not moving my feet, turning my head in different directions, listening for signs of life. I sniffed the air for perfume or food smells.

Nothing.

I took a couple of steps, passing between the bathroom on the right and the closet on the left. If anyone were hiding, now would be the time he would jump out.

Nothing.

I wished I were anywhere but in David Bridges's suite, the possible scene of the crime. I sniffed the air again, this time for the smell of blood.

Nothing.

The entry led to a large sitting area with a round table and chairs, a sectional sofa, and a television set. A doorway next to the television stand opened into a bedroom with two king-size beds. The drapes and comforters were more colorful than those in my room, but still unmistakably hotel décor. The bedroom drapes were open and I wished I had the time, and the right, to reflect on the magnificent view, looking northwest toward the Golden Gate Bridge.

I walked around, careful not to touch anything. There was no sign of life. Or death. The room was stripped bare, even the usual coffeemaker and basket of expensive snacks gone from the dresser.

I'd done something foolish, and indeed for nothing. I needed to get out as inconspicuously as I'd gotten in.

As I headed for the door, I saw a quick flash. A stream of light coming through a small opening in the otherwise closed drapes had hit a bright object. I traced the line of the reflection and found the object in the narrow space between the carpet and the wall in the entryway. I bent down and picked it up: a tiny oval mirror, about a half-inch long, with a thin gold rim.

A layperson might think of the item as a bauble loosened from a piece of jewelry, or a bit of broken glass. A miniaturist would know it was a mirror from a dollhouse dressing table set. A miniaturist in my crafts group would recognize it as a mirror from Rosie's locker room.

I held the mirror by the gilt edges, between my thumb and index finger. It was impossible to see my reflection in the small area, but I knew my eyes looked weary, my face drawn, sad, and confused.

I dropped the mirror into the same pants pocket that held the key card. Did such a tiny article count as evidence? The police had obviously left it there. If a tree falls in the forest . . .

I almost laughed out loud. But another sound kept me in check.

A rattle! The doorknob was moving. Someone was trying to get in. Someone who also had the right key card?

I held my breath. I didn't dare walk the two steps to the door and check the peephole. I had no confidence that those things worked only one way.

Tap, tap. Not too loud. A woman's knock?

No one is here, I wanted to shout.

Another rattle, another knock, and he or she was gone.

I stepped to the door and looked out the peephole. This action unnerved me; I wouldn't have been surprised to see the nose of a gun pointed at me. Could a bullet penetrate a peephole lens? All was clear, however, except for the room service tray still in place across the hall, outside the door. No other person or thing filled the cone of view.

I wished the room were closer to the elevator so I could hear a ding that would tell me when or if the knocker had left the floor.

I waited until I couldn't stand it any longer. I opened the door a crack and looked up and down the corridor.

No sign of movement.

I slipped under the tape and walked as fast as I could toward the elevator. I kept my head high, my walk confident, as if I'd just exited a room that was legitimately mine.

In my pants pocket were a life-size key card and a miniature locker room mirror that made my face flush at the thought of them.

I came to the corner. One more lap to the bank of elevators. I felt more than saw another presence. A wave of fear came over me as I passed one door after another, staying as close to the center of the hallway as possible, lest I be easily dragged into a room on one side or the other.

I had only two more rooms to go when a door behind me opened and closed. I stepped up my pace. A tall hulk of a man passed me on the right, then turned, stood, and faced me, stopping me in my tracks. If he hadn't been so well groomed and dressed to the nines, I might have fainted, instead of just freezing in place.

"Did you find it?" he asked. His sharp dark suit spoke of wealth and power; his heavy whisper carried authority and threat.

My heart pounded; the tiny mirror in my pants pocket seemed to be rendering the fabric transparent so that my accoster could see its outline. "What — ?"

"I know you were in Bridges's room. Did you find it?"

My gaze followed his right arm down to where his hand was hidden in a bulging pocket.

"Excuse me," I said, moving to the left to pass him.

I knew he'd block my way. I thought this might give me an excuse to scream. He hadn't touched me, but I felt as though he had me in a choke hold.

"Look, I know you're from Callahan and Savage," he said. "Tell them we're looking for it, too."

Wonderful. I took a breath. It was simply a case of mistaken identity. I could clear this up in no time.

"I've never heard of them. You have me confused with someone else. I'm here with the reunion. The Abraham Lincoln —"

"Listen," he said, closing the already small gap between us. He gripped my arm.

I opened my mouth to scream.

Ding, ding.

The elevator doors opened and a crowd of teenagers came out. The group was loud and loaded down with packages and shopping bags. I was relieved when they headed in our direction, taking over the hallway with their different-size purchases. I looked at the red logo souvenir bags and translated the slogan to "I <3 SF." I was delirious.

When the kids started up a chorus of the song I nearly joined them. They sang out, "I Left My Heart in San Francisco."

The thought of my granddaughter and her <3 symbol gave me a burst of energy. I rushed past the hulking man to the elevators and slipped into the car with its doors still open to accommodate a straggler who had dropped her bundles. Frantic, I edged the teen away from the doorway, slammed in the CLOSE DOORS button, and pushed the button for the third floor. (I hadn't sat through James Bond movies with Richard and Ken for nothing — when being pursued, never choose your actual floor on the elevator panel.)

I got off at three, found the stairwell, and ran up two flights. I arrived breathless at the door to my fifth-floor room. I knocked, said, "It's Grandma," and searched for my key card, all at the same time.

Maddie opened the door, the ever-present white earbud wires around her neck.

"You're out of breath, Grandma." She laughed, as she always did before one of her own jokes. "Was someone chasing you?"

"Very funny, sweetheart. Let's get ready for dinner."

CHAPTER 7

I hoped dressing Maddie and myself for a banquet would take my mind off the near mugging (albeit by a designer-clad attacker) on the eleventh floor. The image of the man's threatening eyes stayed with me, however, as did the specter of his no-neck strength.

There was one thing I could do that might put the matter to rest.

When Maddie went into the bathroom, I pulled her laptop toward me. I was a Luddite in many ways, but I knew how to Google.

It took me a while to cut through Maddie's technology camp software and get to a clean, white Google page. I entered "Callahan and Savage" and pushed Google Search.

The first link on the list was for Callahan & Savage wholesale refrigeration equipment. After that, there were links that had

Callahan and/or Savage in the description but not together, such as "Mary Callahan wrote a savage attack on the latest novel by . . ." I didn't bother with those links. I'd learned a lot from Maddie.

I sat back. *Refrigeration equipment.* Why would a refrigeration company send me on a mission? Did I look like I needed more than one fridge? We'd considered buying an upright freezer for the garage in the days when Richard and his friends could put away several pounds of meat and a few loaves of bread in one sitting. But that was the extent of my involvement with refrigeration, other than keeping the freezer compartment cold enough for ice cream.

I felt a little better since my mission had nothing to do with wholesale or retail cooling and freezing. I was sure the hulk in fine clothing would find the Callahan and Savage representative he was so concerned about — somewhere else.

On the other hand, it nagged at me that he'd known I'd been in David's room. If David had recent (and contentious) business with the hulk or with Callahan and Savage, or both, maybe the police should know. If a company representative hoped to find something in David's room, after it was public knowledge that David was dead, maybe whatever he was looking for had something to do with that death.

On the other (third) hand, if one of them were the killer, why wouldn't he have just taken the item at the same time? Aha, I answered, because he killed David in Lincoln Point and the item was still in the Duns Scotus suite.

Too many possibilities. I made a mental note to seek Skip's input on the matter, in such a way that my trespassing wouldn't be part of the exchange.

I'd tried Rosie's cell and her shop phone off and on throughout the day and left messages but had no response. I looked over at her twin bed, still made up. The maid had folded Maddie's roll-away cot and pushed it against the wall. I had a feeling we wouldn't be needing it tonight.

We had a few minutes before our scheduled meeting with Henry and Taylor in the lobby. Maddie decided to check her e-mail once more, in case a boy named Doug had answered a question she had about something called "flash animation." She'd mentioned Doug a lot in the last weeks. He was her camp lab partner, she'd explained.

"You seem to like Doug," I said.

"Yeah, I like him because he gets my

jokes, but I don't *like* like him," she said.

Strangely, I knew what she meant. I wasn't sure I'd ever be ready for the day when "like" became "like like" and the chance of hurt and disappointment hung inevitably in the air.

I'd taken the opportunity during Maddie's shower for another look at the spiral-bound "yearbook" Rosie had produced for her reunion class. I hoped to be able to greet as many of my former students as possible by name, without looking at their badges.

Rosie had done an impressive job on the book, using fancy fonts and color graphics throughout. For each classmate, she'd juxtaposed a senior photo with a current one and added an updated biography, plus a space to "please share your funniest experience since high school."

I flipped through the pages, stopping to read about students who no longer lived in Lincoln Point, which was a considerable percentage. Many entries brought a smile of recognition. The unfortunately named Mathis Berg, "Math Bird" to the C students, had survived the nerdy label and now taught math at a college in San Diego. Billy Anderson, who was the shortest guy in the class and suffered accordingly, now operated a chain of health clubs. Fran Collins, voted Girl Most Likely to Succeed, ran a travel agency, her funniest experience being the European cruise she organized for single people and their pets.

I paused at David Bridges's page. Rosie had already told us most of what it contained, especially his management successes. David used his anecdote section to describe his first day on the job as hotel manager-on-duty. He'd had to deal with hundreds of geeks (his term) in alien costumes, at a science fiction convention. One night the geeks descended upon the hotel pool, all of them nude, and David had to round them up and send them home.

"Funniest thing I'll ever see in my life," David wrote. My eyes teared up at how true that was. He'd never see anything again.

Cheryl Carroll Mellace's page was lacking in much text, but included a half-page photo of her in an ALHS maroon-and-gold cheerleading outfit. She had married young, into the family of the locally famous Mellace Construction Company. The Mellaces lived on a villa-like estate on the outskirts of town. This wasn't Rosie's description of their residence, but my own interpretation of their home, which Ken and I had visited on a benefit tour. I'd never had the occasion to see the couple around town, and I imagined they did their shopping elsewhere.

I learned that the Mellaces had three children and that Cheryl had never worked outside the home but devoted a lot of time to charity. Besides the open houses for children's causes, they were active in all manner of good works, from organizing blood drives to paying for a bookmobile for shut-ins. There was something good to be found in everyone, I guessed.

It was hard to reconcile the two Cheryls, the one who shared her wealth so generously and the one who displayed low-class rudeness on the other. I looked at her photo again, arms waving pom-poms in exhilaration. I couldn't help turning her lovely smile of thirty years ago, one I'd seen often when she sat in my class, into the twisted face that ousted Rosie from David's doorstep last night.

Rosie's own page made no mention of her brief union with Ray Normano, a transient worker in the fields outside Lincoln Point whose principal method of communication was violence. The marriage was annulled, but she kept a shortened version of his name as her own. "I just want to keep some memory of him," she'd said at the time.

I didn't understand the logic of that decision, but now I saw it as a pattern of Rosie's

— to hold on to men who weren't good to her. I hoped no licensed therapist ever heard me offer my diagnoses of my family and friends.

"Hey," Maddie said, looking smashing in her new bright green pants and top. "What's Callahan and Savage? Are you Googling without me?"

I'd forgotten that what you did on a computer, stayed on the computer.

"Nothing important, sweetheart. Just satisfying my curiosity about something."

"And you didn't ask me to do it?"

She made it sound adulterous.

The mood was subdued in the banquet hall. The only light touch was the favor at each place: a hard rubber Abraham Lincoln pencil topper, about one and a half inches long. I turned the likeness over and over in my hands. Lincoln's signature black top hat sat on a bearded face, the whole affair cut off at the neck.

"You're trying to figure out where you can use this in a room box, aren't you?" Henry said.

He knew me well, already.

We'd started the evening with a moment of silence for David, during which the small band played a cheerless version of the class song. There was no word yet on the exact time and place for the memorial service, except that it would be in a few days, in Lincoln Point, where his parents still lived. President Barry Cannon had led the program and closed now with the hope that we'd all try to attend the service.

Once the banquet got under way our table was busy as Henry and I were flooded with compliments from our former students who stopped to visit. The ones who hadn't liked us stayed away, we decided.

"My mom still has that end table you helped me make," from Mark Forbes to Henry.

"I saved all my Steinbeck texts for my daughter who's an English major at UC Berkeley," from Catherine Jackson to me.

"I used to do my shop sketches in English class and read my crib notes for English in shop," from John Rawlings to both of us.

"That makes it all worthwhile," Henry said. I wondered if John caught the sarcasm, delivered so smoothly.

I looked in vain for Rosie. In case she changed her mind and came to the banquet, I didn't want her to be without company. Other than that, plus planning a call to Skip with a heads-up on Callahan and Savage, worrying about how to return the key card

I'd confiscated, wondering what to do with the miniature oval mirror, and questioning the motives of the hulk who accosted me in the hallway, I enjoyed the meal.

And deep down, I was grateful for the company of Henry and the girls.

"The only way to tolerate 'You Light Up My Life' is to dance to it," Henry said, offering his hand.

He was right. It had been a while since I'd danced with anyone other than the men in my family and Maddie. I pushed away any comparisons and went with the music.

On the dance floor I spotted Cheryl Mellace, in cream-colored chiffon that set off her chestnut hair, dancing with Barry Cannon. As they came close I noticed Cheryl was still wearing an eye patch, this one also seeming to blend in with her outfit. I'd heard of women who had dozens of pairs of shoes, but a wardrobe of matching eye patches seemed excessive. Where would one even shop for them?

We were back at the table in time for dessert, cheesecake with blueberries. I enjoyed the taste of the scrumptious, creamy wedge. Until a shadow crossed my plate.

I looked up to see the hallway hulk.

My throat went dry as he hovered over the table. Was he part of the reunion class?

He looked vaguely familiar, but I was certain he hadn't been my student. He wasn't wearing a name tag — maybe he'd crashed the party to find me. His thin smile did nothing to encourage me that I was safe. I surveyed the banquet room, about twelve tables with eight to ten people at each. Plus, there was a crew of waitpersons carrying heavy trays and coffee carafes, in case I needed a weapon.

The hulk had timed things perfectly, coming up to my chair while Henry was talking to the girls. "I'm sorry I strong-armed you that way in the hallway. Mrs. Porter, isn't it? Barry pointed you out. I'd had a little too much pre-banquet refreshment, if you know what I mean, and I thought you were someone else."

"Someone who found something in David Bridges's room?" I asked. A poorly phrased question, asked in a near whisper, but I was in a state of high anxiety.

He laughed, his expression changing from relatively sweet to bordering on sour. "It's not your problem, Mrs. Porter." He reverted to sweet again. "I don't even remember what I was babbling about in the hallway, but I'm definitely going to have to lay off the three-martini business meetings in the afternoon."

I should have felt relieved. My mugger was just a poor soul who had a bad habit and failing eyesight when he drank too much. I could put the whole incident to rest now. No harm done.

I wished I believed it more firmly.

Henry, who must have heard part of the conversation (or else had a sixth sense for questionable characters), stretched his arm across the table. "Henry Baker, retired ALHS shop teacher," he said, shaking hallway hulk's hand. "And you are?"

Good move, Henry. Why hadn't I thought of getting his name? I might need it for a police report.

"Walter Mellace," he said.

"Mellace Construction?" Henry asked.

"Cheryl Mellace's husband?" I asked.

"Guilty of both," he said.

And what else? I wondered.

I couldn't wait to get back to Google.

I did my best to pay attention for the rest of the evening at our table, my mind wandering off now and again to Cheryl's eye patch and wondering what she was doing in David's room if she was still married to Walter, who would always be the threatening hallway hulk to me. Had Walter found out where his wife spent the evening and used force to win her back?

No wonder the hulk had looked familiar. I'd never met him in person but he looked enough like the grainy newspaper photos I'd seen of him. I knew his interests extended far beyond our town and he wasn't one to be strolling around Lincoln Point eating Willie's bagels, or even greeting its citizens when he offered his home for a charity tour.

I hoped my immediate table partners weren't aware that my thoughts were elsewhere. I did pick up on an enjoyable thread that included the girls and their hobbies, plus teasing about their names.

"Imagine a name like Taylor," Henry said. "It's an occupation. And her parents are my daughter, Kay, and my son-in-law, Bill."

"And Madison is an avenue in Manhattan," I said. "Her parents are my son, Richard, and my daughter-in-law, Mary Lou."

"Maybe that's the problem," Maddie said. Taylor gave her an obliging smile and a thumbs-up.

Maddie had a new inventory of computer jokes, thanks to her e-mail correspondence with Doug. We limited her to one per twenty minutes, which she deemed unfair.

I almost hated to leave such pleasant company, but I had a couple more things to accomplish on what was probably my last night at the Duns Scotus. Unless the San Francisco Police Department, on the recommendation of the Lincoln Point Police Department, called me back for my expert advice.

As we broke up, Maddie gave us one more laugh. "What did the computer say as it was leaving the party?" she asked.

We shook our heads. "I'll bite," Henry, the good sport, said.

"Thanks for the memory," she answered.

We rolled our eyes and said good night.

As I'd anticipated, Maddie got to use what should have been Rosie's bed. On the writing desk was an unopened box of candy. I'd first noticed it this morning and assumed it was sent on Friday evening to Rosie by David or whoever might be pretending to be David. Like my Wednesday-night crafters, I'd had my doubts about the origin of the presents. After last night's episode, I no longer had doubts, but simply a question about who had sent the gifts.

Other than the candy, there was no sign that Rosie had been my roommate. On a whim, I picked up the box and turned it over. The sticker on the bottom identified it as sold at the hotel gift shop. I stuffed the box in my tote for further consideration.

I felt I'd let Rosie down. She'd counted on me to support her in her reunion with David. I wasn't sure what I could have done to make the weekend turn out differently, but I had that feeling nonetheless. I'd also been enjoying myself with Henry and the girls and former students who flattered me, while Rosie was probably depressed and frightened out of her mind somewhere. I wished I knew where.

I needed to get serious about this investigation and do better for my friend.

Friends, in fact, were the last thing Maddie talked about tonight.

Maddie always referred to Devyn, her classmate at her old school in Los Angeles, as her BFF, her "best friend forever."

"I think Taylor could be my BFF, too," she told me, her voice sleepy. "Do you think Henry could be yours?"

The light in the room was too dim for me to be able to tell from her expression whether she was serious, teasing, neutral, or talking in her sleep.

I thought back to Maddie's shorthand lesson and pulled out an appropriate response.

"GGN," I said.

■ ■ ■ ■

What a terrific grandmother I was. I waited until Maddie was asleep, then slipped out of the room. I wished I had something like the pink-and-white baby monitor I used when she was little. Once again I tugged on the door handle three times to be sure the door was locked, hoping that would count as "good grandmother."

I took the elevator to the lobby floor and walked through an elaborate junglelike area with a small tile footbridge across a stream that was generated by a waterfall. I hoped the system worked with recycled water in our drought-threatened state. On either side of the tile bridge were oversize houseplants and atrium-friendly trees. Large, leafy ficus and ferns lined the ends of the walkway and arched over the short stairway at the point nearest the front desk.

The registration desk had more clerks than customers at eleven o'clock on a Saturday night. I saw no sign that the hotel was any different for the loss of its chief engineer. In fact, many of the staff were gathered at the concierge's desk enjoying a laugh. In the group were several uniformed men whom we used to call bellboys and two or three others in the gray uniform I'd seen on Ben last night at the cocktail party.

It never seemed the right time and place to call Skip, but I needed to know what if any of the facts of David Bridges's death were known to the public. I moved to an alcove off the lobby, one that formerly held a bank of pay phones, and a place I had every right to occupy, so there'd be no hint of guilt in my voice. I leaned against the counter, took out my cell phone, and speed dialed Skip. It was late, but I reasoned that cops were always on the job, protecting and serving.

"Aunt Gerry," said my nephew with caller ID. (At least that told me he chose to speak to me.)

"I hope I didn't wake you, dear." I used my "remember all the times I baked you cookies" voice.

"No, no, dear. I was just going to call you and give you an update on all my cases, as I do for my other fellow sworn police officers."

"No need to be sarcastic."

"Where are you?" Skip asked.

My dime, as we used to say. My questions. "I need to know what you've released about David Bridges's death."

"Are you still at the hotel?"

None of the old rules seemed to work anymore. "Yes, I'm still at the Duns Scotus with the reunion class and it's very awkward not knowing how much information is public."

"Aren't all the festivities over?"

Good point. "There's breakfast tomorrow."

"Ha."

After years of teaching adolescents, and raising one, I had a large inventory of tones of voice. I now brought up the rhythm that was the equivalent of stamping my foot. "I need to know, Skip."

"Okay. I was going to call you first thing in the morning anyway. We've been holding off on releasing cause of death. I gave you that heads-up only because I thought Rosie Norman was with you at the groundbreaking."

"So everyone now knows that David was murdered?" I'd lowered my voice so much that I had to repeat the question to Skip.

"They will by morning. It'll be in all the papers, I'm assuming."

"And it's your case?"

"Mostly. We're now certain the crime scene was here in Lincoln Point, but Bridges worked in San Francisco and spent his last night there, and he lived in South San

133

Francisco, which is a whole other police department from SFPD. But yes, it's our case."

It sounded like a complicated problem of jurisdiction. I wasn't sure why it mattered, except that if Lincoln Point had no responsibility to investigate, it would be harder to obtain information I needed to help clear Rosie. Skip was right; when a good friend was suspected of murder, I did have a twisted notion that I was part of the LPPD, with the associated right to enter a taped-off area, for example.

"And Rosie?"

"You tell me."

"I have no idea, Skip. Honestly."

"I believe you, for some reason. I guess she's in the wind."

"That's bad, isn't it?"

"Let's just say the less cooperative she is, the more guilty she looks."

"I have things to share with you," I said, mentally trying to decide how much.

"Me, too."

"Really? Are you going to be in your office tomorrow?" I asked.

"Tomorrow's Sunday. In fact, it's almost tomorrow now."

"I'll find you," I said.

I hung up, wishing I were there now to

hear what it was Skip had to share. I was frustrated about my own lack of progress. I'd hoped to learn something I could take to Skip that would exonerate Rosie. I thought of the tiny, gold-rimmed mirror, which I'd hidden under my nightgown in the drawer upstairs. So far, all I had for my trouble was a piece of evidence that made it seem likely that Rosie had gone back to David's room later last night.

Not a good thing, but the night was young.

There was only one other person I knew would be up and ready to chat at this hour. I speed dialed my friend Linda Reed, who would be answering from the on-call nurse's nook at the Mary Todd Home, a high-end assisted-living facility.

"Gerry, it's been ages since I saw you. I had to miss crafts night last Wednesday because they called me in to substitute for someone here, and it's extra money, which you know I can't turn down since Jason has so many activities coming up his sophomore year."

I knew better than to interrupt Linda's flow too soon. She was by far the best crafter in the group, eschewing kits of any kind. She had the patience I didn't have. I'd been known to ruin a piece because I didn't wait long enough for glue or paint or a coat of varnish to dry. Linda, on the other hand, adopted the strategy of Abraham Lincoln: "Give me six hours to chop down a tree and I will spend the first four sharpening the axe."

Over the din of my own mind, I heard Linda still offering details of Jason's classes that I didn't need. Time to cut in. My mission was to find out how far and wide the news had spread in Lincoln Point, if there was talk of suspects, if she'd seen Rosie, or any other juicy bit Linda might know. With her years of experience at every medical facility in Lincoln Point, and her current position at the Mary Todd senior residence, Linda was an indispensable source of information and a font of gossip that nearly always proved to be true.

"I'm glad Jason is doing so well this summer, Linda," I said. "I'm still here in San Francisco at the ALHS reunion, by the way. You probably heard about the great tragedy, David Bridges's death. That's what I want to talk to you about."

Linda gasped. I pictured her eyes widening. "How did you know?" she asked.

"How did I know what?"

"Never mind," she said, but the pause was too long and her voice too high-pitched.

"Linda."

Linda was even more vulnerable than Skip was when it came to responding to my stern teacher voice. Only a few years younger than I was, she still afforded me a certain respect. I pictured her adjusting her beehive hairdo and nervously smoothing her uniform over her wide hips.

"That . . . that . . ."

"That what, Linda?"

I heard a deep exhale, then a whisper. "That Rosie Norman is here."

Sometimes, when investigating, you get more than you bargained for. If it weren't for Maddie sleeping peacefully upstairs, I'd have gone straight to the Duns Scotus garage and driven back to Lincoln Point.

CHAPTER 8

"Rosie Norman is at the Mary Todd?" I needed to hear it again to believe it.

Linda was a first-class resource, having intimate knowledge of everyone in Lincoln Point who needed medical care or had a relative who needed it. She was one of the least adventurous people I knew, however, and I never dreamed she'd harbor a fugitive.

"She's technically not hiding from the law," Linda said, as if I'd spoken out loud.

I felt I was hearing one of my own oft-given excuses to Skip, bending the truth, rationalizing, mentally reserving certain facts. Was I responsible for this personality change in Linda? Had I taught her the many uses of the word "technically"?

"The police need to talk to Rosie," I said, lowering my voice as two young men in cargo pants entered the alcove and headed for the restroom.

"I didn't know that. When she first came in, I had no idea why she was asking about our guest rooms. Her grandmother used to live here in the assisted living wing and we do offer that accommodation when relatives visit from a distance. Remember that time old Mr. Mooney's niece from Kentucky came to see him?"

"Kentucky is almost across the country, Linda. Rosie lives on Joshua Speed Lane in Lincoln Point. It's less than ten minutes to the Mary Todd. And her grandmother died two years ago."

"Rosie was desperate, Gerry. She told me she had to get away for a while because things went bad with David at the reunion. I knew how much she was looking forward to seeing him again." I heard a heavy sigh and pictured Linda's plus-size body being taxed with the effort. "Then I heard David was murdered, and I didn't know what to do. Technically —"

"Never mind technically. What else do you know about David's death? I haven't seen a South Bay paper or heard any news."

"He was hit on the head with his own football trophy." Though this wasn't news to me, Linda's words sent a shiver through my body. The nurse part of Linda took the facts further. "That external trauma would

139

likely have caused his brain to strike his skull and ultimately rupture blood vessels. The intracranial pressure would block the flow of oxygen —"

"Okay, Linda. I'm not sure I need that much detail. I heard he was found in Joshua Speed Woods?"

"Yeah, one of the EMTs I know was in the crew that went to the scene. He said not to spread it around, but David's lips —"

"Never mind, Linda. Will you please tell Rosie to call me on my cell?"

"I don't know. She said not to tell anyone she was here. She won't even call her father, and you know how close they are, like Frick and Frack."

Linda was right about their being close, though I wasn't clear on the reference to the comic ice skaters. Larry Esterman had raised Rosie, his only child, after her mother died.

I was about to bring out my commanding-officer voice but thought better of it. I didn't want to precipitate Rosie's leaving the Mary Todd, where she was at least safe, and force her to be "in the wind" as Skip called it.

"Fine, Linda. I'll keep the secret."

"Really?"

"Uh-huh. I'll let you know when I'm back in town."

I could hear a deep sigh of relief. "So otherwise, did you have a good time at the reunion?"

"It's been a blast," I said.

Finished with Linda for now, I walked back toward the front desk. I scoped out the late night staff and hung back until I could be served by a pimply young man who looked like a trainee. Chances were he was still under the influence of his mother or his teachers and I could exploit that.

I approached him and read his shiny new name badge. "Good evening, Aaron. I'd like to talk to a member of your maintenance staff," I said. I aimed my tone somewhere between authoritative and nurturing. "His first name is Ben and he was working last night."

Aaron's skinny neck seemed to roll around in the collar of his dress shirt. I was sure he looked better in a tank top. "Is there a problem?"

"Yes, I'm Mrs. Porter, in charge of the Abraham Lincoln High School event" — here I coughed to muffle the little white lie — "and I'd like to speak to Ben, if you don't mind."

"We have lots of people on duty all the time. The Duns Scotus is proud to have a full staff twenty-four-seven for your convenience. There's a carpenter, a locksmith, a plumber —"

Aaron looked over my shoulder as he recited the list. He might have been reading a teleprompter version of his employee orientation notes.

"The staff member I'd like to speak with is named Ben." I came close to spelling it for him. "He came into the ballroom during our cocktail party last night. That would have been somewhere around seven fifteen. I need to talk to him."

Aaron drew in his breath. "Ooh, that's tricky. Kind of on the cusp of the shift change." He straightened up, apparently remembering another part of the front desk employee handbook. "You know, you're supposed to call from your room if there's a problem with maintenance."

I let out an exasperated sigh, sending what I hoped would be a subliminal message: *don't disappoint your mother figure.* "Aaron," I said. "My granddaughter is asleep in our room, and I don't want to disturb her, which is why I came all the way down here in the first place." I paused for another well-placed sigh. "Our group has more than one hundred guests in your hotel and I'd really like to get this off my list of things to do

142

before I can call it a night."

Aaron cleared his throat; a low whistle escaped. He tapped his temple with a hotel pen. "Okay, let me see. I should be able to check for you."

Aaron left his station at the high, sleek, marble counter. I hoped it wasn't to consult his boss, or anyone else over eighteen. Fortunately, there was no one waiting behind me. This not only relieved me of some guilt, but also decreased the chances that my cover would be blown by the person who really was in charge of the ALHS reunion. The stresses of undercover work were enormous.

While Aaron was gone, I tried to put my mind in order. I had a few more things to take care of before checking out in the morning. Besides chatting with Ben, I needed to determine who had bought the chocolates for Rosie in the hotel gift shop. I also wanted to talk to whoever had delivered food to the room across the hall from David's. He or she might have seen or heard something unusual. Other than the outright rejection of two women on his doorstep.

I thought of Rosie and how frightened and upset she must be. I wondered how many other Alasita devotees had experiences so diametrically opposed to the dreams and miniatures they put their hearts into. Not many, I decided, or the tradition would have died long ago.

I was relieved to see Aaron come back to the counter alone and with a long printout. He spread the sheet in front of him. "Okay, looks like the Ben who was on duty at that time was Ben Dobson, and he actually quit this morning. Isn't that a coincidence?"

I doubted it. "Did you know Ben?"

Aaron shook his head; his collar didn't move. "Nuh-uh. When someone has a maintenance problem, like with the plumbing or the air-conditioning, we just enter a work order on the computer and they take it from there."

I tapped my fingers on the counter: very disappointed, said the gesture. "I really need to talk to another staff member, then. How about someone else on the maintenance staff? Or housekeeping. Or room service."

Aaron scratched his head. "Those are all different departments. This is a big hotel. Each department has its own supervisor and all. We have an IT person, licensed mechanics and electricians, the works. If you could just tell me the nature of your problem."

"And if you could just direct me to someone who was around last night. Should I be speaking to your supervisor?" I sincerely hoped not.

Aaron held up his hands. "No, no." I knew it — no trainee wants to admit he can't handle a simple request from an old woman. Not so old, especially in my banquet attire, but to anyone Aaron's age, I might as well have been an octogenarian, instead of closing in on sixty, from the young side.

"Well?" My challenge voice, spoken often to those students who were not working to their full potential.

"Okay, here's what I'm going to do," Aaron said, his fingers working the keyboard. Talking and clicking was the top-ranking multitasking scenario these days, I noted. "I'm going to call down to Maintenance and have them send up Mr. Conwell, one of our electricians, and you can have a chat with him right here in the lobby. Just wait right over there on that couch and I'll have him here in a few minutes."

I put my hands together, in prayer formation. "Thank you, Aaron. You've been a big help."

I kept my eye on the "waiting couch," a paisley U-shaped sectional, but walked over to the gift shop, which, as I suspected, was closed. I looked through the all-glass walls and door. For a shop in a major hotel, it seemed rather small, with only a shelf or two of T-shirts, plus some snacks, drinks, and magazines. One trip down to the nearby Market Street was all anyone needed, however. A multitude of vendors would be happy to sell a tourist not only souvenir T-shirts and baseball caps but also a shot glass with an image of the Golden Gate Bridge or a spoon rest with an imprint of the pagodas of San Francisco's Chinatown.

Small was good (wasn't it always?) since it was more likely that the shopkeeper would remember the customer who purchased the chocolates for Rosie. I noted the hours of operation for Sunday. Seven to seven. I'd have to come back in the morning, preferably without Maddie. I hoped the pool also opened early.

I spotted a short, weathered-looking man in a gray jumpsuit, a match to Ben's last night, lurking near the couch I'd been sent to and rushed over.

"Are you Mr. Conwell?" I asked him.

"Mike," he said, keeping his hands in his pockets. "What's the problem?"

Mike wasn't going to be the pushover Aaron was. Maybe it was the names. "Mike" had a strong ring to it, whereas I thought I remembered correctly that the biblical Aaron had made a few lapses in judgment and had to keep being forgiven by God.

"Hi, Mike. I'm Geraldine Porter. First, I want to express my condolences on the death of your boss, Mr. Bridges. It must be a great shock and a loss to you and the whole staff."

Mike looked at me sideways. I couldn't figure out whether he was chewing gum or working his jaw. "Yeah, a great loss. What's the problem?"

"As a matter of fact, I wanted to talk to Ben Dobson, but I understand he's quit his job. He came into our cocktail party last night and caused quite a disturbance, arguing with Mr. Bridges."

"Nothing we can do now," Mike said. He licked his lips. I caught a whiff of tobacco.

I struggled to maintain the composure I'd had while I was dealing with Aaron the novice. I tried the one-hand-on-hip signal. "How can I be sure no one else on your staff will do the same thing at our next gathering, Mike?" I paused, hoping Mike wouldn't ask when that would be. (In five years, unless you counted an ad hoc breakfast get-together tomorrow morning for anyone who hadn't already checked out.)

"Huh?" Mike asked, understandably confused. But Mike was the kind of guy who led you to believe that any confusion on his part was your fault, due to your inadequacy, not his.

I weakened in the face of his confidence, and my voice faltered. "I just thought maybe Ben had a particular grievance with Mr. Bridges?"

"Lady, are you a cop? You asking me, did Ben have a reason to kill Bridges? You look too old for a cop, but you're asking cop questions."

I wondered what Skip would say about that. Not that I planned to ask him. I didn't care much for the observation that I looked too old for a cop, either, but I couldn't let it distract me. "You mean the police have already asked you about this?"

Mike shook his head and turned to leave. "I think we're done, lady."

I considered threatening to complain about his attitude on the "How was your stay?" survey card in my room.

I threw my shoulders back. "I am not a cop, but I know cops, and I thought it would be better to get some answers from Ben before I call my friends on the force." Talk about flailing around. It was all due to Mike's ill-tempered attitude. I resolved to be more appreciative of the friendly electricians of Lincoln Point.

Mike stepped toward me and leaned in

close. "Look, lady, friend of cops, or whatever. I'm an electrician and I got work to do. You got a fuse blown, I'll replace it. Your lamp don't work, I'll fix it. Anything else, you're on your own."

Mike tromped back to wherever Duns Scotus maintenance people lived, and I headed for the elevator. I walked down the short flight of stairs that was part of the pathway through the jungle. I'd learned nothing and been put in my place by an electrician with tobacco breath. I was through with the lobby for the night.

But the lobby wasn't through with me.

Halfway down the row of potted ferns and ficus, a figure jumped out from the mini-woods and landed in front of me. This was becoming a Duns Scotus pattern. Before I could react, the person, a man I was sure, knocked me into a large planter, grabbed my purse from my shoulder, and ran down the path, off to the left, where there was a stairway to the parking garage.

"Stop," I called out, as I tried to right myself. I was so startled it took me a moment to react. I thought I heard something comic book–like, "Help, help, police!" but I couldn't be sure the words made it out of my mouth.

In a flash, he and my purse were across

the bridge and through the stairwell door. I struggled to my feet and followed, screaming (I thought) all the way, at a disadvantage with my dress heels instead of tennis shoes, which I'd have bet the thief was wearing. Besides that, my left side hurt where my hip and thigh scraped against the ceramic pot.

Was every Duns Scotus guest asleep? Where was its staff? Where were all those men in red who were eager to help get your bags to your room and collect their tips? Couldn't Aaron at least hear me from the desk or Mike from his maintenance post? Apparently I was on my own, as Mike had decreed.

I ran down one long flight to the garage, which was full of cars of all types, smelling of fuel of all grades. The man who assaulted me was nowhere in sight. The garage had a hollow sound as my footsteps echoed. I expected at any minute to hear dramatic music and see the muzzle of a gun.

I wanted to be out of there before that happened. I had no business chasing a robber anyway. I should be grateful that he wasn't interested in injuring me any more than he had. I went back up the stairs, my body smarting in new places. I made my way back down the tile path toward the front desk, where I planned to report the incident, once I caught my breath.

I mentally cataloged everything that was in my purse. The only good news was that I'd been carrying my dressy evening bag and had left my thick wallet with most of my cash, my driver's license, and all my credit cards in the room. I was ready to relegate the matter to the "no great loss" category. The sorry bandit was about to be treated to a lipstick, a fold-up hairbrush, a package of tissues, and about fifteen dollars in bills.

And the key card to my room.

I felt a wave of nausea. The room where Maddie was sleeping. The key cards didn't have numbers on them, but it was possible that this was not a random pilferer, that the thief knew which room I was in, and he was headed to it right now. He simply had to board the elevator at the parking level and go up to five.

I looked in panic at the bank of elevators, about thirty feet away to my left, and at the front desk about the same distance on the right. Counting time for waiting and the trip to the fifth floor, my best bet was the desk.

I pushed my way in front of a family of travelers who were at the counter. (Where were they when I needed them?) "Sorry, this is an emergency," I said, out of breath.

"My purse was just stolen, and I'm worried that the thief will head for my room." Everyone cleared out of my way, and I supposed by now, after sprinting down and up a flight of stairs and across a bridge through a jungle, with a tear in my pants, I looked like the kind of woman you'd make way for.

I faced Aaron, the only one on duty now. I felt like the lady who cried wolf. If Mike had by any chance reported on my real reason for wanting to talk to maintenance, there was no way Aaron was going to believe this story.

I plunged in anyway.

"Aaron, did you hear me? Someone just knocked me over and took my purse. I'm in five sixty-eight. Can you send someone from security up there right now? I'll meet him there."

Aaron shuffled some papers on the lower level of the registration desk. "I'll have to fill out a report."

I looked at Aaron, this time with true urgency. "Please," I said. "My little granddaughter is in that room and I think someone may be breaking in right now."

The man of the family group, who had no reason to doubt me, spoke up. "You know you can just have him change the code from here and then the guy won't be able to get in." I shot Aaron a questioning look. "Unless he's already in the room," the man added.

Not comforting.

Aaron picked up a phone and punched in a number. "But that means Mrs. Porter won't be able to get in either, so if the guy is already in . . ."

"Aaron!" I heard my voice reach an eight on the Richter scale.

"I'm sending someone up there immediately," he said.

"Thank you, thank you." I turned and darted back toward the elevators.

"Don't you think you should wait here for security?" Aaron called out.

No, I did not.

The fifth floor was quiet, except for my clomping down the hallway toward room five sixty-eight. Hotel security must have had its own elevator since, much to Aaron's credit, a tall, husky man wearing a dark jacket with a patch on his sleeve approached my room from the other end of the corridor. Indistinct radio chatter echoed down the hallway. I pictured guests being awakened from sleep, making their way to the peephole to see what was causing the commotion.

We arrived at the door at the same time.

153

"Thank you so much for coming. Please open the door. Please." I heard my voice crack, all composure abandoned.

"Stand back," the man said. He didn't draw a gun, and a closer look at his face, with lines of maturity around his eyes, told me he was probably a retired policeman. He was fit enough to take care of himself, I hoped. And Maddie, too.

He inserted his keycard, a passkey I assumed, into the slot and pushed open the door. Against his wise advice, I slipped past him. I'd left the desk lamp on so I saw Maddie immediately, snuggled in her bed. I went over to be sure she was breathing. Then I took a breath myself.

Meanwhile, the security man — I needed to learn his name, to thank him for his speedy response — checked the bathroom and the closet, behind the heavy drapes, and even used his extra-long flashlight (which could double as a weapon, I noticed) to look under the beds.

"All clear," he said.

"Thank you . . . ?"

"They call me Big Blue," he said, smiling and extending his hand.

"Now I'm sure you were a cop," I said.

I slept only fitfully, though Big Blue had

promised that the entry code for the room had already been changed and said he'd come around often during the night to be sure all was well. Still, I shoved the desk chair under the door handle, hoping to get to it before Maddie woke up and saw it. I didn't need to worry her. About every hour I thought I heard the doorknob rattle and reached for the phone, only to determine that it had been a dream, or the door to the next room, or a noise from outside. Or nothing at all.

Big Blue had given me the choice of going downstairs to file an incident report tonight, thus leaving Maddie again, or waiting until morning. I chose not to leave my grand-daughter this time, even though he himself offered to stay with her.

Maddie had awakened briefly and accepted the explanation that I'd stepped out of the room for a minute and forgotten my key, so the nice man from the hotel let me in. She'd dropped back on her pillow and seemed to be off to sleep in a minute.

I wondered how many years before she wouldn't be able to do that.

It wasn't hard to talk Maddie into one last hour at the pool with Taylor before we checked out. So far I'd been able to shield her from the events of last night and I planned to keep it that way.

The interview with hotel security was brief and relatively useless. As luck (for the thief) would have it, not all the lights in the garage were working last night. Thus, the security camera had only the fuzziest image of someone exiting the stairwell and running across the garage floor within a half hour on each side of the time I specified. Other than that, no one could say what had happened to the robber.

By the time I'd repeated my story three times, to different personnel, none of whom were SFPD, my purse had been located in a trash can outside the exit door from the garage. The shiny beads on the black silk purse, put there myself in a fit of macro-crafting one day, had caught the eye of a hotel custodian.

The purse was empty. I imagined the thief, tossing my lipstick and sundries aside, frustrated when he found little cash and no credit cards. The other option was too hard to accept: that all he'd wanted in the first place was the key to my room. And that one of those middle-of-the-night rattles was not a dream.

CHAPTER 9

Knowing that I'd left Maddie at the pool for a supervised kids' water ballet class with her BFF temporarily set my mind at ease.

"Most of your body is in the water," Taylor had explained to Maddie, and then Maddie to me. "It's mostly just kicking your legs up and flopping your arms around, in tune with some music," Taylor assured me, as if I were the one who needed to be talked into it.

With not a lot of time to waste before checking out, I headed for the hotel gift shop. Walking through the quiet lobby, I had an uneasy feeling, which wasn't surprising after last night's ordeal. Again, I wondered where everyone was. I thought San Francisco was one of the most visited cities in the country. Not this weekend.

I bypassed the tile bridge that ran through the faux jungle and took the longer route, through a seating area for the hotel's coffee shop, called Friars Minor. Only low-level plants lined this wide-open area. No place for someone to hide. Or jump out from.

I approached the gift shop, hoping that an Aaron-like person had the early morning shift. It bode well for the success of my mission that there were no other customers at this hour.

I knew as soon as I entered the shop that getting what I wanted from the bored-looking young woman filing her nails behind the counter would require only a small percent of my talents. I imagined her sitting at the back of a classroom, tapping her desk, longing for something interesting to come her way. I'd seen the likes of her many times over.

From my tote, I pulled out the unopened box of chocolates and the updated "yearbook" Rosie had produced. "Hey," I said. "I wonder if you can help me with some romantic detective work I'm doing."

She looked up from her nails (that was a start) and raised her eyebrows. "What's up?" she said, sounding like Skip and the rest of the twenty-to-thirty crowd.

"Well, I got this nice box of chocolates from your shop" — I placed the box on the counter — "and I think it's from an old flame." I flashed a coy grin. "But, you know,

I'm going to be really embarrassed if I have the wrong guy." I flopped the spiral-bound yearbook over the box and tapped the cover. "His picture would be in here."

"Yeah?" she said, brightening. "When did you get the candy?"

I wasn't sure, but I knew the box hadn't been in the room when we checked in. I couldn't remember if it was there after the cocktail party. I was sure Maddie would remember, however, and wished I'd asked her when it first appeared. But then, it was never possible to ask my granddaughter a question without giving her the background she'd insist on.

"Sometime late Friday evening," I said, which I felt was as good a guess as any. "I just opened my door and there it was. There was a message on a card, but no name." I tried to fake a blush.

"Mmm," she said, rubbing her palms together. The young woman had rings on every finger except her ring fingers. A wide silver thumb ring with a large turquoise stone was especially eye-catching. "I was here from four to midnight on Friday. I have to do inventory after we close. You're lucky because, you know, the guys that work here . . ." She whooshed her hand over her head to indicate how clueless her male colleagues were. "Who do you think it is?"

I'd already stuck a piece of hotel notepaper in page thirty-six, toward the back of the book, where the faculty photos were laid out. A random choice. I opened the book to the spot and pointed, again at random, to Joel Mullins, who'd taught history at ALHS during the eighties. As far as I knew, Joel and his wife were happily married and traveling the world together. "I think it might be Joel," I said.

She held up the book for a better view and shook her head. "Nuh-uh. I've never seen this guy."

Good sign. She'd passed the "trick question" test.

A young couple in nearly matching sweats came through the door. I was worried that their presence would end our research session, but my new BFF, the clerk with spiffy nails, handled their transaction quickly, telling me, "Don't go away, okay?"

She was mine.

As soon as the couple exited with newspapers and trail mix, the ringed clerk rushed over to me. "Let's start from the beginning," she said. She held out her hand. "I'm Samantha."

"Mary Lou," I said. Maddie's mother's name was the first to come to my lips once

I made the quick decision not to use my own. Just in case my real name was on a hotel watch list somewhere, or Skip was monitoring my activity.

Samantha, whose morning I was salvaging, I knew, took the book from me and opened it on her lap. Apparently her "Let's start from the beginning" meant not only a name exchange but going to page one of the yearbook.

She flipped pages, uttering sounds like "nuh-uh" and "mmpft" now and then, while I stewed and hoped no one I knew came into the shop. I imagined Henry Baker coming in with "Good morning, Gerry." Which reminded me — Maddie and I were due to meet him and Taylor for brunch at ten when the girls had finished swimming.

"Bingo," Samantha said.

I came to the present. "You found him?"

"Yup. Here he is. I remember because he was carrying this big trophy, like for football or basketball or something. And I stored it in back here for him while he looked around and made up his mind." She folded her arms and stepped back to admire her work. "Yup, it's him."

I was glad she didn't feel it necessary to point out the age difference between me and my Romeo, found early in the reunion class pages. On second thought, as with Aaron, we probably all looked the same vintage to Samantha. I was glad it wasn't someone whose name began with Z; the shop couldn't stay empty too much longer.

I turned the book around to see whom she'd fingered.

"Barry Cannon," she read, as I was processing the photograph and caption. "Wow. He was senior class president."

I gulped. "So it was Barry?"

"What? Is he married or something?"

I shook my head no, though I wasn't positive. I closed the yearbook before she could verify his marital status.

"Sweet, huh? He's cute. Did you guys date back then or something?" Samantha asked.

I couldn't disappoint her. "Yes, it was a long time ago. I had no idea he still cared after all these years."

"So maybe you'll get back together now? Woo-hoo!"

"Thanks a lot, Samantha," I said, packing up to leave. "You really helped a lot."

"You made my day," she said, in a convincing tone.

"I'm glad."

I'd reached the threshold between the shop and the lobby when I heard Samantha's voice again. "Hey, Mary Lou?" I almost blew my cover by not responding. "Go for it, okay?" she said.

I planned to.

I took a seat in a cozy corner in the lobby. I sat on a wide easy chair with my back to the tile bridge, the boulder, and most of the jungle area with their unpleasant associations. I needed to review everything I knew and try to make sense of it.

I had about a half hour before I should pick up Maddie and get ready to meet Henry and Taylor for brunch. I took out my small notepad and pen. I knew that most of my notes would be mere doodles as my brain worked over bits of information, but the physicality of the writing and scribbling helped me focus in situations like this.

I decided going backward would be the easiest process. I called up the image: Barry Cannon with a sports trophy, buying candy for Rosie and delivering it in David's name. I thought it was a safe bet to believe Samantha, who had passed too many other tests to have made an error identifying Barry. And if nothing else, I had a sense that she was very good with people and faces.

First task: find out if Barry had ever won a sports trophy of his own (I doubted it) or if he'd been carrying David's trophy, the murder weapon, into the shop. For now, I'd have to assume those two options were the only ones. I couldn't remember whether there had been a trophy on the stage at the ALHS groundbreaking ceremony. Barry himself was small-framed, not an athlete, unless it was at a sport that got less attention at ALHS than the big three of football, basketball, and baseball.

At the very least, Barry seemed guilty of overseeing the delivery of the presents to Rosie, leading her to think David was courting her, with or without David's knowledge. It was a slim motive, but a motive nonetheless, to think that David found out what Barry was up to and a fight ensued. *Slim,* I repeated to myself, but not zero.

I found Barry's page in the yearbook to see what he'd been up to since his well-written Dickens paper. I did a quick read of the text and saw no mention of participation in sports. I moved on to Training and Education — it seemed Barry was a CPA. He now worked as the chief financial officer in the accounting office of Mellace Construction Company.

Small world, and not just for miniaturists. I filed the information under "what a coincidence" and moved on.

More accurately, I moved back, to my conversation with Skip, who had claimed to have more to share eventually. I had a sinking feeling that whatever it was, it wasn't good news for Rosie. I had to decide whether to add to his arsenal by producing the tiny locker mirror I'd found in David's room after the murder.

If I were a trained interrogator, as he was, I'd skirt around how I found the mirror and get him to tell me how and where he located the vandalized version of the miniature locker room Rosie had built.

I tried to weave in the loose ends — a disgruntled (based on one interaction) employee who quit the morning David's body was found; Walter Mellace wanting something from David's room. For a moment I considered that it might have been Walter who stole my purse, thinking I had that "something" he'd hassled me about on the eleventh-floor hallway, in my purse (could the something be that small?) or in my room. Given Walter's heft, however, I guessed I'd still be unconscious in the Duns Scotus jungle if he'd been the one to bump into me on the bridge.

I had Callahan and Savage to fit into the scheme also. The only connection I could put my finger on was that both they and

Walter Mellace were in professions associated with buildings. I thought of my crafts rooms. So was I, you could say.

Another loose end fluttered to the front of my mind, demanding attention. I remembered what Rosie had told me when we woke up in adjacent beds on Saturday morning. She'd come in at two, she said, after a workout at the hotel's fitness center.

This one was easy. I didn't even need Aaron or his equivalent. I went to the concierge's desk and picked up a hotel brochure from a pile in the corner. I ran my finger down the list of amenities and hours of availability. Room service was offered twenty-four hours; same-day service laundry pickup was before seven in the morning; the fitness center — my heart sank — closed at midnight.

If I were the police, one lie would be enough to discredit Rosie completely. But I was her friend; I had to give her the benefit of the doubt in spite of the trashed locker room, the tiny mirror in David's suite, and the failed alibi.

The concierge came back to his desk and I made one last stab at rescuing my faith in Rosie. "Is this brochure up-to-date?" I asked him.

Young enough to be Aaron's twin, he

scratched his stylishly bald head. "Yeah, pretty much. Something in particular you're interested in?"

"What time does the fitness center close?"

"Midnight."

A sigh escaped. "Thanks."

"That do it for you?"

"I'm afraid so."

I was in dire need of someone to talk to. That person had always been Ken's younger sister Beverly, Skip's mother. Now that she was "going steady" with a retired cop friend of Skip's, I saw her less and hesitated to bother her.

"Nothing has to change," she'd told me. "I'm always here for you."

True theoretically, and I thought Beverly believed it, but in fact, much had changed. No more late-night tea klatches, no more last-minute taking care of Maddie. This weekend, for example, when she would have been an enormous help to me, she was in Seattle with Nick's family.

What hadn't changed was that we were a close family and wanted the best for each other. I had pangs of guilt over my selfish thoughts and was glad she wasn't aware of them. I knew that if I really needed her and told her so straight out, Beverly would be at my side in a minute.

It was hard to ask for more.

The Duns Scotus brunch buffet was as lavish as any I'd ever seen outside of pictures of Victorian-era banquets. A beautiful table was spread with breads and fruit; at a separate station a chef made omelets to order; at another station one could be served slices from an enormous leg of lamb, roast pork, or a side (it seemed) of beef. As Ken would say at a feast like this, "Many a man would call it a meal."

"Wow," said Taylor and Maddie almost in unison as they saw the oversize éclairs. Taylor's blond pixie cut was wet, as Maddie's red curls were, from a quick after-swimming shower. The girls sent sprays of water drops onto their shoulders in their excitement.

The éclairs and other pastries could each feed a family of four. I made a note to leave room for a dessert or two and therefore skipped the carnivores' table in favor of a mushroom-and-cheese omelet. Calorie for calorie, there probably wasn't a lot of difference.

"Isn't it funny?" Taylor asked Maddie. "Your grandma and my grandpa only live a few blocks away from each other in Lincoln

Point, but we're all hanging out in San Francisco."

The thought had crossed my mind, too.

"Why did the witch need a computer?" Maddie asked, out of context.

"You'll have to tell us," Henry said.

Taylor and Maddie burst out laughing.

"We planned it," Taylor said. "We're not going to tell you the answer until next week."

"When we have lunch together in Lincoln Point," Maddie said.

Henry and I glanced at each other across the table, both seeming to catch on to the ploy — the two girls plotting to get together. I worried about Maddie's becoming too attached to Taylor when she had just a few weeks before she'd be leaving Lincoln Point. Would this be another wrenching separation, like when she had to leave Devyn and her other friends in Los Angeles?

It was only ten miles to Maddie's home in Palo Alto, I reminded myself. We could have playdates. Not the same as being in the same school and joining clubs and teams together, but we'd make it work.

There were many fewer reunion people here than at the banquet. I imagined many had been anxious to get home and get ready for the workweek. A couple of students we

169

hadn't seen yet came over to chat, but otherwise there were no new incidents. No one fighting, no one jumping out of bushes. Still, I kept my everyday shoulder purse on my lap instead of hanging it from the back of the chair as I usually would.

"It's a real shame about David. I keep thinking about him," Henry said, during one of the girls' trips to look at the dessert table. "And poor Rosie, caught up in it all."

"What have you heard about Rosie?" I said, jumping past sympathy to detective mode.

"I called my daughter, Taylor's mother, this morning to give her our timetable and apparently it's all anyone's talking about in Lincoln Point. Way more than yesterday. She says she heard that the police want to talk to Rosie and she's nowhere to be found."

"I don't think for a minute that she's guilty," I said, skipping over the part that I knew where to find her.

"I'm sure you're right. I used to do business with her father, Larry Esterman, when he had his own place in town. At the time, all of us trades teachers used to get together and pool resources and network with the Lincoln Point tradesmen. Larry was always ready to take on a promising student as an intern and I placed a lot of kids with him. Most honest guy around."

My experience complemented Henry's. I'd had many dealings with Larry during Rosie's high school years. He was as dedicated a single parent as I'd ever met. I now saw him occasionally in the bookshop, though we never had extended conversations.

"I don't remember exactly what business Larry was in," I told Henry. "He's retired now, isn't he?"

"Refrigeration," Henry said.

I gulped. "Refrigeration?"

"Uh-huh, good-size company, too. But he retired and now he works off and on for Callahan and Savage."

"You don't say."

For a minute I reverted to Maddie-land and wondered, how many refrigerators does it take to cool a town?

Back in our room, packing to leave, I had a brainstorm. With Maddie distracted by last-minute computer work (a drag-and-drop interface, she called it), I went into the bathroom. I pulled all of the tissues from the box on the sink and unrolled a long strip of toilet paper. Together they made a wad I hoped was big enough to stop a toilet.

Then I threw the wad into the bowl and flushed.

I was surprised that I got it on one try. The water rose to the rim and stayed there.

Oops. Time to call a plumber.

"We're about to check out," I told the woman who took my call. "But we still need to . . . you know."

"Oh, of course. I'll send someone right up."

When the knock came less than five minutes later (something for the plus column on the Duns Scotus evaluation card), Maddie went to answer it. She knew enough to ask who it was and check for my approval first.

"He says he's a plumber," she called back.

"It's okay, sweetheart. I forgot to tell you the toilet is plugged up."

Maddie opened the door. I was relieved to see that Mike the electrician didn't double as a plumber. Rather, a gentle-looking Enrico introduced himself and entered the room with a large toolbox.

"Thanks for coming," I said. "This just happened a few minutes ago." I left out, "by my own hand."

Enrico looked at the mess and produced an industrial-size plunger and a gallon of something apparently toxic enough to require a skull and crossbones on its container.

I suspected it wasn't often that Enrico's clients stood over his shoulder while he worked. "Such a shame, losing your boss yesterday," I said. The concerned guest.

"Yes, yes, it's a shame, very sad. A young man, Mr. Bridges."

"I'm surprised at your quick response to my little problem this morning, since I also heard that someone quit yesterday?"

"Yes, yes, Ben, he walk out with no notice."

"Was he a plumber, too?"

"No, Ben was what you call a supervisor."

I laughed. "I'll bet he didn't work as hard as you do."

I tried not to pay too much attention to the details of Enrico's recovery program at our toilet, but I noticed that he never turned to me, nor did he lose his work rhythm as he talked.

"I wonder if Ben and Mr. Bridges got along. I guess that's not unusual, though. For a boss and an employee to have disagreements." No comment from Enrico. "You're such a good worker, I'll bet you get along with everyone."

"I mind my business, you know? But Ben, he's what you call ambitious."

"Ah," I said, with a small tsking sound. "And Mr. Bridges didn't like that?"

"I mind my business," Enrico said again. "All done here." I had the feeling he was referring to more than the plumbing.

Thwarted.

It made sense that the electricians and plumbers of the Duns Scotus wouldn't share company politics with guests. Too bad for me they all took their training to heart.

Enrico stood up and did a test flush. All went smoothly. Next time I'd have to create a bigger problem. All I'd gotten from this little exercise was news of Ben Dobson's ambitious streak and his position as supervisor.

Enrico packed up his tools and glanced back at Maddie, still deep in the computer zone. "Gotta watch these kids, huh?"

I smiled and threw up my hands. "What are you going to do?"

I didn't tell Maddie she'd been blamed for a problem she knew nothing about.

"You didn't get to see my apartment building that Grandpa made me when you were in the shop last time, Mrs. Porter. You should come by and see it."

That was Taylor, trying to prolong her departure from Maddie as we piled our two cars with duffels and garment bags.

I couldn't believe we'd spent the better part of a weekend in San Francisco without seeing any of the sights outside the hotel. No Golden Gate Park, no Coit Tower, no Ghirardelli sundae, no ferry to the redwoods of Marin. Not even a cable car ride to the bay. Checking into things here and there, though not all that productive, had eaten up all the time I'd had in between reunion events. Not to mention having my personal space violated a couple of times.

I needed a new hobby.

Maddie took a turn at securing the four-way friendship. "My grandma has lots of crafts rooms, Mr. Baker. You should see the furniture she has."

"We get it," I said.

"And we like it," Henry added.

I felt a twinge of pleasure. Because Henry might be able to help me figure out connections between Mellace Construction and the Callahan and Savage refrigeration business.

That was the only reason.

CHAPTER 10

We left the San Francisco skyline and the clanging cable cars behind and drove home to Lincoln Point, Maddie now happily old enough and heavy enough to sit in the front passenger seat and not relegated to the second-class, as she thought of it, backseat. My pangs of guilt intensified as the wharf and Ferry Building, along with Ghirardelli's earthquake sundae receded. I resolved to take Maddie back for a fun-only weekend.

"I'm ready for an update," Maddie said, her posture erect, eyes straight ahead.

"What's that, sweetheart?" As if I hadn't heard her.

She twisted to face me. "C'mon, Grandma. Do you think I don't know why I was dropped in the water so many times?"

"You make it sound brutal. Like child abuse. I thought you liked the hotel pool. Wasn't Taylor with you a lot of the time?"

"Yeah. But she's a little young and I didn't

want to talk to her too much about the case."

"Isn't she the same age as you?"

Maddie grinned. "I'm four months older. I did most of the case stuff on my own."

My granddaughter made a criminal investigation sound like child's play, like making miniature furniture or wallpapering dollhouse rooms. "What kind of case stuff did you do?" I asked her, gritting my teeth. Images of her parents scolding me loomed before me.

"The *Lincolnite* is lame," Maddie said, referring to our once-weekly newspaper. "They don't even have their own website. They're just online with a whole lot of other small newspapers so you only get a summary, not full stories, and you don't get to see any archives. But I read a little about the case. I know the man's body was found in the woods out past the high school, and he was beaten."

I didn't like hearing crime scene words from my granddaughter. I felt irresponsible that I didn't monitor her computer use more carefully. Or at all. That I didn't know a lot about how to do that was no excuse. Standing over her shoulder, instead of wandering around as if I had a PI license, would work.

"What else?" I prodded. At least I could find out after the fact what she already knew before being pressured to dole out bits of information of my own.

"Mostly, I worked on the computer while you were out snooping at night."

"I was in the ballroom, dancing."

Maddie coughed, pretending to be choking on that tidbit. "And drinking at the bar, too, right?"

We were in stop-and-go traffic on the 101, giving me a second to glance over at her. "You got me."

"I found out all kinds of things about Callahan and Savage. The stories were in the big newspapers so you could actually read the articles online."

I'd planned to search through Google again for more information on Callahan and Savage, and to talk to Henry about them, but as expected, those who were born into the electronic age worked much more quickly.

There were worse sites that Maddie could have been browsing, I guessed, than the San Francisco and greater Bay Area newspapers. If Richard or Mary Lou looked back on Maddie's history, I hoped it wouldn't be obvious that their daughter had been searching for information on a murder case. I imagined having my grandparent visiting rights revoked until Maddie turned thirty.

"Did you find anything interesting?" I asked.

"Lots. Like, did you know that construction companies compete with each other for contracts to do buildings and stuff? I found a list of the contests, which ones they won and lost and who beat them."

I couldn't imagine more interesting reading outside of a Great Books class. "Did you save the information?"

Out of the corner of my eye, I saw a vigorous nod. "I'm going to give it to Uncle Skip when he takes me on the tour of the police department after we get home."

I checked to see if Maddie, the great negotiator, had her teasing grin on. Sort of.

"I'd like to see the list," I said. "And I'm the one who's going to get you home in the first place." I could negotiate, too.

"And?"

"And get us pizza for dinner."

"And?"

I wondered who taught her these skills.

"And if you cooperate, I won't send you back to Palo Alto early before computer camp is over."

"Technology camp. Okay, I'll show you. I was going to anyway."

I knew that.

I was still waffling about whether to talk to Linda and take a look at the Callahan and Savage data before seeing Skip. I came close to letting Maddie extract a promise to take her with me so that she could have her tour of the police station, but I was saved by a phone call.

"I'm home," Beverly said. "We took a really early flight this morning. I'm exhausted, so I'm just sitting here getting reentered." I pictured her with her long legs stretched out on the lounge chair by her pool, a glass of ice tea in her hand, a luxury she allowed herself only after a string of stressful days.

"How did everything go?" A silly question when asked of funeral services, but somehow obligatory.

"It went as well as it could have. You know, everyone was sad. Old Saint Nick, that's what they called Nick's grandfather, was ninety-seven years old."

"That's a lot of life to celebrate."

Beverly and I knew each other so well that we were able to cover a lot of ground in a few minutes, from the family gathering in Seattle to the tragic death of David Bridges in Lincoln Point.

"Nick, my Nick, that is, was so glad I was with him, Gerry, but I'm sorry I couldn't be here to take Maddie, especially after what happened."

"You can make it up to me right away," I said.

"It's hot in here, isn't it?" I asked Maddie once she'd had a snack. I was too full from brunch to think about another bite, but Maddie had apparently worked off her three desserts in the car on the way home. "Too bad the air conditioner isn't working."

"I'm going to Aunt Beverly's pool, aren't I?"

Such a bright child.

Only time with her Aunt Beverly could bring on such good spirits from Maddie when she knew she was being left out of the loop on an interesting project. (I hesitated to say "case" lest it seem, even to myself, that I was doing unsolicited police work.)

Once Beverly and Maddie went off together, I called Linda.

"Rosie's still here," she said. I could almost see her wringing the starched collar of her white uniform or twisting the ends of her hair. That seemed to me the only purpose of the long, stiff coils she arranged below the beehive on top of her head. "It's pretty tense, Gerry."

"I'm coming over," I said.

I couldn't take the chance that Rosie would go somewhere out of reach. Or that Linda would have a crisis of conscience and — dare I say it? — do the right thing and turn Rosie in before I got to talk to them.

I changed into hot-weather clothing and drove the short distance north of my neighborhood to the Mary Todd Home. I was very familiar with the residence facility, having taught seniors crafts classes there since it opened a few years ago.

I entered the ornate front lobby (too rococo for Lincoln Point, was architect Ken's judgment), greeted Olara and Tim at the front desk, and asked for Linda. I knew where the guest wing was, where relatives of residents could stay for short periods, but preferred not to attract attention by walking back there myself.

Linda came to greet me in the lobby. With her level of nervousness over these relatively low-stakes circumstances (no global nuclear implications, that is), she'd never graduate from spy school.

"Gerry, let's go have a chat. Just the two of us," she said, her forced, louder-than-necessary communication causing raised eyebrows at the desk.

"You're inviting suspicion, Linda," I said, in a whisper that probably also did.

I had to admit I was no better than Linda at an undercover operation. Anyone listening would have wondered what we were up to. Fortunately the two at the front desk had gone back to paying more attention to each other than anything happening in the lobby.

Rosie had aged ten years. She was dressed in a nurse's uniform, presumably Linda's, a bad fit even though she and Linda were both on the chubby side. She'd exchanged her dressy black patent sandals for blue paper booties. The cocktail dress she'd worn on Friday night lay folded on a chair. I wasn't proud of the fact that I wished I could surreptitiously check it for blood-stains.

A side table held several plastic containers that I was sure were from Linda's cupboard. I was glad Rosie didn't have to count on the vending machines for her nutrition.

The guest room itself was cheerless, only a cut above descriptions I'd read of thirteenth-century monks' cells, minus a cross over the bed. Instead, a stern Mary

Todd Lincoln, her hair tightly braided, looked down on the twin bed outfitted with white-only linens. There was a small bath and shower off the room, probably more than the medieval nuns and priests could say, but my guess was that the administrators of the home didn't want the nonpaying guests to get too comfortable.

Linda had done her best, it was clear, to house, feed, and clothe her friend, but she could do nothing about the depression that caused Rosie's face to sag, her eyes to be rimmed with red.

When Rosie saw me she gasped, then rushed to embrace me and cried softly. I let her stay as long as she needed to. She smelled of stale makeup. When she relaxed a bit, she said, "Someone killed David, Gerry."

Only then did I realize I hadn't seen Rosie since David's body was discovered. We'd left the Duns Scotus in separate cars on Saturday morning — me for the ALHS groundbreaking ceremony, Rosie for . . . here, apparently.

I found myself questioning the timeline. What was the time of death for David? What time did Rosie arrive at the Mary Todd? Could Rosie's case be so easily resolved — that she was still in San Francisco when he was killed? Nice thought, but I was sure Skip had checked that out. More important, why in the world was I giving any credence to the possibility that Rosie was guilty of murder? I was falling into the bad habit homicide detectives had of gathering evidence and alibis before making a decision on a suspect.

I needed all the information I could get, just to keep even with my nephew.

"What else do you know about David's murder, Rosie?" I asked.

Rosie pushed herself away from me. I barely kept my balance. "I didn't do it. How can you think such a thing?" Her voice was a hoarse whisper, a sad croak. "You know how I felt about him."

"I only meant, what other news have you heard?" realizing too late that my question sounded like an accusation. You'd think a former English teacher would be more careful with words.

I chose not to remind her that great love was often the source of a crime of passion. And I did think that bludgeoning a man to death with his own trophy eminently qualified as a crime of passion and, if I weren't such a highly moral person, as an example of poetic justice.

■ ■ ■ ■

A pitcher of Linda's special mix of ice tea and lemonade brought us a measure of refreshment. Just as we settled down to talk, Linda was called to a patient, which suited me very well. It saved me the trouble of finding a diplomatic way to get rid of Rosie's protector and sole support.

"Let's start from the beginning, Rosie," I said, in the most comforting tone in my repertoire. "What did you do after you left David's doorway?"

"I went down to the —"

"And please don't tell me you stayed at the fitness center till two in the morning. They closed at midnight." Not so comforting a tone, but I didn't have a lot of time to waste. The police might be screaming down the street toward us with an arrest warrant, sirens blazing, right now. Or was that my vivid imagination after two nights on a busy street in San Francisco? And those sirens more likely came from fire engines, anyway.

"I'm so embarrassed to tell you, Gerry."

We sat across from each other on uncomfortable straight-back chairs, making it easier for me to remain firm. "It won't be as embarrassing as being carted off to jail, believe me."

"You're right." Rosie took a long swallow of her lemony tea drink; I did the same. She worked the corner of a tissue around her eyes. I didn't want to tell her it was a hopeless gesture if she meant to fix her makeup.

"Take your time," I said, willing her to hurry. The small quarters were already beginning to close in on me. I wondered how Rosie had stood the cell-like room for a day and a half.

"I rode down to the lobby. I was going to go out, but I had on those uncomfortable heels and I wasn't crazy about walking around the city alone. I'm sure it was safe, but I didn't want to risk it. And anyway I wanted to see David. I went upstairs to eleven again and listened at David's door. I could hear David and Cheryl. Not what they were saying or doing exactly, but I knew they were still together." Another long swallow. "I figured since Cheryl had come to the reunion with her husband, sooner or later she'd have to leave and go back to her own room."

I could believe that marriage to Walter Mellace would be a strong motivation to at least appear to be a faithful wife. Thinking of Cheryl's eye patch — which might have come from a visit to her ophthalmologist, I realized — I wondered again if Mrs. Mellace had failed to pass the fidelity test.

Rosie had come to a halt, her eyes tearing up again. I tried to ignore it. Empathy would get us nowhere. I prodded. "And then?"

"Okay, you know where the ice and the vending machines are in the little alcove by the elevators?"

"You hid there?"

Full-out tears now as Rosie nodded. "I wanted to wait until Cheryl left. I had the thought that if I showed David the locker room, it might, you know, soften him and make him remember our first kiss and all."

"You came into the room while Maddie and I were sleeping?"

She nodded and dabbed her face again. "Uh-huh. I forgot to tell you, I stopped in our room first. The room box was right on the corner of the dresser near the door, so I just slipped in and got it. I knew you wouldn't have chained the door and locked me out."

I had a hard time processing that Rosie had come and gone while we were sound asleep, but she had no reason to lie about that.

"Then?" I prodded.

"I went to the eleventh floor. It was almost

one in the morning. I was so stupid, Gerry. My legs were cramped and every time someone came for ice, for real I had to pretend I was getting some ice myself, or a soda, or tossing a bag of trash. I hid the room box behind the big drink machine. One guy must have come in three times while I was there. Who knows what he thought. And Barry Cannon came in. He was in the room right across the hall from David's. He . . . oh, never mind what he said."

"Rosie, I'm so sorry you had to go through all this."

"I thought, you know, maybe the reunion had reawakened feelings in David, and if I had a chance to talk to him alone and show him the lockers . . ." She shook her head, as if trying to get rid of silly dreams. "I can't believe I was such a fool."

"It's not going to do any good to think that way, Rosie. We need to go on and cover the rest of your night."

"Here's the worst part." *Uh-oh.* Did I want to hear this? "Cheryl came out for ice, right when I'd taken the room box out from its hiding place, to make sure it hadn't gotten too dirty behind those machines. She was wearing a robe, one of those thick white hotel robes. I didn't want to think about why. She laughed her head off, Gerry. She knew right away why I was there. I've never been so embarrassed in my life. She called me pitiful, and she was right."

Once again, I couldn't disagree, so I simply uttered a sound between a cough and a grunt.

Rosie wasn't finished reliving the traumatic episode. "Cheryl grabbed the room box from my hands. Roughly, Gerry. She started to pull at the pieces, but you know how carefully I attach everything. She was getting frustrated and finally she was strong enough to deflate that football I made out of leather."

Linda came back with another pitcher of ice tea and lemonade, just in time to hear Rosie finish her story.

"I was so mad I hauled off and hit her in the face with my purse. I didn't even care that the scene fell to the floor."

Linda stopped in her tracks. "I guess I missed a lot."

An eye patch zoomed into focus on the white wall of the Mary Todd guest room. "Did you injure her?"

"She was bleeding, from her forehead, I think. I guess the heavy rhinestone buckle on my purse caught her in the wrong place. She started to scream, but we couldn't exactly yell at each other in the middle of the night in the hotel hallway. She just whispered something very crude and ran back to David's room."

"And you?"

"I waited . . . not long . . . and finally decided it was no use. The great David Bridges didn't care about me thirty years ago, and he never would."

"The room box?"

"I just picked it up and took it back to our room. Some things were broken, but I didn't care."

Rosie seemed to collapse on the straight-back chair, as if she had just entered room five sixty-eight at the Duns Scotus and flopped on the bed next to me.

Was this the point where an LPPD interrogator would apply further pressure, taking advantage of her exhausted state?

I had question after question on the tip of my tongue. If she never entered David's room, how did she explain the presence of the tiny oval mirror from the door of the locker? And what was the meaning of the trashed room box? Although Skip hadn't told me where or how the police had found the piece, I knew the ugly changes — the graffiti and the bottle of poison — were certainly made by the hand of a miniaturist.

I could simply ask Rosie where she thought the scene was now, but my mind was in a spin trying to figure out what to settle first.

I was eager to know if Rosie was aware that it had been Barry Cannon who sent her the chocolates, and probably all of the other presents, and not David. If so, did that make her angry? How angry?

A cop would know the right order to pursue these questions.

"Rosie, you need to talk to the police," I said, not for the first time since I'd entered the room.

"I can't," she said.

"Why not?"

"I can't tell you."

Here's where I should deny the suspect water or a chance to visit the bathroom. I looked at my friend, ragged and vulnerable, and threw back my shoulders.

"Let's take a break," I said. "Have some more ice tea, Rosie."

When Maddie's call came in on my cell phone, I was alone in the tiny bedroom. Rosie was in the bathroom; Linda was back on the floor, as she termed it, with patients.

"Where are you, Grandma?" Maddie asked.

"I —"

"No, wait. Let me guess. You're doing er-r-r-rrands."

I smiled at the way she stretched out the word, rolling the *r*'s as if she were practicing a romance language. I couldn't deny my overuse of the word, whenever I was looking into matters I thought too risky for Maddie's involvement.

"Are you having a good time with Aunt Beverly?"

"Uh-huh. And with Uncle Nick."

Nice for all. I was just getting used to Nick's being part of the family. Beverly had met him in her work as a civilian volunteer for the LPPD and they now seemed to be inseparable. She'd been a widow much longer than I had, since Skip was only eleven years old. On days when I wasn't completely selfish, I was happy for her.

"And Uncle Skip is here," Maddie said.

Not so nice. I had a reaction similar to the one I'd have if I were cruising down the 101 and saw the black-and-white California Highway Patrol car in my rearview mirror, even if I wasn't exceeding sixty-five miles an hour.

"How's the pool?" I asked Maddie.

Maddie laughed. "No stalling around, Grandma. Uncle Skip wants to talk to you."

The odds seemed stacked against me. My

Nancy Drew granddaughter, my homicide detective nephew, and retired homicide detective Nick Marcus were all at the other end of the phone line. Not a line, exactly, since it was cell phone to cell phone. Maybe an electric wave of some kind.

In any case, this time I was speeding.

CHAPTER 11

In the approximately ten seconds it took for Skip to assume control of the phone at Beverly's house, I ran through my options for truth or consequences. What if he asked whether I knew where Rosie was? How could I get around that? I could use his technique and ask another question. I could —

"Is Rosie Norman with you?" Skip asked, without prelude.

I swallowed hard. Then, aha! I heard water running in the bathroom, behind a closed door. "No," I said, with the ease of the just.

"If you find her, will you advise her to come in immediately?"

"Of course," I said with great confidence. No lies so far. If he'd phrased his question as "Do you know where she is?" I'd have been stuck. I couldn't believe my luck. And it was my turn. "Is Rosie a fugitive from justice?"

195

"Technically, no."

Whew. I was home free. "When can I talk to you?"

"Besides right now on the phone?"

"Yes." (Because the water had stopped running and technically, I would be *with* Rosie in about one minute.)

"I'll meet you at my office in ten," he said.

"How about twenty? And, Skip, can you leave —"

"Without the redheaded squirt."

"You mean the other redheaded squirt."

I was glad we were a close family.

I knew the LPPD would be looking to make an arrest soon, partly to give David's family some comfort as the time for his memorial approached. The sooner Rosie talked to them, the better.

My strategy with Rosie hadn't worked so far; I had to try a new tack that I hoped wouldn't upset Linda even more than she was already. Maddie's term "freaked out" came to mind, and I had to say, though I admired and taught proper English, that some of my granddaughter's current favorite expressions had more impact than the classics.

"Rosie, you know Linda's job is on the line here, if not worse." I didn't mention that I was prepared to take the full blame, telling whoever needed to know that I'd forced Linda into this position, on threat of . . . something. I'd work it out.

As I feared, Linda gasped. She had a habit in times like this of grabbing the front of her uniform, already stretched across her full bosom, as if she were having a heart attack. Before she lost her composure completely, I told her that I had it on good authority that, technically, she was not harboring a fugitive.

"But you might be one soon, Rosie. The longer you put this off, the more guilty you look. I'm going downtown to talk to Skip, to clear the way for you, but you have to promise me that you'll go to the station and talk to him before the day is over."

Rosie nodded, her sad eyes drooping.

"Now, I have only a few minutes to clear up some things." I dug in my tote and fished out the tiny mirror, which I'd wrapped in tissue, having thought of preserving fingerprints only after it was too late. "No beating around the bush, Rosie. I found this in David's room on Saturday afternoon."

Rosie took the mirror between her thumb and index finger. Neither she nor Linda asked what I'd been doing in the murdered man's hotel suite. Apparently my friends took my investigative privileges for granted. Rosie peered closely at the mirror. The shiny gold edge seemed to blink on and off as it caught the late afternoon sun, now directly, now through a waving tree branch. She squinted, missing her magnifier, I was sure. I had one in my tote but decided against offering it to her. Either Rosie knew where the mirror had come from or she didn't. It didn't take close scrutiny for her to figure it out.

Rosie looked confused. "It looks like one from the set I used in my room box, for the locker doors. But I swear I don't know how this mirror got in David's room, Gerry. I was never in there, just at the doorway, with you."

And lurking in the hallway, I added, but not out loud. "You did take the scene to the hallway while you were waiting, though."

"I told you, I thought it might take him back to high school, to those old hallway lockers, in a good way. Remember I told you how it was in front of the lockers when he kissed me and asked me out that one time? But, I never got to show it to him on Friday night." She looked at the mirror again, as if in wonder. "The only time I actually laid eyes on David that night I was with you. Where would I have put the room box then? I had that tiny evening purse."

"With a big buckle," Linda said, reminding us she was there, with a slightly wrong-time, wrong-place joke. She cupped her hand over her mouth. Linda couldn't know how relieved I was that she wasn't still gasping in terror over the possibility of being arrested herself for her Good Samaritan gesture.

"One more thing, Rosie." I took my time describing how the scene was trashed. I wrote out the words in the air between us: *I hate David.* I could tell from Rosie's expression that she herself was the vandal. "Remember, no skirting the truth," I reminded her.

"I trashed it. I was so angry, Gerry. I was in our room after you and Maddie left on Saturday morning. I'd shoved it in a drawer the night before. It was already broken in a lot of places. Everything was loose. I started to put the scene back into its carrier while I was packing up and I went nuts. I shaved a point on my lipstick and used it to write that graffiti and then I had this thought of making a bottle of poison. That part calmed me down in a strange way."

It was not a pretty sight — Rosie madly writing her hate message on the miniature lockers, then, with great concentration, gathering materials from hotel supplies and fashioning the tiny bottle.

"Then you — what? — threw it away?" I was still trying to figure out how the police got hold of it. Rosie blew her nose and nodded at the same time. "I was on my way out and I started to feel so angry again. I just shoved it in the wastebasket in the room. Who needed it? I'm surprised it survived at all."

"Good glue comes through again, huh?" I said, wondering at what point the police got hold of it.

A brief, thin, but welcome smile crept over Rosie's face at my glue comment.

Linda kept extra clothes in her locker at the Mary Todd, a storage place much more elegant than the rusted old gray ones that ALHS provided its students. Rosie was invited to borrow any of Linda's pants and shirts, and she started to clean herself up. The easiest logistics would have been for Rosie to show up at the police station soon after I'd had a chance to talk to Skip.

"If you leave here an hour after I do, that should do it," I said.

"Don't let me go alone, Gerry," Rosie said, reminding me of her plea before heading for David's fictitious private party. "I'm not sure I'd be able to get there."

This time I held firm. I needed to reclaim my family life and spend some time with Maddie and Beverly. (Oh, and Nick.)

"I'd rather not come all the way back here to get you. It might be good if you drive your own car to the station," I said, thinking, It's the grown-up thing to do.

Rosie didn't look happy about that arrangement but before she could speak, Linda rescued her. "I'll take her," she said.

Usually moody and often disgruntled, Linda came through big-time when anyone appeared ill or needing help. I learned that firsthand when she dropped all extraneous life tasks and helped me care for Ken during the last weeks of his life.

I gave Linda a smile that she probably thought was for only her present kindnesses.

I had one more question for Rosie, a speciously easy one. "I've been meaning to ask you about your dad," I said. "How's he taking this?"

"I haven't talked to him. Isn't that awful. But he never liked David back then because of, you know, the date."

"The date gone bad." I had no idea exactly what had gone wrong but now was not the time to ask.

Rosie took a seat on the bed. She had a

pair of Linda's elastic waist pants in her hands. If she tried to hang her head any lower, she'd have swept the floor with her hair. "Uh-huh."

"Your dad still works, I understand. For Callahan and Savage?" Just evaluating Henry Baker as a possible future source of information.

"He consults for them, mostly. He prepares bids, things like that."

"Why are you asking about him now?" Linda asked. I knew she meant "on my time."

I patted Rosie's head. "I'm just trying to get Rosie back to normal and remind her that many people love her."

Not bad for a quick cover story.

Linda walked me to the front door, leaving Rosie to finish dressing in her clothes. Once we entered the main wing of the home, we ran into a few people I knew, mostly seniors who were enrolled in my crafts classes. We got away with a quick wave at Emma and Lizzie, veritable twins they were such close friends, and one of the best woodworkers I'd ever met, Mr. Mooney.

Seeing the old man in his trim cardigan reminded me of Henry, my newest woodworker friend. I found myself planning a way to initiate another visit to his shop. So that I could see the apartment complex he'd built for his granddaughter, and so that Maddie and Taylor could play together. There was also that unresolved computer joke begun at brunch this morning in San Francisco: why did the witch need a computer? I was eager for the punch line.

Those were the only reasons I could think of for contacting Henry Baker.

"I have news from the front," Linda said, sounding like a war correspondent from the forties. "I was chatting around while I was on the floor and found out the memorial service for David will be next Saturday at St. Bridget's. Kind of funny, huh? I mean Bridges and Bridget?" Linda's nervous laugh trailed off for lack of company. "What is it with me today, Gerry? You know me, I never make this kind of joke."

"We're all a little off this weekend," I said.

"But there's more," Linda said. "His classmates have decided to have a memorial service tomorrow morning so people who came from a distance would have a chance to participate. They won't have the . . . uh . . . deceased, of course, but his friends will be able to say good-bye. The announcement made the local news."

"It sounds like something not to be

missed."

Linda put her hand on my shoulder to slow me down to her walking pace. "I'm not through. I heard that the Mellaces — really Cheryl, because Walter didn't go to ALHS — are paying for everything."

"Nice of them."

"Plus they're making a second donation to the new athletic field for a special plaque with David's name."

Linda had truly become the eyes and ears of the world.

"They already had a little program for David at the banquet and special mention of him at the groundbreaking," I told her.

She shrugged. "I guess when you're a VIP in the class, you get as much attention when you're dead as when you were alive." Linda's hand went to her mouth to stifle another shaky laugh. "Sorry," she said.

I patted her shoulder. "Rosie will be out of here soon," I promised.

Skip wasted no time getting the upper hand at our meeting. He slid a multipage printout across the newly polished table. The police building had only a skeleton crew on Sunday afternoon, so we appropriated the conference room for our tête-à-tête. Not that it was much more attractive than Skip's cubicle. The no-frills space, with room for about eight people around the table, had the same muddy colors on its walls as the cubicles' partitions. The big luxury was that the room had four walls and a door, and a working air-conditioning unit. Skip had also managed to have cans of ice tea available. Not as good as Linda's concoction, but refreshing nonetheless.

"What's this?" I asked him, though the headings on the sheets said it all. *RFPs. Bidders Awards.* Names like Mellace Construction and Callahan and Savage Refrigeration stuck out as if they'd been written in a crafter's glittery marker or puff paint.

"A little something Maddie showed me. She doesn't know what connection this all has to the Bridges case, and neither do I. It's just a little something she printed out."

I couldn't believe Maddie had . . . what . . . flipped on me? Gone over my head? There must be a popular term for what she'd done. Engaged in a little passive-aggressive attention getting? Gotten even with me for dumping her yet again at a pool, this time at Beverly's?

Given up on me and gotten her hooks into her uncle was probably a good-enough description.

I didn't know the connection of this

information to David's murder any more than Maddie or Skip did, but the links I did know made me uneasy. In my mind I saw a straight, incriminating line leading to lockup, with yours truly on the wrong side of the bars.

I now realized what Maddie had done: my Internet search for Callahan and Savage was what had alerted her to my interest in them, and she'd probed further. Maybe this was what could be called hacking?

The rest of the thread was unsettling. Working backward: my Internet search had been sparked by Walter Mellace's near assault and outright accusation in the hallway, that I was representing Callahan and Savage when I was snooping around the late David Bridges's suite.

And said snooping had been a direct result of my pilfering of the Duns Scotus key card from Skip's desk yesterday.

If I answered the Google search question for Skip, it was a slippery slope back to a very bad decision on my part, in the office down the hall.

I took a long drink from my can of ice tea, aware of Skip's gaze boring down on me. Technically (I was beginning to like that word), he hadn't asked me a question and I didn't have to talk.

I wished I'd had a chance to look at Maddie's data before now, but what was done was done. I wondered if I were strong enough to reduce the size of Maddie's ice cream portion as an incentive never to do something like this again.

As usual, Skip won the silence contest. I cleared my throat and answered a nonquestion. "I think there was some competition between Callahan and Savage and the Mellace Construction Company, and I was checking it out."

"What's the connection with Bridges? Because I know you wouldn't have been looking into this unless there was one."

"You don't think I might just have been browsing, getting familiar with the World Wide Web?"

Skip rolled his eyes. "Can't we do this the easy way for once?"

I took a breath. The easy way for Skip was the hard way for me. "Let's look at the printout," I said.

"I guess the answer is no, we're not taking the easy route."

"Bear with me," I said, not knowing what that meant, other than a major stall tactic.

The printout had a list of recent contract awards for major facilities, including several hotels and office buildings in San Francisco and in the East Bay. I scanned page after page titled Request For Proposals, with the project name, such as a remodel or an equipment overhaul. The forms gave the names of the primary companies bidding for the job, a reference to what the companies had offered by way of promised work and expected compensation, and a score for each company. The winning contractors and the dates of the awards were also indicated.

"I did a quick review of these RFPs," Skip said. "All of these are for works completed. Nothing newer than last spring."

"Where did Maddie get these?" I wondered aloud.

"I'm guessing she went into the building commission's site. Some of this has to be public information."

"She's a whiz, isn't she?"

"Yeah, I'm glad I'm not dealing with her right now."

I gave him an I'm-offended look. No need to prolong that topic, however.

Skip had highlighted the Duns Scotus jobs in yellow. Some were small, for repairs and remodeling, others were large, like a complete overhaul of the hotel's several dining facilities.

I scanned the information on the highlighted jobs. "It looks like Mellace has received all the contracts for the Duns Scotus in the last five years, including all the refrigeration contracts that Callahan and Savage bid on."

"Right. We don't know that these were all the projects, however."

"But even so, Callahan and Savage bid lower on the ones we have here and they still didn't get the contracts," I said. "I thought the low bidder always won."

"Not necessarily. First, not all corporations have the requirement for competitive bidding. Second, even if they do, the winning award has to do with the reputation of the company, the timeline, the staffing, what side benefits they're offering. A lot of things."

"Which is what these scores are all about." I may not have been a whiz, but I could be a fast learner.

"There's a cycle for this kind of thing. Sometimes RFPs go out to third parties, like brokers. The broker will solicit proposals from companies, then sift through all the applicants and try to match the needs of the buyer with the needs of the seller."

My head was dizzy. I wished I'd paid more attention when Ken talked about this part of his business. Not that he was a builder or an expert at trades himself, but as an architect he'd dealt with this network of people and forms over the years.

It seemed that lately I'd been paying the consequences of inattention to things that would turn out to be useful. Like Rosie's ramblings during crafts night and Ken's humble opinions on contracts and subcontracts and sub-subcontracts.

This printout said one thing — either Mellace was the absolute best contractor around, especially for the Duns Scotus, or the Duns Scotus would have no other. It was as fishy as the grading procedures of some ALHS teachers I knew during my career.

"Who decides all this?"

"Good question," Skip said. "Might not hurt to find out."

And I had a good idea where to start. With Walter Mellace, if anyone could get to him. And with Rosie Norman, the daughter of a Callahan and Savage employee, if she would just show up.

It was almost an hour since I'd left the Mary Todd. I expected Skip to get a call from the duty cop downstairs any minute, telling him one Rosie Norman wanted to see him.

The phone in the conference room rang

at that moment.

Good timing, except I could tell from Skip's end of the conversation that it wasn't a Rosie alert.

"Okay, I guess I know where I stand," Skip said in a light tone. "Do I have to serve them ice tea?"

A soft laugh and Skip hung up.

"We have to move," he said.

"I'm not through with you," I said.

"Back at you. Can you wait for me in my office? It seems some bigwigs want the conference room. I'll clean this up and be right there."

"No problem."

In truth, it had been my greatest wish to be alone in Skip's office. Even as I walked past the empty cubicles I reached into my tote and pulled out the key card to David Bridges's room. I fingered it all the way down the row of offices, my heart racing in time with my quick steps.

I entered the dull orange-and-brown-felt cubicle, relieved to find Skip's desk and extra chair cluttered as usual. I immediately knocked a stack of folders from his visitors' chair. I made sure papers didn't fly too far, just enough distance for me to have to gather them and place them on the corner of the desk, amid other stacks. And in pulling them together, I managed to slip the key card between who knew what case and who knew what other case.

By the time Skip returned, I was settled on the chair. I'd taken out my notebook and pen and was making notes on the RFP review we'd just been through. Calm as can be.

"Turns out the meeting's not just for bigwigs. I need to be at it, Aunt Gerry. We'll have to continue this later."

Another plus. Rosie hadn't shown up yet and I was running out of delay tactics.

I got up to leave. I tapped the stack of folders I'd knocked over and replaced on his desk. "Oh, I dropped some stuff when I moved things from the chair," I said. "So this pile might be a little mixed up. Sorry."

I felt my homicide detective nephew could see right through me. But not directly, because I kept my eyes cast down the whole time I was talking.

I expected repercussions at some time, but for now, he let me off the hook.

CHAPTER 12

My thin towels, with their faded blue stripes, some from the earliest years of our marriage, looked pitiful after the plush vanilla bath sheets at the Duns Scotus. Two nights at a San Francisco hotel made my house, and most of my belongings, look equally shabby. I wasn't usually interested in flowery scents, but I rummaged for the fragrant soap I'd taken (not pilfered, as I do in cops' offices) from room five sixty-eight and put it on my cosmetics shelf. A definite upgrade.

I reminded myself of the trade-off for the hotel amenities: I'd been accosted in an elegantly appointed hallway and had had my purse stolen in their thickly verdant lobby. I resolved to go back someday when I wasn't hanging out with murder suspects.

I was in desperate need of some time at home, mediocre though it was, and of time with my family. I also needed to get to a miniature project soon to help me relax and gain perspective. Very often I solved a problem only when I stopped thinking hard about it and escaped to a different world for a while — a world where a small suction cup could be turned into a bathroom plunger or a bead from a broken necklace could be the base of a tiny lamp.

Today, however, my safe world of miniatures was marred by visions of Rosie's trashed locker hallway. I had to keep reminding myself that the red in the *I hate David* scrawl was only lipstick and not David Bridges's blood.

I had about a half hour alone, enough for a quick shower and unpacking, before Beverly and Nick would be bringing Maddie back. The best of both worlds.

Maddie called from Beverly's as they were leaving.

"Can I invite Taylor to come over tonight, Grandma?"

"Of course."

I wondered who would drive Taylor to my house.

On Sunday evening, my home was just the way I liked it — crowded with family and friends. Beverly and Nick had provided pizza for all and I'd phoned Sadie's for a delivery of enough ice cream for a whole football team. The flavors included Maddie's favorite triple chocolate, though I was still a bit put out about the way she'd wormed herself into the investigation without me.

I needed a serious discussion with my granddaughter about the printout caper. It wasn't clear why it bothered me so much that she'd delivered the material to Skip directly. Unless it meant that I was afraid she was growing apart from me. I waved my hand at an imaginary audience in my head. Ridiculous, I told myself, on both counts.

June Chinn, Skip's almost-fiancée, caught up with me in my pantry as I was searching for a new box of crackers. In faded denim shorts and a black tank top, June could have been a top model in the "short women" category. Her latest style statement was a tattoo on her lower back — the area that was universally visible now on young women as soon as they stretched or bent over. June had chosen a simple design, the Chinese symbol for peace.

She'd brought a large salad with bean sprouts, which she'd prepared in her own kitchen, next door to mine.

"I'm sorry about all that's going on here," she said. "But in a way, I'm glad Skip was called back before the funeral in Seattle. He

215

doesn't do well at that kind of thing. Well, nobody does, but you know what I mean."

I did know. Skip went to his first funeral when he was Maddie's age, for his father, who died in the first Gulf War. That seemed enough to ask of a guy.

"I'm glad you're back," I said, giving her a hug.

"Thanks, Gerry. Skip doesn't talk much about cases with me, as you know, but the rumor going around is that people think your friend Rosie Norman murdered her old boyfriend?"

I took it as a good sign that June posed the idea as a question. I was sure all of Rosie's customers would have an equally hard time believing something so horrible about the woman who loved books and reading enough to open her own shop in a small town. Rosie had reading groups for all ages and was tied into the Lincoln Point library's literacy program, where I tutored GED subjects. I knew she lost money giving students generous discounts on any text related to the GED program.

The question remained, however — why hadn't she presented herself to the police? To my nephew, in fact, which should have made it as easy as it could get.

And where was she now, anyway?

I'd left messages on Linda's and Rosie's cell phones inviting them to the impromptu party, presumably after Rosie talked to the police. I hadn't heard from either of them. Nor from Skip, either, in the last couple of hours.

Were they all on the run?

Henry and Taylor were due to arrive any minute. I wasn't eager to have Henry see my crafts room with its amateur miniature projects. He had shown no tendency toward being judgmental but I was conscious of the comparison between my crafts and his wonderfully artistic woodworking.

I decided my Bronx apartment might be an acceptable piece to show him. Ken had built the miniature structure, a replica of our first residence (a term that glorified the six-hundred-and-fifty-square-foot flat) and Maddie and I worked on the interior off and on. I was proudest of its lived-in look, with "clothes" peeking from the drawers of a messy dresser in the bedroom and a "dirty" towel hung over the bathtub. Maddie wanted cracker crumbs on the kitchen counter, so we'd found a way to model that, too.

Beverly caught me brushing my hair in my bedroom. Served me right for leaving the door open.

"I know what you're going through," she said, with a wide smile. Her red (augmented a bit by chemistry) Porter hair looked beautifully layered as usual. "Maddie told me about Henry Baker. I don't think I ever met him. Which is a good start. It means he never got a traffic ticket, violated the seat belt law, or abandoned his car on a city street."

I laughed at Beverly's reference to her job as LPPD's much-loved civilian volunteer. "What could Maddie have said? There's nothing to tell."

"Uh-huh," Beverly said, stepping behind me and massaging my shoulders.

I didn't know how much I needed it.

We'd all decided to give Nick plants to take home for his garden, in memory of his grandfather. Nick was an avid gardener and seemed genuinely moved by the gesture.

"This is just what I need," Nick said, the sweep of his arms encompassing all of us and the plants, too. "The best comfort is another great family."

Henry and Taylor had contributed to the array, arriving with two pots of orange and yellow marigolds, one for Nick's garden, and one for mine.

"How did you know about our plan for Nick?" I asked him.

"You know how it is. Maddie told Taylor; Taylor told me." He shrugged, as if every man was quick to pick up on social protocol.

It was so delightfully noisy as seven of us passed salad, pizza, and drinks around my large dining room table, I almost missed the doorbell.

Maddie, always first to jump up for a phone call or a knock, ran to the door and came back with Linda.

"It's Mrs. Reed," she said, bounding back to the dining room. She pulled a chair from the kitchen into a spot at the table. "You can sit next to me, Mrs. Reed."

Maybe I was just easy to please, but I felt a burst of pride — it was a small accommodation that Maddie had made for our guest, but she'd thought of it on her own and made a friend feel welcome.

Linda, in anything but a bounce, trundled into the room. She looked haggard and exhausted, but managed a small smile for everyone and took the seat suggested by Maddie.

"How's your mother, Henry?" she asked.

"Not too bad, thanks, Linda."

I guessed that Henry's mother was in one of the three assisted living facilities that

Linda had worked in over the years, but not the Mary Todd, or it would have been Henry asking the question of a dedicated nurse.

Was that a twinge of envy I felt — that Linda seemed to know more about Henry's family than I did? Like Beverly, she knew almost everyone in town; in Linda's case, either as patients, or as children of patients. On my side, I knew only those with an ALHS diploma obtained between three and thirty years ago.

I wondered if everyone at the table could tell how distracted I was, my perpetual state it seemed, since Friday night. I kept asking myself, *Where's Rosie?* as if a corner of my mind might shout out an answer. It was clear to me that Linda was dying to tell me whatever she knew of Rosie's current location. We exchanged glances frequently, with slightly lifted eyebrows and twitching facial muscles.

Before we had the chance to chat in private, however, my landline rang.

I excused myself and took the call in the kitchen. I stretched the cord to the back hallway, out of earshot. It was testimony to how involved I was in the case that I hoped it would be either Skip or Rosie.

It was only my son. Richard and Mary

Lou called from Lake Tahoe, elevation approximately seven thousand feet, to see how things were going in the lowlands.

I was glad my call-waiting signal came before I passed the phone on to Maddie, who was prone to giving too much information to her parents.

"Can we call you back, Mary Lou? I should take this other call," I said. Not my usual telephone protocol, but once I recognized Rosie's cell phone number, my son and daughter-in-law were immediately relegated to second place.

"No problem," Mary Lou said. "We're in for the night." I pictured their cozy retreat on the beautiful lake, far from the murky waters of Lincoln Point.

I clicked the button on my phone and heard a cough and a sniffle.

"I can't do it, Gerry," Rosie said. "Not until tomorrow afternoon."

I didn't have to ask why she needed the extra time. Rosie wanted to attend the memorial for David and was worried that she'd be arrested if she went to the station today. I couldn't blame her for wanting to pay her last respects first.

"Where will you be until then?" I asked.

"It's probably better if you don't know."

I couldn't argue with that.

■ ■ ■ ■

Linda stayed long enough for me to pull her aside and let her know that Rosie called. She breathed a sigh of relief.

"I didn't know how I was going to tell you that she escaped," she said. She threw up her hands. "She's wearing my clothes, Gerry." As if that was the biggest problem in either of their lives.

Beverly, Nick, and June followed soon after Linda departed. Linda did seem less tense than when she'd arrived with her burden of information about Rosie's change of plan.

It seemed strange not to be able to brainstorm with Beverly, but her life had changed for the better and I was happy for that. At the door, she leaned over and whispered in my ear. "Good luck," she said, a slight nod in the direction of Henry, who was being led by Maddie and Taylor toward the crafts room.

"No, no. It's not like that," I assured Beverly. I waved at Nick, waiting at the car, and at June, turning up her driveway. "Henry and I have a lot in common, and we might become friends," I said.

"Uh-huh," she said, her grin spreading.

"Well, let me know how that goes, okay?"

I hoped my face would return to its normal color by the time I got to the crafts room.

Maddie seemed to be doing well with her tour of my crafts room. I joined them and took in the utter disarray, with more works in progress than finished pieces. In one corner was a room box, newly painted in blue and gold, the colors of the University of California, Berkeley. (Richard, formerly a big fan of their football team, was now torn since he worked at Stanford, their great rival.) The scene was on its way to being a miniature dorm room. I hoped to have it finished for one of my GED students whose daughter would be starting at Cal as a freshman in a couple of weeks, the first in her family to go to college.

My Christmas scene, the one I was working on for our Alasita project, stood pitiful and boring in the center of the table. Sure, the stockings hanging on the faux brick fireplace looked decent, especially after I'd nearly lost the tips of my fingers embroidering our names on the tops, and I'd started to add toys — a wagon and a large (relatively speaking) doll. But it needed something to make it different from the low-end greeting cards of the season, sold in all the chain card stores. I didn't have any ideas about what that could be.

Here and there on the work surfaces in my crafts room were tiny easy chairs piled with miniature books. Lamps, coat racks, teacups, and snacks were scattered around each chair, the raw material for separate scenes, about seven in all. My process was to add a rug or an afghan and other accessories to the centerpiece chairs and let the arrangements sit for a while before I committed to them. I liked to look at the various compositions over a period of days or weeks and see which combinations looked best. Once a particular design stood the test of time, I sealed it with glue, forever.

With Henry standing next to me and Maddie prattling on about each scene, the unfinished room boxes looked even more pathetic. As did the chaotic assembly of pieces of yarn, toothpicks, body parts (of dolls), and fabric scraps.

When Henry turned to address me, I wanted to close my ears against the remark.

"I've never seen such a happy and creative workshop," he said. I wished I had the presence of mind to say "thank you."

Henry fingered a small, white plastic cylinder, one of dozens on my table. "These silica gels are everywhere. They come with everything I purchase lately, even a pair of shoes. Are you collecting them?"

In answer, I reached behind to my sparsely populated "finished" shelf and picked up three of the tiny cylinders, known formally as moisture absorbers. I'd printed food labels from an Internet site of "printies" and wrapped them around the cylinders. I painted the top gray to complete the fiction.

"Presto. We have cans of diced tomatoes, sliced beets, and marinated peach halves," I said, wondering why in the world I'd said "presto." Henry's presence seemed to bring out unusual responses in me. "I was determined to do something with these, so I'm collecting them to put on pantry shelves in my next general store or kitchen."

Henry shook his head. In admiration, it seemed. "I can't wait to see that."

"Wow," Taylor said.

Maddie beamed, and I felt a little less ashamed of my crafts room.

"I'll tuck you in," I told Maddie, who was sweet enough to let me use the phrase long after she'd outgrown it. Eleven o'clock bedtime was much too late for a "school" night, I knew, but I was a weak grandmother. Also a sneaky one. I'd conveniently waited until now to tell Maddie about her parents' phone call. Buying time.

"I didn't think you'd want to tuck me in tonight," she said, a sheepish look on her adorable, freckled face. "I thought you might be mad at me."

"Were you mad at me?" I asked, perched on the side of her bed. She always used her father's old bedroom on her visits and had been sorry to see his original preteen bed go a couple of years ago when it became nothing more than a board and a few feathers.

"You mean, did I give Uncle Skip the printouts because I was mad at you?" Maddie asked. "Maybe a little." She pouted. Still adorable. "You kept leaving me and going off to do interesting things."

Like being run down and having my purse stolen. Maddie didn't know about the former incident, and was only vaguely aware of the latter, since Duns Scotus's gallant security man, Big Blue, had interrupted her sleep.

"I thought you were having a good time with Taylor and the other kids in the program. And you had a lot of homework to do on your laptop for camp."

Something like "Pssshht" came out at the

mention of homework. Apparently the little Porter genius could manage a lot more than homework on any given day.

"You know I love to investigate with you. Then even in Lincoln Point, you dropped me in a pool." She hardly finished the sentence without breaking up in laughter.

"Sometimes it's too dangerous, sweetheart. And I do tell you everything eventually." Almost everything.

I could always tell when Maddie's waking minutes were numbered. Her speech slurred a bit and her eyelids fluttered, as if she were trying valiantly not to miss anything. She looked now as though her time was about up. I kissed her forehead and got up to leave.

Early as it was for those of us who didn't have school or camp in the morning, I was ready to turn in myself.

"Grandma?"

"Yes?"

"I didn't give everything to Uncle Skip."

I perked up. "What else do you have, sweetheart?"

But Maddie had nodded off for good, leaving me hanging.

Which was just as well, since I could hear my phone ringing in the other room.

A phone call this late at night wasn't likely

to be a casual "hi" or a quick chat to set up a lunch date. Or Cindy at Cooper's in Benicia calling to tell me the miniature armoire and new brand of glue I'd ordered had come in. I'd already returned Richard and Mary Lou's call. Who else was left?

I recognized Skip's cell phone number, then his voice.

"Remember I told you I'd have more evidence soon?" he said. "Well, that's what the meeting was about this afternoon. So, now I really need to see Rosie, and if you *really* don't know where she is, I'll have to put out a warrant to bring her in for questioning."

My heart skipped. "What's the new evidence, Skip?"

"What does it matter?"

"Skip?"

He let out a loud sigh. "It's about the glue."

"The glue?" Was this, after all, a call from Cooper's?

"We believe that the glue Rosie used on the things in the little box matches the glue used . . . elsewhere."

Things in the little box? When this case was closed, I'd have to give Skip a refresher course on miniaturists' jargon. "Elsewhere? You mean at the crime scene?"

"In a manner of speaking."

Something was off about my nephew's communication skills tonight, but that conversation, too, would have to be put on hold. There were more pressing questions. "How in the world did you get that information so fast? You're always reminding us how crime labs are understaffed and underfunded, how they don't come up with results in a jiffy like on television or in crime fiction."

"That's absolutely true. Some of the fancy equipment you see doesn't even exist, let alone in regular police labs. And the backlog is beyond anyone's imagining."

Uh-oh, I opened one of Skip's favorite topics. I had to move fast. "So what happened here? It's Sunday night, maybe forty-eight hours since David was murdered and you have a DNA match for glue?"

"Cute, Aunt Gerry. Glue DNA. But, hey, go figure. They train the lab rookies on weekends and this looked like a more interesting, quick little task than the other three hundred jobs in backup. That's why it's preliminary, but it's enough to pick Rosie up for questioning. Now, do you or do you not know where she is?"

"I don't, honestly. But . . ."

"But?"

I couldn't take the chance that Rosie wouldn't show up tomorrow afternoon as she promised. She wasn't herself. "I know where she'll be tomorrow," I said. "And you probably do, too."

"Why would I?"

"I assume you're going to the memorial for David? I thought cops always went to memorial services, expecting the killer to show up. Or is that another myth like the modern crime lab with instant turnaround time?"

"The funeral's not until Saturday."

I told him about the special service on Monday, to give out-of-town classmates the chance to pay their respects.

"You're going to earn a badge, yet," Skip said.

"Not if it means working this late all the time."

CHAPTER 13

What grandmother takes advantage of a little girl?

Much as the idea appealed to me, I stopped short of withholding breakfast from Maddie if she didn't tell me what it was she'd held back from her uncle Skip.

"Remember, just before you fell asleep you told me you discovered something else while you were searching the Internet?"

Maddie grinned, sedately, since her mouth was full of a very bad sugarcoated cereal that Mary Lou would never buy. "I was going to use it later."

"You mean to strike a better bargain?" I asked, working my tickling magic on her skinny torso at the same time.

My finger work had the desired effect. Maddie went to her room and came back with a sheaf of papers that looked like e-mail printouts. A quick look showed they were all from David Bridges, to various contractors and subcontractors. I recognized some of the same names that were on the material she'd given to Skip. I tried not to show my disappointment that what Maddie had kept from Skip, to give to me, was just more of the same, except that it was correspondence about the contract awards.

I asked my routine question of the whiz kid. "How did you get these?"

Maddie shrugged. Just another day in the life of a young detective. "It was part of what was there, like official correspondence for the awards, I guess. I figured if I gave some to you and some to Uncle Skip, we'd all be working together," she said. "That's the only reason I didn't give everything to the same person."

Awkwardly put, but on further thought, I realized Maddie wasn't trying to get even with me for dumping her at a pool every chance I had since Friday; she wanted to be seen as helpful to all.

The family that investigates together, stays together?

"Thanks, sweetheart," I said. "This is very useful."

I pulled out of the Rutledge Center at eight in the morning, after dropping Maddie off for day camp. She was excited about what she was learning, but vague about the details.

"We're making up games. You'd be bored," she'd said.

By which I guessed she meant I wouldn't get it, as I'd demonstrated all month. I shuddered to think what she'd be able to pull off with even more computer knowledge.

My cell phone rang, throwing me into confusion about how to access the call. I had a new Bluetooth contraption on my ear and could never remember the sequence of pushing buttons to answer a call.

It had taken three tries to find a design that fit and I still couldn't use it with the abandon I saw young people using it. The robot-like units on their ears seemed to survive stretching over the counter for their lattes or bending to pick up a dropped set of keys, whereas I could barely move my neck and still keep it on. But "hands free" was the California driving and calling law and I was nothing if not law-abiding.

Most of the time.

I was pleased to hear Henry Baker's voice, though any voice would have spelled my success at using the new technology.

"I hope I didn't wake you up," he said.

"Not at all. I'm downtown in my car."

"I was thinking — why don't I pick you up and we can go to David's service together?" Henry said. "I don't have grandfather duty today and it seems silly for us to drive separately."

Which we'd been doing the last few decades, I thought. I liked the flexibility of having my own car, in case . . . well, in case something came up on The Case.

"It's a great idea, but I have some errands to do before and after," I said. Errands. The term I used on Maddie. Maybe I should think of another term for adults.

"Right," Henry said, as if he didn't believe me.

"Otherwise, I'd love to," I said. "Some other time."

He laughed. "Sure. Some other memorial service, okay?"

"I didn't mean that."

We hung up on cordial terms but I had the feeling I'd disappointed him. Too late I remembered that it was Henry who'd first mentioned that Rosie's father was a subcontractor with Callahan and Savage. Maybe he knew more. I was sorry I'd missed an opportunity to talk to him about that.

And maybe other opportunities as well, but I was busy enough as it was.

On the way home I did the one legitimate errand I had for today and drove through the Lincoln Point Library book drop station. I'd checked out several history and English books to review for Lourdes's use and I wanted to return the ones I thought were inappropriate for her current level. It gave me some measure of satisfaction that I was doing my unquestionable duty for my GED student, as opposed to the wild physical and mental meanderings I'd been involved in, in an effort to free my friend from suspicion of murder.

I always craned my neck when I passed Sadie's Ice Cream Shop. Even at this hour of the morning, milk shakes beckoned. Milk was a breakfast food, was it not? Sadie's looked dark, however, as on most days before ten o'clock. I considered stopping and looking in the window. I knew from previous experiences of these off-hours cravings that, if she or Colleen were working in the back, there was a chance I could rouse them and gain admittance.

I slowed down and pulled over to the right on Springfield Boulevard, across from Sadie's, intending to cross the street and scan the shop for movement. This put me almost directly in front of Scrap's, Lincoln Point's worst fast-food restaurant. (You'd think if you were going to serve inferior foodstuff, you wouldn't make it so obvious by the name of your establishment.)

Scrap's opened very early to serve the breakfast-bacon-to-go crowd, a few of whom were exiting now with white paper sacks. I could almost see the grease leaking through from where I sat in my car, exchanging glasses and gathering my purse.

I was about to exit when a family group caught my eye. On closer inspection — not a family group, but Cheryl Mellace, Barry Cannon, and a little boy about four years old. I pulled my leg back in and snapped the visor down in front of my face.

Was the woman who could buy and sell the entire town of Lincoln Point a closet junk-food junkie? Neither Cheryl nor Barry had a to-go sack, so they must have eaten inside the restaurant. Who could guess that Scrap's was the in place for celebrity sighting?

The group stopped only a few yards from my car. Cheryl and Barry, her husband's CFO, were engaged in animated conversation, but not arguing, as far as I could make out. Cheryl held fast to the little boy's hand.

I'd read that her children were grown and figured this to be a grandson.

I thought of rolling down my window but didn't want to make the slightest noise, lest they see me. My plan for that contingency was to wave and pretend I'd just arrived. I was torn between clandestine observation and full-fledged interaction. Why wait until the service, almost two hours away?

Before I could make my choice, the group broke up. Cheryl had picked up the little boy and walked north toward Hanks Road. The toddler nuzzled his face on Cheryl's shoulder, as Maddie used to do. Cheryl patted his back and nuzzled him back. It was the first soft gesture I'd seen from her and I had to rethink my view of her as cold and witchlike. Grandmothers could dump their grandchildren into pools, I knew, but they couldn't be killers, could they?

Barry came toward me. I turned my back to the sidewalk, using my purse to shield my profile. Barry walked quickly, looking straight ahead.

The moment was gone to speak to either Cheryl or Barry. My reaction time had been too slow. If I'd already had a milk shake, I might have done better.

I decided against Sadie's also, however, and headed for home.

I thought back to the muted conversation between Cheryl and Barry. I hadn't seen any sign of mourning or grief. Not that outward manifestations were necessary, and not that life had to stand still when a friend died. But having seen Cheryl with David on Friday night, I expected less normalcy in her behavior just two days after his death.

I replayed the scene. Had there been any clue of a romantic connection between the two? I didn't think so. Surely, it would be too soon for Cheryl to replace David in that way. But maybe she had the ability to bounce back emotionally the way she bounced on the football field with her pom-poms.

Alas, none of this was my area of expertise.

When I returned home, I found Skip at my kitchen table with a mug of coffee, toast, and a half dozen of my ginger cookies.

"Why do you bother with the toast?" I asked him.

"Appearances."

I poured a cup of coffee for myself and joined him.

"I thought we could chat before the service," he said. "It would help a lot if you could give me your version of the relationship between Rosie and Bridges."

I felt a conundrum coming on, like the hint of a headache when I didn't get enough sleep or when I didn't switch from coffee to tea early enough in the day. If I told Skip of the obsessive nature of Rosie's attachment, real or fictional, to David Bridges, and her deep-seated anger after his rebuke, it would make matters worse for her.

I related the story in as neutral terms as possible, making it sound like high school–style unrequited love. "We've all been there," I ended, as if I myself had once staked all my happiness on the off chance that someone I hadn't talked to in thirty years was now longing for me.

"Hmm," was all Skip said. Maybe, unlike me, he had been there.

"Can we review the other suspects?" I asked. "For example, have you looked into the man named Ben whom I told you about — David's employee?"

"The SFPD might have picked up on that."

"Might have? Don't you share?"

"They wouldn't necessarily share that. They interviewed a lot of the reunion class and even other guests who were at the hotel that night. I'm assuming if the fight was that public, one of them would have remembered, too."

"They didn't interview me or Rosie, so on that alone we know they're not being thorough."

Skip shrugged and left the table. He pulled a plastic storage bag from a box in my kitchen drawer and filled it with ginger cookies. From the number he took, I guessed he was planning on a long, tough day.

I was thrown back in time to the young boy, newly fatherless, who visited Ken and me (mostly Ken) more and more often, falling asleep on our guest bed or on the floor in his cousin Richard's room, treating our home as his. They were difficult days for all of us, especially for Beverly, who drew comfort from her brother's near adoption of her son.

I was almost surprised to hear the voice of the grown-up Skip as he addressed me now, back at the table, notebook and pen ready.

"This is what happens sometimes when there's questionable jurisdiction at the beginning. I hate to say it, but now and then things fall through the cracks."

It bothered me that a murderer might go free because of a breach of continuity in an investigation from one city to another less than an hour away. It didn't seem a very thorough way to do police business, but I resisted complaining to Skip. I knew his job was hard enough.

"And when it's early in a case, no one knows exactly what will matter in the end and we try to cover all bases," Skip continued, while I pondered my next move.

"Can't you go to San Francisco and find out more about this maintenance supervisor, Ben Dobson? It's peculiar that one minute he's fighting with the victim, and the next he quits on the spot." I thought back to my own inability to get anything out of Mike the electrician and only the vaguest mention of Ben's temperament from Enrico the plumber.

"How do you know he was a supervisor?"

"My toilet got stopped up," I said.

Skip gave me a confused look, then laughed as if I'd told a joke. I let it go at that.

It was time I came through for my nephew, and did something that would benefit Rosie also. The sooner Rosie showed up for the police, the sooner we could get to the bottom of the case and clear her. It wasn't as if Rosie were doing any good out there, now technically in the wind, since neither Linda nor I knew where she was holing up. She wasn't in any shape to investigate on her own, but maybe the police would get a tidbit from her that would help.

I decided to come clean (almost) about my recent brushes with assault, in case there might be a useful tidbit buried in the incidents.

Skip jotted notes and kept any responses to himself while I talked. I described Walter Mellace's stopping me aggressively in the hallway. I was a little vague on the timeline and on what you might call . . . ahem . . . trespassing, but I had the feeling Skip was able to put it all together nicely. He remained surprisingly restrained.

"Doesn't that sound like you should look at those RFPs and why Callahan and Savage gets the short end all the time?" I asked.

Skip nodded. "I already put someone on that. It turns out that Bridges did have decision-making power on that stuff. He was only one vote on the hotel's executive committee, but when it came to anything related to maintenance or upgrades, they essentially followed his recommendation."

"There's more." I braced myself for the purse-snatching story. "But it's probably completely unrelated," I began. By the time I got to the act of theft itself, however, Skip had dropped his pen and his eyes had widened. I feared he was going to call an ambulance.

"Did you report this?" he asked. *Why not to me?* was in his voice.

"Yes, yes, and I didn't lose anything." I thought of Big Blue with his crooked nose and gentle manner. "They took all the information, and I got my purse back, but no one expects the thief to be caught. I'm telling you this because I think it's possible that he was also looking for something I might have found in David's room."

Skip relaxed, realizing I guessed, that since I had no visible bruises, there was nothing to worry about. I waited while he doodled and wrote a few notes.

Our session would have to come to a close soon. David's memorial was at ten at Miller's Mortuary, near the main commercial district of Lincoln Point.

I wanted to leave Skip with a final thought before he considered handcuffs, for Rosie or for me. Fortunately he never pushed me on how, when, or why I got into David's room.

"Rosie isn't capable of murder," I said, my final word as I got up to clear the table.

Skip looked at me, a mixture of sadness and frustration in his expression. "Have a seat, Aunt Gerry."

I sat. "What?" I knew that nothing good

243

could come from his tone. I sipped my coffee.

"I didn't want to be too graphic before, but you ought to know this." He took a breath. "About what the killer did to David's body."

"Do I need to hear this?"

"I think so. David Bridges's lips were glued shut, Aunt Gerry. That's the glue we matched to the pieces in the mini box."

It took a few seconds to register, then I grasped the edge of the table and hung my head. My breath felt heavy in my lungs. I fought down an acidy taste in my mouth. The last mouthful of coffee now seemed like a big mistake.

I had a flashback to my conversation with Linda — I'd interrupted her when she tried to describe what an indiscreet EMT friend had told her.

I pictured David's lips . . .

"Excuse me," I said and headed for my bathroom.

Who could do such a thing? I didn't for a minute think that a miniaturist could use her craft in such a horrible way. Certainly not one who came to my house once a week for an uplifting evening of shared creativity. Although in Skip's mind, the awful detail was further proof of Rosie's guilt, to me it was the clearest sign that Rosie had been framed.

Miniaturists treasured their craft, the fruits of their labor, even their glue. I tried to hold fast to this belief even as the awful image flooded my mind — a vandalized room box with hateful words, destroyed property, and a tiny bottle of poison.

CHAPTER 14

To some it might seem disrespectful, but I planned to take full advantage of the memorial service for David Bridges, using it as a tool to make progress in finding his killer. From what I'd heard from Skip, I wasn't convinced the police would do anything but settle on Rosie.

My views might have come from too much exposure to television dramas (though real-life drama seemed to have taken over my time lately), but I believed that David's killer would show up for this service. Moreover, if he was from out of town, this might be my last chance to have a close look and a talk with him. Or her.

As I got ready for my visit to Miller's Mortuary, deciding to wear a jacket in spite of the heat, I made a mental list of whom to look for and try to console.

In my mind, the Mellaces were the prime suspects. Walter's motivation could be simply that he'd found out about David and his wife, who seemed to have enjoyed at least one exclusive party together, if not a longer-term arrangement.

Cheryl's motivation, according to self-appointed Detective Gerry Porter, could be that she became uncontrollably upset when David rejected her offer to leave her husband for him. I worked out a standard scenario in Movies of the Week: now that her children are grown and out on their own, Cheryl can be with David as she's wanted since high school. But David never intended to be committed to her in that way; he was never serious about her.

I wasn't sure how Cheryl managed to carry the trophy from San Francisco to Lincoln Point or lift it high enough to kill David, but I had to leave something for the police to figure out.

I found myself casting the movie version of the triangle, with perhaps the petite Holly Hunter playing Cheryl.

David's fictional rejection of Cheryl loomed larger and was more of an issue in my mind than his real rejection of Rosie, which I'd seen with my own eyes. My mind was a marvel. "Anyone but Rosie Norman" was its theme.

I wished I were confident in my ability to

recognize Ben Dobson without his gray jumpsuit. I had no idea where he lived but guessed it was San Francisco. Maybe there would be a revealing decal on his car: A monk in a habit and the words *Duns Scotus Supervisor.* It was possible that Ben wouldn't come to this unofficial service, however, in which case I'd have to nab him at the funeral on Saturday at St. Bridget's, assuming he'd go to that. I hoped the case would be solved by then. I had a life to get back to. Sort of.

Barry Cannon, sure to be in attendance, as class president, also had to answer for his elaborate fraud, sending gifts in David's name. I realized I was leaping from a box of chocolates (if Samantha's ID was correct) to a shower of jewelry and flowers over the past weeks, but it seemed reasonable. If nothing else, the ID by Samantha, the lovely gift shop clerk, gave credibility to Rosie's claims that she received a series of presents. It told me that at the very least Rosie hadn't sent the chocolates to herself — ashamed as I was to acknowledge that I'd given that idea some thought, as I was sure some members of the crafters group had.

I tried to work through what Barry's scenario could have been. To lead Rosie into thinking David was wooing her, so as to get her mad enough to kill him? Why? Because Barry wanted David dead but didn't want to do it himself? Rosie as hit woman. The idea sounded silly even to me, its originator.

Barry was the CFO for Mellace, who did business with the Duns Scotus, and therefore with David. If only I knew more about white-collar crime, I might be able to put together a business-related motive for Barry.

The simple version might involve kickbacks. I played it out: David uses his influence on the hotel's executive committee to give contracts to Mellace, no matter what the competition. When Barry finds out, he blackmails David, the meeting goes wrong, and David is killed. Lots of holes in this plot, thanks to my ignorance of the ways contracts could be manipulated.

After this morning's sighting at Scrap's, I couldn't rule out a coconspiracy between Barry and Cheryl. So they could take over Mellace Construction? I wondered if Maddie could use Google to find out what the insurance policy on the company looked like. If only she were an adult and I didn't have to feel so guilty about these thoughts.

I'd checked out Barry's marital status in Rosie's updated yearbook — he was a bachelor. It crossed my mind that he himself might have wanted to connect with Rosie and was too shy, so he used David's name as an intermediary.

I regretted that I had no brilliant suggestion as to who might be a good choice to take on the movie role of Barry Cannon.

It was disheartening to think that my students of thirty years ago seemed stuck in high school, in terms of the dynamics of relationships.

The logistics of David's murder were still fuzzy in my mind. Did someone lug a cumbersome trophy to the murder scene, or did David carry it into the woods himself for some unknown reason? It was Barry who toted David's trophy into the hotel gift shop. He was much more capable than Cheryl Mellace, for example, of transporting the heavy object and using it on David's head. But why would he be walking around with something he intended to use as a murder weapon?

I'd meant to ask Skip about David's estranged wife and son. Didn't investigators always focus on immediate family first? It was possible that either David's wife or his son was in custody now. I hoped that if that were the case, my man inside the LPPD would certainly alert me and spare me a lot of trouble and anxiety.

I thought of the other one hundred or so alumni who had gathered for the weekend, and the myriad of friends, relatives, and business contacts — Larry Esterman, Rosie's father, and the rest of the personnel of Callahan and Savage, for example — that David had accumulated over the last thirty years. Any one of them could have had a better motive than those on my personal suspect list.

The awful use of glue brought ugly images that I tried to shuck, but it was a clue that had to be accounted for and didn't fit with any suspect other than my miniaturist friend.

Here again, I'd have to leave something for the LPPD to do to earn their large salaries.

Miller's was old school from start to finish, the kind of mortuary I was used to seeing when I lived on the Grand Concourse in the Bronx, but not in sunny California where funeral homes were as likely as not to have skylights. The building was set back from a row of stores along Springfield Boulevard.

Stained-glass windows depicted pastoral scenes, and Gregorian chant from a hidden source greeted the guests as we took our places on Miller's dark wood pews. Except for the absence of statuary and incense, the room could have passed for the interior of a Catholic church, like those I'd seen when Ken and I toured Italy.

I chose a seat near the back of the room, the better to survey who came and went. Especially Rosie. I flopped my large purse next to me, to save her a seat, though the room could easily have held twice as many as the hundred or so people I estimated to be present.

I admired the floral arrangements surrounding the lectern at the front and wished I'd thought of sending one myself. This was not the official funeral service, I remembered, and there was still time for me to contribute.

I'd picked up a flyer, tasteful, but clearly done in a hurry, with a recent photograph of David Bridges, with his birth and death dates, juxtaposed with the original yearbook photograph and write-up for him: "Our own strong, handsome BMOC, sure to succeed in life as he has on Abraham Lincoln High's football field."

A feeling of sadness overtook me, perhaps because of the simple prose or the dejected faces of David's peers all around me, or because it dawned on me that I hadn't taken any time to grieve for a former student who died a violent death in my own hometown.

I'd been so busy trying to protect Rosie, first from the disdain of the living David and now from being named his killer, that I'd forgotten who was the real victim.

I hung my head, reflecting and feeling the loss.

During the forty-five-minute service, while I listened to eulogies and sang "Amazing Grace," I scanned the crowd, looking for Rosie and the other, more worthy suspects.

I spotted the Mellaces, hand in hand a few rows in front of me. It was impossible to tell from their body language that they were anything but a devoted couple. I supposed that Walter and Cheryl might indeed have a happy marriage — on Friday night on the eleventh floor of the Duns Scotus, Cheryl and David might have been playing a friendly game of chess, and today on the sidewalk in front of Scrap's, Cheryl and Barry might have been talking over old times.

How did Cheryl keep her men straight?

After eulogies from principal Frank Thayer, Coach Robbins, and Barry, we were all invited to share memories of David. Walter Mellace was first up, though he wasn't even a classmate. He talked about how lucky some of us were to have known David thirty years ago, and how he wished he'd known him.

"So many people, including my wife, spoke so highly of David," he told us from the lectern.

Walter was brief and made no mention of doing business with David himself. I found the presentation odd, but thought maybe Cheryl asked him to represent the family. Her talents in oratory matched her skill at decorating, I recalled.

We heard from other classmates, with the expected praise of David's wonderful personality and great loyalty to ALHS even though he no longer lived in Lincoln Point.

I was too far back to see the front row, where I imagined David's parents were sitting, and perhaps his ex-wife and son. I doubted I'd recognize them but hoped I'd get a chance to offer condolences today or Saturday.

I half expected Rosie to pop up in a front row to proclaim her love of the deceased. I sincerely hoped she wouldn't.

I didn't see Skip or any LPPD presence in the hall. Either they were off Rosie's tail or they'd sent someone I didn't recognize.

As the program came to a close, I listened

for the sound of handcuffs but heard none.

The reception following the service was in a room at the back of the mortuary, a brighter, more airy space with large windows opening onto a neatly manicured lawn.

Miller's employees were easy to pick out, even among so many men wearing black. They stood at the edges of the crowd, hands behind their backs, earpieces showing. I wondered if they'd been alerted that there might be an arrest on their property this morning.

Barry and I arrived at the doorway together. I was ready.

"How are you holding up, Barry?" I asked him. I expected him to tell me he had an upset stomach. His wouldn't be the first Scrap's casualty I'd heard of.

"I'm doing okay, Mrs. Porter. I still can't believe he's gone." Barry seemed genuinely upset, his shoulders slumped and his lips in a downward arc. That could have been from remorse as much as from the grief of an innocent man, I reminded myself. "We go way back, you know. All the way to grade school."

"And you still had business dealings with him, didn't you?"

"Sort of."

I feigned surprise. "I thought it was more than 'sort of.' You work for Mellace Construction, right?"

"Uh-huh. I've been there a long time."

"And your company has received a number of contracts lately for work at the Duns Scotus, hasn't it?" Barry opened his mouth to answer, but I ran on, intending to provoke him if possible. "Networking with friends is always a plus, isn't it? I mean, for mutual benefit." I held back on winking, hoping the inflection in my voice carried the message.

Barry squinted at me, as if he was having trouble making the shift to the new topic and to the sarcastic tone of his former, reserved English teacher. "You'll have to pardon me if business isn't the first thing on my mind right now," he said.

"I understand, Barry. I just want to make sense of what happened to David and to figure out who could have done this terrible thing. I'm trying to think of why anyone might want to kill your friend and business colleague."

It seemed to take a minute for Barry to digest what I was saying. He straightened his shoulders, which kept him still shorter than me, however. "With all due respect, Mrs. Porter, this is probably not the best time for a conversation like this."

"You're right. But I value your input, Barry. I wanted to get your opinion also on who might have been sending presents to Rosie Norman, using David's name."

Barry's lips tightened, in anger, I thought, not in sadness this time. "What are you talking about?"

"I'm referring to candy, flowers, a bracelet." I let that sink in. "Can we set a time to meet?" I asked him.

"I don't think so." Barry tugged on his suit jacket, gave his neck a brief roll, and walked away.

On the whole, I wasn't proud of my first interview. Barry's response left me as suspicious of him as I had been since Samantha identified him from his updated yearbook photo.

If one of David's best friends was innocent, however, I'd just done a rude, heartless thing.

The tables were turned during my second try at information gathering, this time with Cheryl Mellace. Walter had evidently had enough of me in San Francisco: as I approached, he turned his back and busied himself serving punch to guests who'd lined up.

"I know how close you both were to David," I said to Cheryl, with a tsk-tsk sound. It occurred to me that I'd already used that line on her, but if she was guilty it might just make her nervous, which might prove to be a good thing.

Walter kept his back to me, ladling a very pink punch into glass cups, engaged in chatter with a couple I didn't know but recognized from the cocktail party and banquet.

Cheryl yanked on my arm with what felt curiously like a pinch, through my beige-and-white seersucker jacket. A mild pain ran along my upper arm. She pulled me to the side.

"Listen, Mrs. Porter. You're not my teacher anymore, okay? And I don't need you sniffing around or whatever it is you're doing." Cheryl's eyes darted from me to her husband, still working intensely, like hired help, at the punch bowl. "I know Rosie was always your favorite pet and you're trying to pin this on someone else. But just face it. She did it. I saw that stupid little dollhouse thing she made. She had it while she was stalking David in the hallway on Friday night. And she all but confessed when she wrote all over that thing and destroyed it."

I bristled at "stupid little dollhouse thing," but kept my cool. "I thought you were the one who destroyed it," I said.

"I'm not the one the police are questioning. The police have their ducks in a row; they pulled her out of a hat, not me."

Cheryl never was any good at figures of speech. By the time I untangled the message enough to ask what she meant, how she knew the police had questioned Rosie (had they?), she'd walked away, the sound of her high heels ringing out on the hardwood floor.

I was left convinced that a woman who called a room box a "dollhouse thing" was capable of murder and deserved her high place on my list of prime suspects.

Two lines had formed in the room, one for the buffet table and one that ended at a couple who looked bereaved enough to be David's parents. I saw no sign of a man young enough to be David's son, but perhaps he would make an appearance at St. Bridget's on Saturday.

I clicked my phone back on, in case there was breaking news from Rosie, Linda, or Skip. I was concerned that I hadn't seen Rosie, though that didn't mean she wasn't present in the crowd.

Before I could decide which line to join first, I saw another attraction — standing by himself looking as though he didn't know

259

anyone in the room, was Duns Scotus maintenance supervisor Ben Dobson. I was 95 percent certain it was Ben, especially when I caught him in profile. Ben had an unusually large, hooked nose, all the more pronounced on his small frame. I edged closer on the pretext of getting into the Bridgeses' reception line. I needed another view of him to be sure this was the employee who'd argued with his boss, David Bridges, on the night before he was murdered.

I moved ahead in the line of people waiting to offer sympathy to Mr. and Mrs. Bridges, all the while keeping my eyes on the man I was increasingly sure was Ben Dobson. When I left my house I knew it might come to this — disrespect of a solemn occasion for the sake of an investigation. I hoped it didn't show.

I was framing an opening line for Ben, hoping to do better than I had with my approach to Barry, when I heard, "May I join you?" I hadn't noticed that Henry was several people ahead of me in line. He had left his place and walked back to greet me.

I started to answer Henry when a call came in on my cell phone and Ben Dobson left his post. I almost lost track of Ben. My abilities were strained by the need to triple-task.

"Hi, Henry," I said, clicking on my phone and watching Ben over Henry's shoulder. My height made it slightly easier to accomplish all of this.

"Go ahead and take that call," Henry said.

"Do you mind? I'll just step over here for a minute."

Henry left the line also and stood far enough away to give me privacy. "I'll wait," he said.

I wished it were Ben who'd said he'd wait. I could see him survey the crowd, much the same way Rosie had at the cocktail party. Was he also looking for an old flame as she had been? I doubted it.

Worse luck, Ben Dobson was now headed toward the exit door. I glanced at my caller ID. Linda. One of a very short list of people whose calls I felt necessary to answer today.

I smiled at Henry, picked up Ben's retreating back, and clicked my phone on.

"I didn't want to interrupt you during the service," Linda said. "I hope I waited long enough."

"It's over. What is it, Linda?" I kept my eyes on Ben. I hoped the urgency I put into my voice would be Linda's clue not to give me her customary long lead-in to a status report.

"Rosie's at the police station."

I glanced over at Henry. He stood where I'd left him, to the side of the line for David's parents, arms crossed. I figured he'd planned on having me join him for what could pass for lunch at the buffet table. A pleasant enough thought, if I weren't so busy.

Ben was less than twenty feet from the exit.

Back to Linda. "I'm glad to hear that, Linda, but I'm surprised Rosie skipped the service for David."

"She didn't have a choice. They picked her up in Miller's parking lot as she was going into the mortuary."

And Cheryl had seen the action, I realized. Her twisted metaphor had made no sense at the time.

My heart sank, my eyes focusing now on Henry, now on Ben, and back. "They arrested her?" I asked Linda.

"No handcuffs or anything," Linda said. "She just got in an LPPD car."

"How do you know this?"

"I know people." We both laughed at the sinister implication. "I mean, there's a lot of business between us and Miller's."

"Of course there is." I pictured a large black van making not infrequent trips between the Mary Todd assisted living facility and Miller's Mortuary.

"It's awful, Gerry. What are you going to do?"

"It might not mean anything, if they weren't arresting her. The most they can do is cite her for being uncooperative," I said. I had to check that little detail in the police handbook, if there was one.

Ben closed in on the exit to the parking lot. I carried my phone with me as I followed him, keeping stragglers between us whenever possible.

He took his keys out.

I took mine out. *What was I doing?*

"I'm sure Rosie would like it if you went down to the station right away, Gerry."

Ben approached a late-model sedan at the edge of the lot and got in.

I approached my Ion and got in.

I seemed to be on autopilot as I put my key in the ignition, turned on the engine, and started backing up. "I'll get to the police station as soon as I can," I told Linda, breaking the California hands-free law for a car in motion. "I have an errand to do first."

I turned my head to look over my shoulder as I rolled out of the parking spot in reverse.

Henry Baker was standing in the doorway, his hands in the pockets of his light summer jacket. I couldn't see the details of his face, but his posture seemed dejected, as if he'd been given a brush-off, not that different from the one Rosie had experienced from David.

It couldn't be helped, I told myself.

CHAPTER 15

Miller's Mortuary predated the row of stores on the east side of Springfield Boulevard. Its asphalt driveway was now wedged between a card shop and a do-it-yourself ceramics shop. I drove out, allowing about three car lengths between Ben and me. I was confident that he wouldn't think it unusual that someone would leave the mortuary at about the same time that he did.

I pulled out onto Springfield and turned left, following the dark blue, ordinary-looking car. A Toyota? A Ford? I'd never been good at identifying a vehicle unless it was a limousine or a pickup truck.

I questioned my decision-making process. Faced with the choice of, one, comforting and aiding Rosie, who might be arrested at any moment; two, having an appealing repast with Henry, whom I was growing to appreciate as a friend; and three, tailing a man I thought might be a killer, I'd chosen the last. If nothing else, Ben Dobson was the only person in my recent history who'd shown a temper. And I'd elected to follow him to places unknown.

My only defense was that finding who killed David was the best thing I could do for my old friend; then I'd have time for new friends.

I'd hung up on Linda unceremoniously, telling her I'd call her right back, though the promise went out of my mind immediately. At almost noon on a workday, there wasn't much traffic. This was a good thing in that I was not an experienced follower and might have lost my target, but a bad thing in that it might be obvious to Ben that he had an unwelcome visitor in his rearview mirror.

Ben took a right on Civic Drive, just past the site of the ALHS groundbreaking ceremony, and continued following the drive, looping around until he was headed for the parking lot that surrounded the gym behind the high school. A circuitous route.

There were easier ways to get to this spot from Miller's Mortuary — by cutting into the gravel drive next to Bagels by Willie, or even circling behind Sadie's Ice Cream Shop. I wondered if his choosing the long route meant that Ben was not a local boy.

I stayed a reasonable distance behind him as Ben drove to the far north end of the back ALHS lot and parked. Fortunately the high school held summer classes, making the area moderately busy and allowing me to blend in with the other red cars. (More than once, even in non-surveillance situations, I renewed my grudge against my son for talking me out of a bronze Taurus, and into a bright red Saturn Ion.)

I parked under a tree, behind Ben's car, so that if he backed up far enough in a straight line, he'd ram his rear bumper directly into my front end. When Ben exited his car, I slumped down in the seat and watched him through the space in the steering wheel between the rim and the horn. I hoped I didn't activate it now by accident.

Ben looked around, but I was fairly sure he hadn't seen me. He had no reason to expect that he was being followed. He threw his jacket onto the backseat of his car, hitched up his pants, and walked straight ahead.

Into Joshua Speed Woods.

I felt my face flush and my arms slacken. I watched Ben walk deliberately down the trail that led into the woods known as a picnic grounds during the summer weekends, a teen lovers' hideaway at night all year, and most recently, the place where David Bridges's bludgeoned body had been found.

A repulsive image came to me, of David's lips, glued together. Wasn't glue a staple in a maintenance department? I couldn't remember if Rosie used the very tough carpenter's glue on her project. Many of us did, depending on the materials we were trying to fasten together. I doubted that every single container of a particular brand of glue was different. The rookie forensics person could have made a mistake when he thought he matched the glue from Rosie's room box to . . . I shut out the image.

Ben walked slowly, head down, kicking the gravel now and then. He seemed to be searching for something, scanning the ground on both sides of the trail. I imagined he might be looking for evidence he thought he left behind, or for a place to plant a miniature tool, to further implicate Rosie.

I shuddered at the thought that Ben had seen me and was now scoping out where to drag my body once he silenced me. I consoled myself with the thought that perhaps Ben Dobson was doing nothing more than exhibiting morbid curiosity about where David's body had been found or that he had a flower in his pocket to lay at the site.

Not long after Ben left my range of view, a minivan pulled up next to me and I started, as frightened as if Ben had materialized next to me, though I knew he couldn't have made it back to the parking area so quickly. My fear was so real, I might have testified (had I lived) that he held a trophy high in the air over my head.

A noisy family of five exited the van. Three high-energy children screaming and laughing brought me back to the present moment. They juggled books, stuffed animals, and pieces of clothing, the way I was juggling all the clues and fears of my last three days.

It had been about thirty minutes since Ben disappeared into the woods. Very few people came into the lot during that time. At one point, I thought I saw Cheryl Mellace enter the lot in her black sports car. She passed close to me but seemed to deliberately turn away when she saw me. I wondered what her yearbook write-up said about her attitude.

Once in a while during my waiting time I treated myself to a few minutes of classical music on my radio. I didn't know enough about car batteries to risk it full time. In spite of my rolling down all my windows to catch the slight breeze, I was beginning to wilt as the sun hit my side of the car. I switched to a "traffic and weather together" station and heard that today's temperature wasn't as high as Saturday's. Maybe not in the weather studio. I knew it wasn't smart to be sitting in a car on asphalt.

I hadn't been in Joshua Speed Woods lately, but I remembered English department picnics there while I was teaching. I pictured the other end of the woods. There was no other trail out that I knew of, besides the trail into the woods, which I'd been watching. The wooded area dead-ended in marshland that filled a large area on the west side of Lincoln Point.

It was nearing one o'clock; I was supposed to pick up Maddie at the Rutledge Center, about five minutes away, at one thirty. I'd hoped to have time to see Rosie at the police station before collecting my granddaughter, but it seemed I'd frittered away the better part of an hour in a fruitless stakeout. On the other hand, maybe it was important to have discovered that Ben Dobson paid a visit to a crime scene in a neighborhood he was obviously unfamiliar with.

In other circumstances, I'd have called Rosie to watch Maddie while I did an errand connected to a police investigation. Rosie's situation came into stark relief now that she was the errand.

By one fifteen, Ben still hadn't emerged from the woods. Why hadn't it crossed my mind before now that he might be a second victim? I hated to think that Joshua Speed Woods, named after a nineteenth-century gentleman who was Abraham Lincoln's best friend, had turned into a killing field.

I talked myself out of making a call that would dispatch an emergency vehicle into the woods. It was more likely that Ben was in there destroying evidence that might incriminate him.

Or was he, like me, unable to leave the investigation of his boss's murder to law enforcement?

I took out my phone to call Linda. I needed a status report on Rosie. Usually I'd worry about waking Linda up, since Monday was her day to sleep in when she'd been on call all weekend. I decided to risk Linda's wrath if she'd gone back to bed after phoning to alert me about Rosie's unwelcome trip to the station.

"Have you heard from Rosie?" I asked, tense about Linda's sleepy voice.

"Aren't you there yet?" she asked, annoyed.

"Not yet."

"Poor Rosie."

"Linda, I'm doing my best for Rosie. It's not as if I went to the movies." Or to lunch with a friend who makes dollhouses, I added silently.

"Oh, then you're investigating?" she said, sounding like Maddie. "I'm worried. I could go down there myself, but really you're better at that kind of thing."

"I can go to the station now if you'll pick up Maddie at the Rutledge Center. Her class is over at one thirty, but she's usually late anyway."

"I can do it. I actually got some sleep last night. The natives weren't as restless as they usually are Sunday evenings."

"They have preferred times of restlessness?"

I shouldn't have asked. Linda loved an opportunity to vent about the families of her patients. About anything, now that I thought of it.

"All the dutiful sons and daughters visit on Sundays for a couple of hours and they get the residents all worked up. They bring their little kids who run around, and they give the patients candy and junk food, which is not good for them. Then, of course, the relatives go home and we're left to calm everybody down. Sometimes I think it would be better if we didn't allow visitors."

"I don't blame you for getting upset at inconsiderate visitors," I said, hoping to move on soon. I was getting hotter by the second, looking around the inside of my car for something that might serve as a fan. I'd already shed my seersucker jacket, leaving me in a sleeveless white blouse. I stretched across the seat and pulled out a map of the San Francisco Bay Area from the glove compartment. I unfolded and refolded it to work as a fan. It would have to do.

"I'm not complaining. You know I love my work, but some of the relatives really tick me off."

"I don't blame you," I repeated, whipping the map in front of my face. "So can you pick up Maddie? If you can do that, I'll go to the station and see what's up with Rosie."

"Done," she said.

I considered calling Maddie to tell her that Mrs. Reed would be taking her home with her for a short while. I knew Maddie would be put out and easily divine what was going on. I planned to get back in her good graces with a waiver of her vegetable requirement at dinner and an extra shake of Parmesan on her popcorn tonight.

If only I could take care of my abandonment of Henry as easily. After rejecting his offer to carpool and running off without explanation when he said he'd wait for me to join him at the reception, I wouldn't blame him if he crossed me off his list of possible new friends. I hoped Maddie and Taylor wouldn't have to break up (so to speak) also.

I decided not to call Skip, either. My "aunt magic" worked better impromptu and in person. I hoped he was tied up as the one interviewing Rosie, anyway.

Time to call an end to the stakeout. Besides my other discomforts, I was starving. I considered going to Sadie's for a malt to go before heading to the police department. I adjusted myself in the seat and prepared to turn the key in the ignition. If I turned the key, it meant Skip's; if I got out of the car, it meant Sadie's, only a short walk away. Wasn't there a child's game with rules like that?

"Something I can do for you?"

I heard a deep voice and saw a sweaty arm on my window ledge.

I jumped and bumped my elbow on my horn, making a noise that caused me to jump again.

Ben Dobson leaned in on my window. His

breath was foul, from a cigar I thought, and his face weathered. He wasn't a big man, but he had a powerful presence.

I surveyed the parking lot. I saw no one entering or exiting a car nearby. My remote control had a panic button. I could push it now, but my experience with false alarms told me that no one paid attention to a blaring horn and flashing lights. I had no reason to think anyone would come to my rescue now. It might simply annoy Ben and provoke him to an unpleasant action.

"I . . . I was just leaving."

"I hear you want to talk to me." Ben couldn't miss my surprise. "Word gets around. I still have buddies at the Scotus. And who else would be following me?"

Mike the electrician came to mind.

I looked around, thinking he might have brought Mike as backup or to help carry me into the woods.

I felt faint, from the heat, from hunger, and from what I sensed as danger.

Ben took advantage of my glaring discomfort and momentary paralysis to come around to the passenger side and get in my car, knocking on my hood on the way. It sounded like a "this is my lucky day" knock, which might have meant the opposite for me. He made himself comfortable, sitting partly on my jacket, facing me, his left hand on the back of the seat. I was grateful for the apparent absence of a weapon.

"I'm here. Talk to me," he said, in an almost casual tone, showing me his palms. It was obvious that he knew how intimidating he was; he didn't need threatening language.

Wasn't this what I wanted, after all? A chance to talk to the employee who'd argued with David on the night of his murder. The trouble was, it might be my last interview.

Might as well get it started.

"You followed your boss into our reunion cocktail party the other night. What were you fighting over?"

"You're really asking, did I kill him, right?"

I wasn't that dumb. There was only one answer. "No, of course not. I was hoping to get a lead on who did."

"You a cop?"

Ask your friend, Mike. He asked me the same question, I wanted to say. Instead I smiled as politely as anyone in a state of quiet hysteria could.

"Not exactly. But my nephew is a cop. He's expecting me any minute."

Ben laughed, before I got to "He'll send out the fleet if I don't show up." A lame survival technique. "Yeah, right," he said, possibly not even believing the first part of what might be my dying declaration. His laugh wasn't as evil as I had imagined it would be. I settled down a bit, though my jaw was no less tight and my hands grasped the steering wheel as if I'd applied tacky glue to both.

"Look, Ben. Right now, one of my close friends is the only suspect in David Bridges's murder. I'm grasping at straws, trying to figure out who really killed him. I thought you might be able to direct me to someone who had a motive. Maybe another one of his employees."

"We weren't that close."

"What about his personal life? I know he's divorced and estranged from his son."

Ben shook his head. "Don't waste your time on them. Debbie has moved on. She's married to a Hollywood pool boy and could care less what Bridges does anymore. And him and Kevin — they're not estranged." He stumbled over the word, as if it were as unfamiliar to him as what a ticket cost to the annual fall miniatures show in San Jose. "Kevin took his mother's maiden name, Malden, and lives in Carmel in some artists' colony. Bridges could never get over that the kid didn't want to play football like his old man, so he pretends the kid is estranged but they still kept in touch from a distance." A little more trippingly that time.

"I thought you weren't close."

I immediately wanted to retract that flip remark, but Ben seemed to let it slide. "Look, I'm in your face for one reason. To let you know that you'd be better off going back to your dollhouses."

I swallowed hard. How did he know my hobby? What else did he know about me and, especially, Maddie? The last thing I wanted was for the conversation, such as it was, to take a turn to the personal.

I cleared my throat. "I'm just curious, Ben. Didn't I hear you tell David that you could" — I drew quotation marks in the hot, still air between us — "burn him."

"I was blowing smoke. He didn't give me a big enough raise and I was mad at him."

My first, unspoken, response was what Ben himself had just said: "Yeah, right."

"Is there anything to the rumor" — I made up one on the spot — "that your boss was involved in some kind of preferential treatment for certain contractors?"

"Who told you that?" Ben asked.

"It's public knowledge that the awards for all the recent projects at the Duns Scotus, like remodeling and equipment upgrades, have gone to Mellace Construction here in Lincoln Point. It's either a coincidence or something shady is going on."

"Shady, I like that. But I wouldn't know anything about it."

Between the miserable weather and the barely abating fear I experienced from having Ben Dobson in my car, I was ready to give up. Maybe my recollection of the incident between David and Ben was exaggerated, made into something it wasn't, out of a desire to lay blame for the murder on anyone but Rosie.

I took a breath, amazingly calm and sure I wasn't in danger from Ben. Not at the moment anyway. "Can you tell me one thing? What were you doing in the woods just now?"

Ben got out of the car, closed the door, and leaned in. He gave me a wicked smile. "You're too much of a lady for me to tell you."

I couldn't help smiling back, though I didn't believe him for a minute.

I wasn't ready to face Skip or Rosie. Thanks to very poor decisions today, I was hot, bothered, and hungry. A quick side trip to Sadie's would take only ten minutes if it wasn't too crowded. I'd get a chocolate malt to go and imbibe while I drove to the police station. So far there was no California law against eating while driving.

My parking spot facing the woods was right behind Sadie's. I got out of my car and left it unlocked, the windows down. There was nothing worth stealing and it would be much better than coming back to an even hotter car.

I wished I had time to get the car washed, inside and out, to erase the presence of Ben Dobson. Though I hadn't been as afraid of him at the end of the exchange as at the abrupt beginning, I still had an uneasy feeling. Maddie would have called the whole meeting creepy.

With long legs and the image of a chocolate malt spurring me on, I reached Sadie's in less than five minutes and joined a short line. I fished my wallet out of my purse, licked my dry lips, and waited, feeling guilty that I wasn't already on my way down Springfield Boulevard toward Rosie.

My turn at last. "The usual, Gerry?" Colleen asked.

"Yes, but I'm on a very tight schedule today."

Most days I enjoyed chatting with Colleen, Sadie's lovely Irish daughter-in-law, especially about her graduate school classes in political science. Today, she caught on quickly to my pressing need and prepared my malt in record time. I couldn't wait to take that first long sip of the thick chocolaty liquid.

"Hi, Mrs. Porter," a girl's voice said. "We just saw you. Where's Maddie? Isn't she out of class by now?" I turned around and nearly tripped over Taylor. I followed her pointing finger to a table in the back where Henry sat with a sundae in front of him. "Come back and eat with us."

Not again. This would be my third strike today if this were a game with Henry Baker. I went back and forth about how I'd spend the next hour. Did Rosie really need me? She hadn't called, so maybe everything had been resolved without me. Didn't I deserve a little ice cream break with friends? But what if Rosie was in custody?

My better self won. "I'd love to," I told Taylor. "But I really can't right now. I have a very important errand to do."

Taylor's face fell. Her pout was a lot like Maddie's — therefore, nearly irresistible. "Just till you finish your shake?"

I hoped she caught the sadness in my sigh. "There's someone waiting for me. In fact that's why I don't have Maddie with me." I laughed and gave her a playful poke in the shoulder. "Do you think Maddie would ever let me come here without her if I weren't on my way to a very serious meeting?"

Her face brightened. She got it. "I guess not. Maybe we'll see you later."

"For sure," I said.

I caught Henry's eye and waved. He gave me a thin smile and waved back, then put his head down and turned his attention to a pile of whipped cream.

I left the shop, still without a sip of malt. I felt I owed Henry an explanation, though I wasn't sure why. It wasn't as if I'd broken a date. Maybe because I wished I'd get a chance to.

I recovered quickly from my stress over Henry, and by the time I reached my car, half the shake was gone.

I placed the rest of my lunch in the cup holder, but only after one more long drag on the straw. I threw my purse on the passenger seat over my jacket and prepared to start the engine. After the fact, I noticed something under my jacket. The sound my purse made indicated it fell on something other than soft cloth. I looked over and saw a manila folder under the jacket, so flat it seemed empty. The folder certainly wasn't mine. Had Ben left it? By mistake? On purpose? No, I was sure I would have seen it, one way or the other, if he'd had it. Besides, Ben and I had already shared so much (a big wink here), he wouldn't have delivered this in secret.

I checked my rearview mirror and my backseat. I wanted no more surprises. I lifted my purse and jacket with care and stared at the folder. Maybe someone mistakenly dropped it in my car, thinking it was someone else's vehicle.

The biggest question was, why was I being so skittish over a simple-looking item from an office supply store? I grabbed the folder and opened it. One sheet of paper lay there, faceup. A bank record of some sort.

I picked up the record, white with a pale blue grid marking rows and columns. It looked nothing like the statement I received monthly from my own bank. There was no name to indicate whose record I was looking at, but long rows of numbers across the top. An account number? A code for the originating bank? One thing was clear, even for someone as finance-challenged as I was, some very large deposits had been made to the account, sometimes only days apart.

Why me? I asked the universe in front of me. Apparently I'd been appointed to follow up on a potential financial motive for

David Bridges's death.

One good thing about this piece of evidence, if that's what it was — as much as I'd snooped around and picked up things here and there in my questionably legal wanderings, there was no way Skip could blame me for this wrinkle.

I had neither broken nor entered into any establishment illegally, and I had an excellent alibi for when the folder was placed on the seat of my car.

CHAPTER 16

The timing was perfect. I arrived at the police station just as I was draining the last bit of chocolate shake from the cup. Since I was alone in my car, I indulged in a final, loud sip, the gurgling sound worthy of a junior high cafeteria.

The first person I saw in the sprawling, shabby waiting area was Larry Esterman, Rosie's father. I sensed that I was about to take advantage of a distraught parent to try to continue my investigation. For his own daughter's good, I reminded myself.

We greeted each other with the usual pleasantries of people who don't see each other very often. I told him he looked good, and he did the same for me.

This seemed to be the week of reunions and the platitudes that came with them.

Larry got quickly to what was on both our minds. "I can't get any information on when they'll be done with Rosie," he told me.

I thought it best to clear this up before I quizzed him on his Callahan and Savage dealings. I figured if I helped him with facts on how Rosie was doing, he'd be more receptive to my questions.

I checked out the officer on duty. What luck. Drew Blackstone had his head down, engrossed in paperwork, so we hadn't noticed each other yet. Sign-in at the LPPD was required only if a person wanted to get past the desk to the interview rooms, offices, holding cells, and other "official places" beyond.

Drew, a former student, was next in line on my list of favorites to catch on duty when I needed a favor, after Lavana and all the other young women who were Skip's groupies.

"Wait here," I said to Larry and crossed the linoleum floor to the high front desk.

"Drew, nice to see you," I said, with my best smile forward, reaching to shake the large man's hand.

"Hey, Mrs. Porter. You, too."

"I've been meaning to give you a recommendation for a book for little Davey. I know how he loves to read. If you have a pen and paper I'll write it down for you."

"Oh, terrific, Mrs. Porter. And he's not so little anymore. He's going on nine."

"Almost as old as my granddaughter. As a matter of fact, it was Rosie Norman who put me onto this book because she knows I'm always on the lookout for good children's literature." I wrote the name and author of the book, addressing Drew at the same time. "I guess you know Mr. Esterman, Rosie's father, over there waiting for his daughter."

"Yeah, he's been really patient, not like some other people nagging about how much longer, like, every ten minutes."

I smiled. "He's a nice man. Do you think you can reward his patience and check out what's happening with Rosie? I know you're swamped here, but —"

Drew waved his hand. "Aw, these forms can wait. Let me go back there for you."

"Thanks, Drew."

I gave Larry a thumbs-up as I walked back to my seat next to him.

"Quite impressive," he said. "Now I know why Rosie called you first and me only second when you weren't answering. Thank you so much. If you ever need a new refrigerator, just give a call."

"Now that you mention it, Larry, I do need information on refrigerators."

Larry sat up, interested, as most people were when you indicated an interest in their

287

business or anything they'd invested a lot of time in. "Oh?"

"Henry Baker mentioned to me that you now work for Callahan and Savage."

"Good old Henry. I don't see much of him since he retired. How is he?"

I wished I knew. I gave Larry the short version of the friendship developing between Maddie and Taylor, and then moved on.

I dragged out a variation of the line I used with Barry. "I've been looking into a couple of things, and I heard something about questionable business dealings between David Bridges at the Duns Scotus and Mellace Construction. Is it true that they're acing out your company, Callahan and Savage?"

Larry Esterman let out a small chuckle. "I guess my daughter was right. You are amazing, Geraldine. How in the world would you know that?"

"I . . . uh . . . I'm just really persistent, I suppose."

"I should tell you, you're not at the shallow end of the pool. You need to be careful."

I was never very good at sports metaphors. In fact, this had not been a good week for figures of speech in general. "So it's true?" was my careful response.

Larry bit his lip. I had a flash of memory

of a younger Mr. Esterman next to my desk in my classroom at ALHS, his teenage daughter, Rosie, waiting in the hallway. Was I sure Rosie was working to her full potential? Could she do more to be sure she got into whatever college she wanted to? Was there a particular school I'd recommend for his motherless, talented child?

He sat next to me now, in a police waiting area, while his beloved Rosie was being interrogated by the police. It was his turn to answer some questions for me if he had any hope of helping his grown-up daughter. He seemed to realize this.

"I'm not as involved as I was when I had my own business, but I've been hearing rumblings about an internal investigation. You're right — C and S is trying to find proof of unfair practices and bring a suit against Mellace and whoever is on the other end. You should know that it's very, very hard to prove fraud. You need hard and fast testimonies, documents, an impeccable witness, or someone who's willing to flip."

I thought of the folder someone left on the seat of my car, the folder now thrust into my tote. "What kind of documents?"

"Bank records, internal memos, that kind of thing. But they play it close to the vest at Mellace. They have so many other businesses going all the way up past San Francisco to Marin County, and then down the other way to Monterey, that it's easy for him to hide money." Larry spread his hands, palms down. "I'm not saying that he does. I'm just glad I don't have to worry about that part of it. That's why I like semiretirement, strictly on a contract basis. I do my job when there is one and I don't worry about the politics."

Rosie was a lot like her father, with a mild temperament and a voice that exuded trustworthiness and honesty, though I sensed the older Esterman was a little more worldly-wise than his daughter. I wondered again how Rosie ever became obsessed with someone like David Bridges. He must have had some charm that I wasn't privy to, to have captured her heart as well as Cheryl's, though I didn't have uncontestable evidence of the latter.

Drew emerged from a door behind the front desk. He met us halfway across the broad expanse of very old gray linoleum. "I rattled the cage back there and found out they're just wrapping up the interview. Your daughter will be out in a couple of minutes, Mr. Esterman."

"When you say she'll 'be out' do you mean . . . ?"

"She'll be free to go," Drew said, "but they'll probably tell her she shouldn't leave town."

The sighs of relief from the two of us were audible.

I debated showing Larry the record I had in my tote. I wanted his opinion on whether the page left in my car would constitute the kind of proof he mentioned. He had enough on his mind with his daughter's future as uncertain as it was, but if something on the mysterious sheet could help Rosie, by pointing to someone else with a strong motive to kill David, we'd all be better off in the long run.

Decision made. I pulled out the folder and showed him the page. "Larry, can you make any sense out of this?"

Larry changed his glasses and peered at the sheet. "Looks like a bank record all right." He pointed to the row of numbers across the top. "This string tells me it's an international account. I did a little overseas business in the old days and this is a familiar template." He pointed to the numbers that had caught my eye the first time I looked at the sheet, the five-digit numbers that stood out in their column. "Are you thinking these large deposits are kickbacks of some kind?"

"I have no idea."

"Whose statement is this?"

I smiled, embarrassed. "I have no idea."

I was grateful he didn't ask how I came by the information, sparing me a third, "I have no idea." I hoped Skip would be equally indifferent to my source.

"I think I know —" Larry started, but we were happily interrupted.

Rosie rushed up and hugged her father. I waited for my hug, but it didn't come.

"What's the story, honey?" Larry asked.

"I'm not arrested, but I can't leave town."

"Was it Skip who interviewed you?" I asked.

Rosie frowned at me. She worked her jaw and took deep breaths, but remained silent. I got the hint that she was upset with me, but I didn't know why. Because I kept my phone off during a memorial service?

"I think you should come and stay with me until all this blows over," Larry told his daughter. He was already steering her toward the exit.

"No, Dad. I'll be fine, and I really want to get back to my own bed. Can you just take me home?"

"Where's your car?" I asked. "I can arrange to get it to your house."

No answer.

I understood that Rosie wanted to cling to her father at that moment, but I had to clear the air. "Is something wrong?" I asked her, hoping she'd know I meant "between us?"

She closed her eyes and bit her lip. "Maybe later, Gerry."

Larry shrugged his shoulders, but seemed equally eager to leave the police station. I couldn't blame them.

I collected my tote from the chair and headed back to Drew, this time to gain admission to my nephew's office. I hoped all would go well there. I already had enough people whom I'd offended today.

"Nothing new," Skip said. "But you know that, if you saw Rosie downstairs on her way out." Skip's short-sleeved peach-colored shirt blended in with one of the faded partition walls, both clashing with his red hair. June must not have seen him leave this morning.

"Rosie didn't have much to say. She was anxious to get home." I took a seat on a formerly peach-colored chair, now an undefined hue. "I wish you hadn't picked her up before the service. When I told you —"

"I know you feel guilty about alerting us

to where she'd be, but believe me, we would have found out anyway. And wasn't that better than interrupting the service?"

"Not to Rosie."

"I'll be honest with you, Aunt Gerry, I feel in my gut that she didn't do it. She's just the closest thing we have now for a suspect. The reunion classmates all checked out."

"Even Cheryl Mellace?"

"Her husband says she was with him in their hotel room from midnight on."

"So they're each other's alibi. Is that legal?"

Skip laughed. "Of course. Maybe not convincing, but legal, definitely."

"They could have been together all night, technically, but wasn't David killed early in the morning?"

"The ME is putting the time of death from about four in the morning to when the kids found him around seven thirty." Not what I hoped — the fact that I could vouch for Rosie's whereabouts at around seven was virtually meaningless.

"And Ben Dobson?" I rubbed my arm where Ben had touched it, leaning on my driver-side window.

"A couple of people at the party corroborate your story —"

"Excuse me?" I folded my arms in mock offense.

"Just an expression. The point is that, yes, it seems they did fight, but we talked to all the maintenance staff, too, and no one was particularly surprised, but neither could anyone think of a motive for murder. Dobson was at the highest level he could go and he got a decent salary."

"What about Barry Cannon?"

"Class president, CPA, works as CFO for Mellace Construction."

"I know all that. What's his alibi?"

"The same as most people's from four to seven in the morning. He was asleep in his hotel room."

What would Skip say if he knew Barry had been sending Rosie presents, in all probability setting her up to be humiliated at the hands of David? I needed one more shot at Barry before I brought this up to Skip. Barry's reaction when I asked him about the presents told me he was indeed guilty — of present buying. Hardly a crime unless I could make a connection to David's murder.

That concluded my list of suspects, but I had one or two more loose ends. "I've been meaning to ask you, Skip, how did you manage to get hold of the locker room scene that Rosie . . . altered?"

"We got an anonymous call that we'd find it in the woods, near the crime scene."

"But it wasn't at the crime scene when you found David's body?"

"No, the call came afterward, later in the morning."

"So isn't it likely that someone planted it there?"

"Not necessarily. Much as we'd like to think we're perfect, the people at the scene don't always pick up everything. The little room was off a ways and in some bushes."

"And the anonymous caller knew exactly where you could find it?"

"Right."

"How would the person know you hadn't already found it unless he or she put it there after you left?"

Impeccable reasoning. But that's not what it was all about.

"This happens a lot, Aunt Gerry. Someone calls in a tip and the timing doesn't always make sense — maybe the person just wanted to make sure we found it — and we just have to go with it. And the locker does exist, and it was Rosie Norman who wrote hate mail on it, that's what's important here."

I wished I could argue with him. Instead,

all I could do was toss other suspects his way. "What about David's son, Kevin Malden? Have you checked out where he was over the weekend?"

Skip scratched his head. "I'm not even surprised that you know his new name. But, yeah, he checks out. He was showing some of his stuff to a few dozen other artists at some kind of fair. And his mother, Bridges's ex, was in Europe. Bridges's family is a dead end."

Police work was frustrating. I might have to think about retiring.

Was this the time when I should tell Skip about Ben Dobson's trek down the path to the crime scene in Joshua Speed Woods? And show him the bank record, which might have been left by Ben?

The bank record was the only lead I had left, if it could even be called that, and Skip needed to see it. "I have something to show you," I said. I reached back into my shoulder tote and found the folder by feel, my normal way of digging things out of the long-handled, oversize bag. I opened the folder and found . . . nothing. No sheet of paper with possibly incriminating bank records, just the blank neutral folder stock.

I removed the bag from my shoulder and sorted through its contents, looking for the sheet, thinking it slipped out of its folder. I fingered a thick wad of scrap fabric, meant to be left at the Mary Todd for my crafts students; a new pair of scissors, still in its shrink-wrap package; and a paperback copy of Edith Wharton's *The House of Mirth*, for discussion at a book club I'd joined recently. I also saw my wallet, brush, and general purse items. No eight-and-a-half-by-eleven sheet of paper of any color.

"Are you looking for cookies or something to do with the case?" Skip asked.

"I had a piece of paper in this folder. I know I had it in the building because I showed it to Larry Esterman downstairs."

Skip picked up his cubicle phone and punched a button. "Hey, Drew, did my aunt Gerry leave a piece of paper or something down there?" Skip held the receiver to his chest. "He's going to look."

I motioned to take the phone from Skip and waited until Drew came on the line again. I had another idea about the record.

"Nothing here, Skip," Drew said.

"It's Mrs. Porter, Drew. Did you by any chance see the folder I was showing to Mr. Esterman?"

"Yeah, I saw you guys looking at it. You know, I think I saw him put something in his pocket, something white, like a sheet of paper. I figured you gave it to him. Shall I put out an APB?" Drew laughed, but I didn't think it was such a bad idea.

"Thanks, anyway," I said.

Larry Esterman didn't have a briefcase or any other kind of container with him, nothing into which a sheet of paper could have fallen accidentally. There was no way he mistakenly walked off with it.

Larry Esterman rushed his daughter out of the building for a reason — he'd confiscated my record. Easy come, easy go, I thought, remembering how the record had fallen into my lap, or one seat over.

A sneaky move on the part of Rosie's father.

Larry Esterman was a man after my own heart.

With nothing much to talk about and no desire to explain my day to Skip, I left the police station and headed for Rosie's house. On the way I called Maddie, who'd been at Linda's for the better part of an hour.

"I just wanted you to know I'll be there soon, sweetheart."

"Okay, Grandma. Don't worry about me. Mrs. Reed let me help her make some leaves and now I'm doing my programming homework for tomorrow."

Huh? No nagging or whining about being left out of my errands?

Not one to question my good fortune, I clicked off and pulled into Rosie's driveway. I was reminded how close her home was to the Joshua Speed Woods. I felt a shiver through my body. Out of the corner of my eye, I thought I saw Ben Dobson strolling down the quiet street, but it was merely a gardener wearing the same color jumpsuit I'd first seen Ben wearing.

I rang Rosie's doorbell, listening for movement inside the small ranch-style home. I was fully aware that I might be waking Rosie up or interrupting a much-deserved bath. We had serious business, however, and any misunderstandings between us had to be cleared up immediately.

I waited and rang again, waited and rang again. Still no action. I sat on the front steps, happily in the shade. One of the benefits of older Lincoln Point neighborhoods was their tree-lined streets, typically large silver maples interspersed with smaller Modesto ash. I didn't think I could live where the trees looked more like miniatures, still tied to what looked like birthing posts.

I didn't have a plan for how long I'd wait in front of Rosie's house, but for now, this was as good a place as any to mope about the case and about how different the week-end had turned out from what I'd expected.

My stay in a luxury hotel had turned sour quickly, starting with David's brush-off of Rosie at the cocktail party. Now one former student was dead and another was accused of his murder. I'd been accosted, robbed, and accosted again. I'd done my share of accosting, also. Of innocent people it seemed. I'd somehow lost Rosie's confidence, abandoned my granddaughter, and made myself scarce to a potential new friend.

I thought about Henry Baker. Now that I'd been reconnected with Rosie's father (resulting in a second robbery, I noted), I didn't need Henry's input on Callahan and Savage. It would have been nice to have his friendship, however, and I guessed he'd decided that I wasn't worth the trouble.

I looked at the enormous fruitless mulberry tree in Rosie's side yard and suspected he was right.

CHAPTER 17

It wasn't my style to mope for too long. Now at four o'clock on a hot afternoon, I felt my waiting time was up. The one positive, useful thing I could do was retrieve my granddaughter from Linda's house. We could work on our room boxes at home, and I'd cook her a proper dinner, preferably including a glass of milk and something that wasn't pizza. I got up, brushed tree droppings from my slacks, and started down the stairs.

That seemed to be the cue for Rosie's front door to open.

"Gerry?"

I turned to see Rosie, freshly showered it appeared, in a deep blue chenille bathrobe that added beads of perspiration to my forehead just looking at it. She held it close around her body and I suspected it was her spirit that was chilled in spite of the high-nineties temperature. We hugged, shoulder to shoulder since I stood one step below her. She smelled of something fresh and fruity, which told me she'd bothered to treat herself to a special soak or shower gel, a good sign.

"I'm glad to see you, Rosie," I said, as we pulled away and entered the air-conditioned house.

Rosie wasn't the neatest person — she claimed that you couldn't really enjoy books if they were all lined up properly and dusted. I'd never seen her living room this disheveled, however. Her suitcases were spread on the floor, half empty, laundry in mesh bags sharing space with shoes and cosmetics. I wondered if there were an emerald and diamond bracelet buried in the wreckage.

I moved a map of downtown San Francisco, with a photograph of the Transamerica building on the front, from an easy chair to a cluttered end table and sat down.

Rosie settled on her couch, upholstered in a light beige leafy design. She was still wrapped in her robe. "I know you had good intentions, Gerry, but I was so mad that I had to miss the special service for David."

"I never intended for that to happen. I thought I was helping you, easing the way for you to go to the police and get started on clearing yourself in this awful case."

"I see that now. I was crazy to hide out as long as I did. I didn't kill David so why am I acting as though I'm guilty?"

"I don't know, Rosie, but the important thing is that you talked to the police and they trust you to stay around in case they need you. You can go back to your normal life."

I wished I believed it. I had an unnerving suspicion that whoever killed David Bridges was not through trying to pin it on Rosie. From the look on Rosie's face, I could tell she didn't see normalcy any time soon, either.

"Who do you think did it, Gerry?"

It was the first time Rosie, or anyone, had asked me that and her question reminded me that I hadn't really settled on one person. Maybe this was like that old Agatha Christie novel where everyone did it. I thought of the mystery play Rosie's class had put on one year. I couldn't remember the name but I'd enjoyed the tricky plot where everyone voted by a show of hands for who they thought committed the murder. The cast took a count and then acted out the rest of the play according to the majority vote. Case closed. They had an ending for every possible voting result. It was a nice fantasy.

"I don't know, Rosie. Maybe we can work it out if we talk for a while."

I took her nod as permission to probe more into Rosie's weekend. I started with something that had been nagging at me since Friday night. "Rosie, what did you and Barry talk about at the reunion cocktail party? You had your heads together for quite a while."

"I suppose it's hard to believe that we were chatting because he enjoyed my company."

"I didn't mean that," I said, though it had crossed my mind at the time. "It's just that I don't remember you two being especially friendly in high school and, as far as I know, you don't see him regularly these days even though he lives in town."

"As a matter of fact, Barry dropped in at the shop a couple of weeks ago, just to say hi."

"He didn't want anything in particular?" Another poorly worded question. I let out a frustrated breath. "I didn't mean it that way this time, either, Rosie. I'm just trying to follow some leads here."

"It's okay. Barry didn't buy any books, if that's what you're getting at. He did ask me if I'd heard from David, and it was right after that that the presents started coming. Let's face it. I was always a wallflower, going back thirty years, and you know I haven't changed much."

"You make friends among your customers very easily, Rosie. They all love you."

Rosie talked right past my compliment. "My parents were divorced at a time when it wasn't so common. I was only nine years old. They had joint custody of me, so I had to shuttle back and forth between their houses and I always felt like an outsider. My teeth were crooked and there wasn't any money to fix them. Remember the lisp I had for most of high school?"

"But look what you've done with your life. Your store, for one thing."

"When my mom died my freshman year, I hid in books, I guess."

"Lucky for Lincoln Point."

"Thanks, Gerry."

"Barry?" I asked.

"You're right that it wasn't what you would call a personal conversation at the cocktail party. There was no 'let's catch a movie sometime.' Barry's a bachelor, you know. He seemed more interested in my father's business, what Dad was doing these days. As if he ever knew my father or cared about my family. It was weird."

306

I'd been processing the weirdness as she talked. To me, interest in Larry Esterman, the petty thief, was interest in the company he consulted for, Callahan and Savage. Walter Mellace thought I represented Callahan and Savage and had found something Walter wanted. Why was the loser in so many recent major bids so popular? And why, other than a genetic disposition for stealing, had a Callahan and Savage consultant walked off with my precious bank record? I'd have to find a way to talk to Larry about that little trick.

For now, I had his daughter in front of me.

"Rosie, remember the box of chocolates you received at the hotel?"

"I was going to throw them away, but I thought you and Maddie might like them."

I told her, as gently as possible, about the origin of the gift. I was ready to support my story with an affidavit from Samantha, the clerk in the hotel shop, if I needed to, but Rosie didn't seem to need confirmation.

"Could it have been Barry who was sending you those gifts all along?"

"I suppose so. I know you and the girls on crafts night tried to tell me that something was not right. I just couldn't listen at the time. But why would Barry send them using David's initials?"

"You talked about, quote, a date gone bad. Are you willing to tell me more about it?"

Rosie bristled. She'd seemed to have matured in her outlook since Friday afternoon. Nothing like a murder to give one perspective. I hoped I hadn't lost her with this question. She'd referred to the date several times, but it seemed the details of its failure were still hard to talk about.

"That was a long time ago," she said.

"That's what reunions are about. A long time ago."

"Do you want some ice tea?" she asked me.

"I'd love some," I said and followed her to her kitchen.

It took longer than it should have to brew two glasses of ice tea, during which time we chatted about decaf versus regular, whether the upcoming week would be as hot as last week, and a special shipment of book club choices Rosie expected on Wednesday. She'd closed Rosie's Books early on Friday and, as far as I knew, hadn't opened it since.

"In some ways, I'm dreading going to the shop tomorrow," she said, once we were finally settled in the living room again.

"It will probably take you all of twenty

minutes to get back in the swing of things. Once you see the boxes of books waiting to be opened and start to work on the details of the fall children's program, you'll be fine."

"Fortunately, not too many of my classmates are customers. I guess we weren't your best readers."

"Except for you."

Rosie's smile was thin, but more than I'd seen for a few days. I felt a breakthrough coming.

"It was a Thursday, before the big Valentine's Day dance. David came up to me in the hallway, where the lockers were."

I knew that. My whole crafts group, including Maddie, knew that. I let Rosie take her time.

"Uh-huh. And then?"

"He kissed me and whispered in my ear that he wanted to go to the dance with me the next night."

"It was pretty short notice, wasn't it?"

Rosie uttered a bitter-sounding laugh. "So? It wasn't as if I had other plans. I nearly fainted, I was so shocked and, of course, deliriously happy. On Friday I skipped classes and went shopping for a dress. I had to beg my father to help me pay for it, and money was very tight at the

309

time. Business was slow and there were so many other expenses senior year."

Rosie was talking so slowly I had time to speculate in between phrases. This time I jumped ahead and figured David stood Rosie up.

"I'm guessing something kept David from showing up."

"It's worse than that," Rosie said. "He asked me to meet him in Joshua Speed Woods, where, you know, kids went to make out."

More interesting. "Uh-huh."

Rosie took several sips of tea, with deep breaths in between. I knew I could end her misery by calling off the question, but I kept my eye on the goal — to have as much information as possible.

"He said he'd meet me in the clearing. I knew where he meant."

"Is that where . . . ?"

"Yes, it's where he was killed," she said, without much emotion.

I expected that David's murder had put an end to romantic assignations in the clearing for the near future. "Did you go to the clearing that night?" Not the night of the murder, I said to myself. That can't be where this is heading.

Another nasty-sounding laugh. "I went all

right, in my new red dress with these little sequin hearts all over it. I got my red heels, which were right out of the box, all dirty, walking down the path, but I didn't care. I was going to meet David."

A long pause. I became impatient. "And he didn't show?"

"Worse than that," Rosie said again. "Do you remember Mathis Berg? He was the school's biggest nerd."

I nodded. "Math Bird."

"Well, when I got to the clearing, guess who was there?"

It started to fall into place. A prank perpetrated by the cool kids on the unwitting wallflowers of the class. "They'd set Mathis up, too? So instead of David, you met Mathis there?"

"Worse than that."

One more time. Rosie knew how to spin a yarn. Too bad she was the victim in this one.

"They were all there to see it. It was dark, just the moonlight illuminating the clearing. Then, suddenly all these lights went on. They'd rigged them somehow to hang from the trees. I picked out the football team and the cheerleading squad, mostly, but it seemed like the whole senior class was there in the woods. Mathis and I were standing there, all lit up. He had on a tux and I remember the collar was so big for his skinny neck. We were both so mortified."

To think I'd taught those students who made up the jeering crowd, probably the same day and the days before and after. I might even have given a couple of them As. Would I have graded them differently if I'd known what shallow lives they led? That was a moral discussion for another time.

I took a cue from Abraham Lincoln: "A friend is one who has the same enemies as you have." Rosie and Mathis should have waltzed out of the woods and gone to the Valentine's Day dance together and had the best time of anyone there.

But that was hindsight, and an adult response, not a high schooler's.

"How cruel, Rosie. You must have felt awful," I said. I moved to a seat next to her on the couch and put my arm around her.

"I wanted to die right there."

"Did you talk to Mathis about it?"

"Never, never. Looking back, I guess he was in his own private agony. I learned that Sheila Philips, who was voted the prettiest girl in the class — do they even do that anymore? I hope not — was the one who invited Mathis to the clearing. It's so dumb, Gerry, what seems important when you're seventeen."

"And you never talked to David about it?"

She shook her head. "Never. But he was nice to me after that. He didn't ask me out or anything, but he would smile and once he picked up something I dropped in class. That made me think the whole setup in the clearing wasn't his idea, that his boorish friends put him up to it. And then this summer, when I started getting presents from him — I thought it was him — I figured he was finally going to make it up to me."

"I'd have been so angry with him."

"My father was the one who was ready to kill him." Rosie stopped and put her hand to her mouth. "I can't believe I said that."

"It's just an expression, Rosie. We don't realize what a terrible thing it is to say, until something like this really happens."

"My father wanted to have it out with him in the schoolyard. Imagine that. He'd have been arrested immediately." Rosie laughed. "Me, I had this fantasy of pouring tacky glue all over David's lying lips."

I withdrew my arm from the back of the couch and sat up. "What did you say?"

"I was into miniatures then, too, remember? So, naturally, that's what I thought of."

"Naturally."

I left Rosie's to go to Linda's where Maddie was hanging out. I was ready for grief as only an eleven-year-old can give it. On the way to her house, I called Linda, using my headset. I wondered if Bluetooth was now a verb — I Bluetoothed Linda. I'd read that the technology was invented in Denmark and named after one of their peacemaking tenth-century kings, Harald Bluetooth. At first hearing, the story seemed like something made up in an eighth-grade creative writing class, but I'd read it enough times from trusted sources to believe it.

I needed to ask Linda a question out of range of Maddie's ears.

"Linda, did you tell Rosie about how David Bridges's lips were . . . how his lips were when they found him?"

"Glued together? Nuh-uh, I thought it was too gross."

I knew that the police hadn't released that detail. Did Rosie know because she did it, or was it one huge coincidence that the killer had used glue, just as Rosie imagined she would thirty years ago. Rosie had told her story with such guilelessness, I couldn't believe she knew the implications.

"Thanks, Linda," I said, though I didn't feel grateful.

My attention switched to Rosie's father. A man who hadn't been in my consciousness for many years now loomed at the front of my mind. He took shape as a former refrigeration specialist who now worked for Callahan and Savage, who stole a bank record from me, and who was angry enough to want to kill David Bridges thirty years ago. Had it all finally come together for him? It was altogether possible that Larry Esterman knew of his daughter's fantasy and carried it out for her. Except that the deed pointed to Rosie and he wouldn't have wanted that.

Every hour today seemed to have created more problems and questions for me. I'd heard many stories, but I was no closer to the truth than I was at noon on Saturday when I heard of David's murder.

I hung up and called Maddie's cell. She loved getting calls on it directly, although lately she told me she much preferred text messages. I had no trouble manipulating two sets of tweezers at the same time, to place a delicate bead on a piece of fabric, but I didn't think my fingers could work the tiny buttons on the phone pad to send a TM.

"Hi, Grandma. I'm helping Mrs. Reed make some ferns like the ones in the Duns Scotus hotel lobby. Remember that bridge and how those trees made it look like you were in a jungle?"

315

Yes, and how the bushes and rocks could hide a mugger and purse thief. I hoped one day I could look at a garden like that and not think of crime. "I remember, sweetheart."

"Look at this," Maddie said, showing me, in person, a miniature version of a large leaf, like the kind you'd see in a real jungle, or in a hotel lobby atrium. "Guess what it's really made of, Grandma."

Linda stood behind her, her look daring me to spoil my granddaughter's fun.

I took the leaf from her and scanned it. "I have no idea."

"It's sticky paper!" Maddie was delighted to have fooled me. Or she thought she'd fooled me. (She'd left telltale scraps of paper backing on the table behind her.) "See how the sides of the leaf stick to each other, and all you have to do is shape it with scissors and snip off little pieces to look like separate leaves."

"Nice work. I'm glad you two had a good time."

"Uh-huh. We had two kinds of Popsicles," Maddie announced.

"The fruit-flavored ones," Linda added, as if to gain health points.

I knew that Linda was addicted to sugary

sweet Popsicles, the kind with a long list of artificial ingredients on the box. I liked to believe Sadie's homemade ice cream was better for Maddie, but if sugar kept her from nagging me about where I'd been, it was okay with me.

After Linda and I made a plan to "talk later," Maddie and I headed home. I waited but never got a question from Maddie about what I'd done during my several hours away this afternoon. Had she learned reverse psychology? Did she think that if she didn't ask me, I'd voluntarily give her an update on the David Bridges case? I wouldn't fall into that trap.

"I'm sorry I didn't pick you up today," I said, turning right on Gettysburg Boulevard toward home.

"No problem."

No problem? No leg-kicking? No bargaining to tag along wherever I was going next? Maddie knew about David's death from the announcement at the groundbreaking ceremony at the high school and she knew of my Internet search for Callahan and Savage. She must have known I'd gone to Skip's office a couple of times since then, and therefore that there was an investigation going on. Where was the whining? Where were the incessant pleas to help?

"You were okay with Mrs. Reed?"

"I told you, we made ferns and ate Popsicles."

"A perfect day."

Why wasn't I happier that Maddie had enjoyed herself, out of harm's way, while I continued to dig around, entertaining strange men in my car near Joshua Speed Woods?

I had to admit I missed Nancy Drew.

CHAPTER 18

Maddie hadn't always loved dollhouses and miniatures. It had taken the Bronx apartment dollhouse to win her over. I'd abandoned the project after Ken died and Maddie started working with me to help me get back to it. It was completely furnished now but there was always something to add, like the cracker crumbs we'd whipped up last night.

As a hobby, miniatures had a lot going for it. Unlike say, golf or skiing, you didn't need to leave home to do it. And you could make progress on a project in as little as ten minutes. Often while heating dinner in the microwave, I'd pop over to one of my crafts areas and apply a quick coat of varnish to a tiny table or bookcase, or I'd test a gluing job I'd done in the morning.

Tonight we worked for a while on our separate Alasita projects, Maddie on her soda fountain, I on my Christmas scene.

Neither was very inspired, I felt, but maybe our real life was so exciting that we needed a stable, boring miniature life.

Maddie added two new flavors to her ice cream parlor tonight, Tasty Taylor and Dusty Doug.

"The dust stands for malt powder, the way Sadie uses it on her sundaes," she informed me — needlessly, because Sadie's dusty road sundae was my favorite after her chocolate malt shakes.

I had some embroidery to finish up on the Christmas stockings I'd bought in Benicia last week, but the whole scene still left me cold. I couldn't remember being so dissatisfied with a project. Certainly not the replica I'd made of Lincoln's Springfield, Illinois, home. Not the street of shops I'd put together, that included a flower stand, a bookstore, and a haberdashery. I hoped something would occur to me before the end of the week when our projects needed to be finished.

"I'd like to make a robe for the Bronx bathroom," Maddie said.

"We can look through our scraps," I said.

It made my heart swell that we could talk like this, each knowing what the other meant. I knew that Maddie didn't mean a life-size robe or the New York borough that was three thousand miles away, and she knew that I was referring to pieces of fabric to put together for a tiny article of clothing.

Terry cloth was hard to work with; the nap was so large and spread out on most selections that the robe or towel wouldn't be able to drape well over a tiny tub or rod. We had several choices, such as dipping the fabric in a glue and water mixture to shape it, or using a thinner fabric with a tighter weave that looked like terry.

We chose the former. I made the glue bath while Maddie rummaged through the box of fabric scraps and found the shade of blue she had in mind.

I heard her groan as she cut the material. "It's picking up everything," she said, showing me what would end up as a sleeve, with tiny beads clinging to it. She had a hard time shaking them off as they clung to the almost magnetic fabric. "It's just like my winter terry robe at home. It's as sticky as tape sometimes."

The revelation flashed in my mind like the only neon sign in Lincoln Point, the one in the window of Jeff's Video Arcade on Springfield Boulevard. Terry cloth picks up things — pieces of thread, hair, lint, and now beads. Why not a tiny oval mirror?

I pictured the hallway on the eleventh floor of the Duns Scotus Hotel. The scene was vivid, playing out before me: Cheryl in her robe, leaving David's room to get ice. Cheryl and Rosie arguing, then wrestling with the locker room box. One of the tiny mirrors, not glued on properly (that was the hardest to imagine) coming off in the struggle and sticking to Cheryl's robe. The mirror finally falling from the robe in the entryway to David's suite.

For completeness, I had to add: Gerry entering David's suite with a key stolen from a Lincoln Point homicide detective and finding the mirror on the floor.

It made sense, and if some variation of my play was true, I could hold onto my belief that Rosie told the truth when she said she never went into David's room.

I was glad I hadn't presented the mirror to Skip.

Had I just cleared Rosie?

I wished it were that easy.

"Can you have two BFFs?" Maddie asked me while we were saying good night.

"Of course. Do you have a new best friend in town besides Taylor?"

"Doug, in my class."

"That's nice. You've told me about him.

He's Dusty Doug in your mini soda fountain, right?"

She nodded. "He's the one who lets me tell jokes and laughs at them."

"Maybe I can meet him sometime."

"Nuh-uh."

Uh-oh. It was too soon in Maddie's life for her to be keeping her family away from her friends. I took comfort in the fact that she'd told me his name. It occurred to me that Doug might be the reason Maddie wasn't kicking her legs anymore when I left her behind.

"I'm sorry to hear that," I said, with a smile that was supposed to tell her I wasn't bothered.

"Grandma, do you have a good picture of me and you?"

"I'm sure I do. What do you want it for?"

She patted a spot next to her clock. "Just to put on my table here. Mine are all on my old computer at home."

"I'll dig one out for you. That reminds me. Why did the witch need a computer? I've been dying to know."

Maddie shook a sleepy head. "Nuh-uh, can't tell you till we're with Taylor and Mr. Baker. That was the deal."

"Oh. Well, that might not happen, sweetheart."

"Why not?"

"You can still have playdates with Taylor, but it might not include her grandfather and me."

"Did you fight with Mr. Baker?"

"No. It's just —"

"Complicated, right? That's what my parents always say when their friends get divorced or something."

"Right. It's complicated."

Usually, no matter how hot the day, nights in the Bay Area were cool. Without even trying to do anything productive, I took a glass of herbal ice tea to the coolest spot in the house — my atrium, one of the features of my Eichler home that I couldn't live without. My house had needed a whole new roof last year, and Richard had suggested an upgrade while I was at it — a retractable atrium skylight. It seemed a luxury I didn't need, but now I didn't know why I'd waited so long to have it installed. When it was closed, the acrylic material cast beautiful patterns of light on the floor; when it was open the atrium was completely exposed to the cool outside air.

I pushed the button and watched the skylight slide back on its track.

I refused to let my recent atrium experience in the Duns Scotus color my pleasure. These were my trees, my plants. I could name every one of them — azalea, mums, cyclamen — and they harbored no danger.

It was the kind of night when Ken and I, unable to sleep, might come out here and chat about the upcoming week or share with each other our own reviews of books and movies. The ferns planted around the edge were a labor of love our first few months and still reminded me of a wonderful time in my life. The multitude of empty pots that I'd neglected to fill were only a mild reproach.

In recent years, Beverly came by often to relate her adventures as a civilian volunteer for the LPPD. She had funny stories about SUVs driving on the sidewalks to get around traffic or about the excuses people came up with for not wearing seat belts. "I'm on my way to get it fixed" was all too common, and "I'm allergic to vinyl" was one of my favorites.

I pictured Beverly on her porch on this warm, windless night, sharing stories with Nick. A smile came to my face. Beverly had contracted rheumatic fever as a child and lived day to day with a damaged heart. We'd had several scares when we thought we'd lost her and never predicted that she'd live longer than her brother, Ken. There was no one who deserved a loving companion more than she did.

Maddie was sleeping in the corner bedroom; that was enough company for me.

Or so I thought.

I heard the faintest knocking on my front door. I put down my glass and turned my better ear to the sound. Unmistakable shuffling noises reached my ear along with another soft tap, tap, tap. Someone was at my door at ten thirty. Not the latest I'd ever had company, but generally late night visitors were expected.

I got up and checked the peephole. Barry Cannon peered back at me from the other side.

My breath caught. Barry looked the most unkempt I'd ever seen him. If peephole lenses could be trusted, he had a miserable expression and a dark shadow on his face. He wore a stretched-out T-shirt with a sports logo on the front.

How did he know where I lived? I wasn't listed in the phone book. I thought back and realized I'd probably put my address in the faculty section of Rosie's updated yearbook.

I debated whether to open the door. I worried about Maddie, in dreamland one room away. Barry shuffled his feet and tapped again.

My ear was still close to the door and I jumped, though the knock was light.

I took a breath. No one who comes to kill you knocks so gently, I reasoned, or looks so downtrodden. Also, Barry was shorter than I was, and even though he was more muscular, I'd always thought that height gave one the edge.

I opened the door.

"I'm sorry to bother you so late, Mrs. Porter," Barry said. "But remember you said you wanted to meet with me."

So I had.

"Come in, Barry," I said, ushering him into the atrium. As he passed by me in my foyer, I'd detected no smell of alcohol, which brought me great relief.

"I know this isn't what you had in mind, but I need to talk to you," he said.

I tried to hide my excitement at having a chance to interview Barry in a better environment than Miller's Mortuary. I recalled his nasty mood at that time and took his presence in my home so late at night as a sign that he was ready to cooperate.

I wasn't completely devoid of fear, however. What if he was a killer? Killing twice wouldn't be a great leap. I wondered if I should slip my cell phone into my pocket and surreptitiously keep my index finger on the speed dial button for Skip. I also thought of saying something like, "I'm not alone, you know. My very tall, husky son is in the next room." Or, to protect Maddie, I might say, "I'm utterly alone in the house."

This was no way to start an interview.

"Can I get you a glass of tea? Or something else to drink?" I asked him.

Barry shook his head, running his hand across his forehead at the same time. When the light from the small lamp in the atrium hit just right, I could see beads of perspiration. "I'm good, thanks. I shouldn't have been so rude to you today."

Barry's manner put me at ease. He seemed as dejected as Rosie when David let her down. "It wasn't the right time to approach you, Barry. I'm really sorry for the loss of your good friend. But I have so many questions about his death and I need to have them answered."

"I'm aware of that. And that Rosie is being accused of killing David. I know you became friends after graduation and I'm sure you want to clear her."

"I want to discover the truth." Wasn't that always what prosecutors said in their opening trial remarks?

"Everyone in the gang is talking about how you're going around investigating and I decided to come here myself and set everything straight. You know, you still have a lot of power over your students, Mrs. Porter. I guess we still need your approval." Not everyone, I thought, calling Cheryl's "you're not my teacher anymore" outburst to mind. "I swear to you, I could never have killed David. He and I have been friends since we were kids."

Barry broke down and I had a moment of feeling sorry for him, but I couldn't let him get away without answering a few questions. He sat hunched on a chair across from me. We might have been in English 1A at the Abraham Lincoln High School thirty years ago. But then all Barry would have had to explain was why his Steinbeck paper would be late.

"Maybe you didn't kill your friend, Barry, but you do have some explaining to do."

Barry nodded. "I don't know where to start, Mrs. Porter."

"Maybe you can begin by telling me why you sent Rosie presents using David's name."

Barry folded his hands, as if in prayer. I could tell he wanted to ask me how I knew about the misrepresented gifts, but thought better of it. He lumbered up from the chair.

"I shouldn't have come. I've said all I wanted to say, and that's it."

"Barry Cannon," I said, in a classroom voice, mindless of Maddie sleeping not far away.

It worked. My roughly forty-eight-year-old former student, whose brown hair was now sprinkled with gray, responded like the well-behaved young man he used to be and sat down again, letting out a long breath. "I'm not proud of this."

I put the best spin I could on the situation. "Barry, someone else's life is at stake here. If you were too shy to ask Rosie out for yourself —"

Barry's loud, rueful laugh interrupted me. I was afraid Maddie would wake. But remembering the drama she'd snoozed through at the Duns Scotus, I relaxed.

"No, no, no," Barry said. I was glad Rosie wasn't around to hear his vehement denial of his wanting to spend time with her. In her fragile state, she would have taken it as yet one more rejection by her classmates. "I'm not courting Rosie. If anyone, I was courting her father."

"Oh?" I hoped for a quick explanation and Barry came through.

"What I mean is, I was trying to get inside

330

information from Callahan and Savage. Her father, Larry Esterman, consults for them now. We wanted David to do it himself — to buddy up to Rosie so we could get to her father. We knew Rosie was still vulnerable as far as David was concerned. She never held him accountable for an incident that happened when we were seniors."

High schoolers and their incidents that "happened." I didn't look forward to the days when Maddie would be in the thick of it. I consoled myself with the fact that Richard seemed to get through those years without trauma of the magnitude Rosie had experienced. But, unlike his daughter, Richard had a steady, nearly unflappable temperament, and took virtually no risks. Good qualities in an orthopedic surgeon, I supposed.

I remembered Rosie's mention of an unexpected visit Barry made to her shop. "You actually did a little research about how Rosie felt about David, didn't you? You went to her shop and tested the waters." If I were standing, my hands would have been on my hips in a how-could-you stance.

"I said I wasn't proud of this. But David refused to try to manipulate Rosie. He said once was enough."

Big of him, I thought. "How did you happen to have David's trophy when you bought the candy in the hotel gift shop?"

Barry looked at me with surprise. I was sure I appeared smarter to him now than I ever had while teaching him the intricacies of literary criticism. "I was responsible for taking it from the cocktail party. You can't imagine how valuable something like that is. I can't believe it's in police custody now, like any other weapon."

"Did you take the trophy to David in his suite?"

"Yeah, he wanted it for the night on Friday. Then I was supposed to pick it up before the banquet on Saturday night."

I gave Barry a few moments to mourn his friend again. I had the idea that in his mind they were seventeen or even ten years old and that he was reliving many of their good times together.

Not by a long shot did I have what I needed from Barry, however, and I started in on a different track. "Why didn't you approach Larry Esterman directly?"

"We thought about it, but he was pretty angry back then at what we pulled on Rosie. We doubted he'd take to our scheme."

"You keep saying 'we,' Barry. I assume you're referring to Mellace Construction?"

Barry jolted his head up. "Are we on the

record here, Mrs. Porter? Because —"

"I'm not LPPD, Barry."

"Close enough. I knew this was a bad idea, but, believe it or not, I want to see David's killer caught. Very badly."

"Without owning up to your part in fraudulent business practices."

Barry took a deep breath. "That about sums it up."

I needed a recap. "Let me see if I have this straight. Mellace Construction, with you as its CFO, goes around finding out what other companies are going to bid for jobs and then bids lower to get the contract. That's why you needed help from a Callahan and Savage insider like Larry Esterman." Barry nodded and I continued. "And when that doesn't work, you simply work a deal with people like David Bridges who are willing to cheat and give you the contract anyway. For a cut, I assume." Another slow nod from Barry. "Is that how Mellace got the contract for the new athletic field? Because our city managers are as unscrupulous as you and your company are?"

"That's harsh, Mrs. Porter."

"So are your practices." I had a brainstorm. "Was it you who stole my purse?"

Barry's head couldn't go any lower. "I never, never would have hurt you, Mrs.

Porter. Walter told me he saw you sneaking into David's room after the murder. He figured you were with C and S and found something damaging."

I was probably more shocked than I should have been, given the events of the weekend. "You knocked me over and stole my purse, Barry."

"Can I get some tea?"

"I'll be right back," I said.

Chapter 19

I hurried the tea preparation because I didn't want to lose Barry. We'd been sitting in a spot past the middle of the atrium, toward the front door, just out of range of sight from the kitchen. I hoped his attack of conscience or whatever had sent him to me wasn't waning.

I carried in a tray of tea and cookies (since Barry had been so cooperative thus far) and asked as I was walking, "What happened with David, Barry? Did he start to get nervous about breaking the law, so someone in your company had to get him out of the way?" The someone I had in mind was Walter Mellace, the hallway hulk, who had accosted me. My theory was taking shape — Walter thought I was from Callahan and Savage, looking for the evidence David had claimed to have to expose Mellace Construction. Why else would anyone be breaking into David's suite?

Barry shot down that theory almost before I'd mounted it. "No way. David was on board. There's a big remodel of the Duns Scotus coming up. He was totally ready to do whatever it took to give us that huge contract."

Barry said this with pride in his voice. It was a depressing thought, that two boyhood friends who had probably shared innocent games were now proud partners in a fraudulent business scheme. Maybe that first not-so-innocent game they played with Rosie's and Mathis's self-confidence was the beginning of their partnership in crime.

I shared none of that musing with Barry.

I thought of Ben Dobson, my recent passenger. "Could someone else have had proof of the fraud and tried to get a cut of the money? Or, possibly blackmail David?"

"I thought of that, but then why kill the person who might be cutting you in or paying you big bucks to keep quiet?"

"Good point."

The way Barry gobbled up my ginger cookies, he would have given Skip a run for his money in a cookie-eating contest. "These are awesome, Mrs. Porter," he said.

In spite of the flattery, I intended to pursue one more avenue. "Tell me about Cheryl Mellace, Barry."

"There's a piece of work, huh? I don't know. I guess it was never really over between those two."

"Do you think David was calling it off and she retaliated? Or she wanted to end the relationship and they struggled, and —"

He shook his head. "I've talked to her. We had breakfast this morning." I thought of scolding Barry for his bad taste in restaurants, but I'd impressed him enough with my extrasensory abilities. "She's devastated over this. And you probably didn't see the side of her this weekend that everyone sees all year. Cheryl's the one behind all the charity giving the Mellaces do."

"That's not an unusual division of labor for a wealthy couple." I wasn't ready to give Cheryl the benefit of the doubt.

"Well, all I know is that Cheryl loved David. I think she was planning to leave Walter in fact. But that's one thing David and I didn't share — our love lives."

I had to be sure Barry wasn't holding out on me. "I thought men friends shared that kind of thing."

Barry swallowed hard. Tears escaped and ran down his cheeks. "That's the kind of guy David was. We made a kind of game of hinting at what was going on with women in both our lives, as if my life were as full as his. But really David knew I didn't have much along those lines, and he did, and he didn't want to lord it over me."

Another dead end. According to Barry, David and Cheryl were both candidates for sainthood.

"I think I'm out of questions," I said.

"I'm not." Barry's frown and abrupt turnaround unnerved me. "What are you going to do with what I told you, Mrs. Porter? About the business."

"I don't have to do anything, Barry. The police are already working on David's financial records, and if everything we've discussed has crossed my mind before tonight, it has probably crossed theirs."

"Believe me, David knew how to cover his tracks." He said this again as a matter of pride in his deceased friend.

"It's only a matter of time, Barry. Your best bet is to go to the police and tell them what you told me. Make it easy for them so they'll be more inclined to go easy on you."

Not that he deserved it.

Barry stood and walked with me to the door. "You may be right, but I'm not ready now, if ever, to go to the police. And anything we've said tonight . . . well, if anyone asks me, we just chatted about old times at ALHS."

I opened the door, and at the same moment the doors opened on a sedan parked outside my house. Three men got out. The street was quiet at this time of night, all residents' cars safely tucked into garages. There could be only one reason for the unmarked car and its occupants.

"You may not have to go to the police, Barry. I think they've come to you."

I was grateful that the LPPD didn't pull out all the stops with sirens and spinning red-and-blue lights.

Something told me that my nephew would be stopping by soon, to explain the quiet drama in front of my house, so instead of retiring my tired mind and body to my bedroom, I refilled the cookie plate and put more water on for tea.

I sat in my chair and tried to put the new information in order. There wasn't much that I hadn't guessed before Barry's visit, but I felt that I could cross Barry off my mental list of murder suspects. His affection for his lifelong friend was obvious, and he seemed as confused as I was about who might have killed David.

Barry would be paying dearly enough for his other crimes. He hadn't directly accused Walter Mellace of orchestrating the broadly applied scheme, but it might be another story once he was under police lights. I wondered if Walter Mellace had made contingency plans in case something like this happened.

I thought of Larry Esterman and his stealing the records that had been left on my car seat, most likely by Ben. What could that mean? I narrowed it down to two possibilities: First that he was going to undertake his own investigation to clear his daughter, and second, that there was something on the sheet that incriminated him.

Barry had confirmed what Rosie had told me earlier — that Larry had been perhaps more angry than Rosie about the so-called incident in Joshua Speed Woods. Could Larry have killed David after all these years? Why wait? It was possible that David's compounding of the insult to his daughter by essentially stealing from Larry's company might have put Larry over the edge.

Fine, I thought, Barry is off the list and Larry is on.

Not what you'd call progress.

As predicted, the next face I saw through my peephole was Skip's. I opened the door and enjoyed his smile when he heard the kettle whistling. "I hope there's food to go

340

with that," he said.

"Of course. But not before you tell me what that was all about." I pointed in the direction of the sidewalk where LPPD plainclothesmen had been waiting for Barry Cannon.

Skip waved one hand at me while the other took up a cookie. "Nothing new. And, I'm guessing, nothing you don't already know. We had our guys look into the construction award records as far as they could without a warrant." He laughed. "Sort of a Maddie approach."

"She'll be thrilled to hear you call it that."

"I know. I get to tell her, okay? It's not open-and-shut, but a little more digging is bound to uncover an illegal scheme to lock out Mellace's competition. Since Barry is Mellace's CFO, we figured he must have had a part in it."

"And you had a feeling he'd be here?" I called from the kitchen where I was attending to the tea.

During the summer especially, I was thankful for a refrigerator that made ice automatically, but lately the process took on a new dimension — I wondered if some underhanded negotiations were involved in the purchase of my home refrigeration system. Had a big company ridden over a

341

small one to get my service contract?

As soon as this case is over, I mused, I really must pursue other interests.

"We've been tailing Barry all day to see what plans he might make now that one of his partners is dead. Imagine my surprise . . . *not* . . . when Drew called in and said he'd tracked Barry to your house tonight."

"He just stopped by, honestly. I didn't invite him. He probably thinks I called you to arrest him."

"Right now, we've just taken him in for questioning. I figure if he ended up here, he must be ready to confess."

I was honored that criminals preferred to bare their souls in my home instead of interview room number three at the LPPD.

Larry Esterman's name was on the tip of my tongue, but I hadn't had a chance to look again at the package of e-mails Maddie had given me, and I didn't want to put Rosie's father in a bad light on the basis of a hunch. I considered telling Skip that the mystery of who mugged me in the Duns Scotus lobby had been solved, but I decided not to complicate matters.

For now, I let it go and enjoyed tea and cookies with my nephew.

■ ■ ■ ■

I had about another half hour before I'd have to crawl into bed, no matter how warm and stuffy my bedroom was. When Skip left, I took out the e-mails. They were useless except as documentation of contract awards. Mostly boilerplate, such as *pursuant to our determination* and *herewith we offer you*. I needed the pages Maddie had given to Skip. I'd had only a glance at them in his office. On the other hand, I thought that even if they were in front of me now, I wouldn't be able to focus. It was time to call it a day.

I turned out all the lights on my way to my bedroom. Only then did I notice the little red light blinking on my answering machine. It was unusual that I wouldn't have seen the light when we got home this afternoon, and even more amazing that Maddie didn't notice it.

Surely I could manage one more task before going to bed. I pushed the button.

"Hi, this is Henry. Sorry we missed each other today, Gerry. Call me when you get in later if you wish."

Four strikes. Was there even a game that allowed that many?

CHAPTER 20

On Tuesday morning at breakfast, I had a treat for Maddie, besides the homemade strawberry preserves crafter Mabel Quinlan had distributed to the group last week.

"How would you like to take a ride to San Francisco this afternoon and finally get a Ghirardelli sundae? I'll pick you up at the Rutledge Center after class and we'll drive right up."

Anyone listening in on our family life would have thought that our diet revolved around ice cream: chocolate malts, caramel cashew ice cream, hot fudge sundaes. They wouldn't be far off.

"That would be cool, Grandma. Do you have more errands to do at the hotel?"

I ruffled her curls. "Why would you ask that?"

I felt I was doing my duty as a good grand-mother by at least starting our afternoon with the promised sundae.

We drove directly to Ghirardelli Square and parked a few blocks away — the best we could do, even on a weekday afternoon. A shopping area at the end of a cable car line, the square offered one of the best views in the city. Using a guide we'd picked up at the Duns Scotus over the weekend, Maddie pointed out the hills of Marin County, the Golden Gate Bridge, and the maritime museum.

For a chocolate lover, the Ghirardelli Chocolate Factory, dating back to the nineteenth century, was the centerpiece of the shopping area. The entire square smelled of sweet, melting chocolate. On this warm summer day, people were lined up around the block on Larkin Street for a chance to eat an outrageously large sundae or soda in cramped quarters.

I held our place in line while Maddie tossed a shiny penny into a fountain already full of coins, each one with a wish attached, I surmised. I never participated in such activities, even as a child. I could never isolate one wish and my parents weren't about to have me toss in enough coins to cover them all.

Today, I'd truly be at a loss to choose among my wishes. The list ran from a healthy, happy life for Maddie, her parents, and all my friends and relatives, to a solution to the David Bridges murder case. If there were coins left over, I'd wish for another trip to England to see Queen Mary's dollhouse.

We chose brownie sundaes, with enormous scoops of ice cream, chocolate sauce, and a large brownie stuck down the side of the bowl, in case the thousands of calories in the sundae weren't enough. We immediately wrapped our brownies in napkins for later. We weren't gluttons, after all.

It was hard to think of much else in the presence of such delicious decadence. Sadie's in Lincoln Point was an outstanding little shop, but the excitement of being in San Francisco and the refreshing, cool air by the bay made everything taste better.

In spite of being in this legendary area, where Tony Bennett had left his heart, Maddie's mind, like mine, drifted to the murder case.

"Grandma, can we work on the information I downloaded about those contracts and things?"

I stirred errant crumbs from the brownie into my ice cream. "We should put brownie crumbs on the counter in the Bronx house," I said.

"Grandma?"

"I'd love to work on that information, but you gave the printout to Uncle Skip, remember?" So there.

Maddie reached into her backpack. "I have copies," she said, with a chocolate-rimmed grin.

"I should have known."

"If you had the e-mails I gave you, we could work on everything right now," she said.

My turn. I reached down into my tote, on the floor by my feet. "I brought the e-mails with me."

"I should have known," she said.

I wondered if anyone could have been as proud of a grandchild as I was at that moment.

We both wanted to work on the contract documents on the spot, but one look at our tiny marble-topped table, and another at the long line of customers waiting for their turn at overdosing on chocolate, and we knew that was a bad idea.

"What about the hotel lobby?" I said. "You don't have to be staying there to walk in and use the coffee tables and chairs. It will be as if we're still registered," I said.

Maddie gave me a sideways look. "You're

not going to dump me in the pool, are you?"

Between bouts of laughter, I made a promise to keep Maddie dry, and she accepted.

I couldn't remember ever being so full as I was driving back toward downtown San Francisco.

"I'll never eat again," Maddie said, both hands on her fat-free belly, though we both knew that sentiment would barely last till dinnertime.

While I drove around the ramps of the Duns Scotus parking garage, I organized my goals for the trip.

I needed to establish the chain of custody for Rosie's locker room scene, tracking its journey from the crafts room in my home to the hands of my LPPD nephew. If I believed Rosie, I could account for the scene up to its fate in room five sixty-eight of the Duns Scotus on Saturday morning, when Rosie unleashed thirty years of anger on it, then dumped it in the trash. The big question: who took the scene from there to the woods of Lincoln Point and then called it in?

I also wanted to study the documents provided by Maddie's Internet search. This task didn't seem as important now that

Barry Cannon had all but confessed the business fraud to me, and was in police custody, but I liked to be thorough.

What to do first? I wasn't eager to take Maddie with me on my mission to talk to housekeeping personnel about the locker scene. She had no idea what had happened to the cute room box she liked so much and I'd hoped to keep it that way. Since we were no longer registered at the hotel, we didn't have access to any of the amenities (that is, I couldn't dump her at the pool even if I'd wanted to).

"How shall we do this?" I asked Maddie. We had the elevator to ourselves as we rode from the parking garage to the lobby floor.

"Just take me with you everywhere and I'll be very quiet, okay?"

A promise was a promise.

"Then, let's say the first stop is the front desk."

Maddie uttered a loud "Whew," which, I guessed, expressed her relief that I had no plans to toss her in the water.

I had to find Aaron. I was prepared to wait a long time if necessary, but good fortune smiled on us, and he was on duty.

Maddie and I joined a short line waiting to check in or out, though I assumed that unlike me, most people checked out through their television sets. I didn't think I'd ever have the confidence in technology that it took to trust a remote control with my credit card.

"Hi, Aaron," I said. "It's Mrs. Porter, remember?"

Aaron's eyes widened, as if he expected an emergency. "Mrs. Porter, I thought you checked out."

Impressive that Aaron would have that data at his fingertips. But then, I knew I'd been a memorable guest, what with maintenance problems and attracting petty crime in the lobby.

"I did check out, Aaron, and it was a wonderful stay," I said.

From a spot down and to my left came another voice, that I didn't expect. "I hope you got our evaluation card," Maddie said. "We wrote nice things about everyone."

I uttered a quick prayer that Aaron's department was completely separate from the evaluation department and that he would have no idea whether we'd filled out the card (I hadn't) or not.

Aaron gave Maddie a big smile. "Thanks, honey." He might have been the only person of his generation to call anyone "honey."

I cleared my throat, preparing for the big

push. "Aaron, you've done so much for us already, and now I need just one more little favor. I need to find the person who cleaned room five sixty-eight on Saturday."

"Did you leave something behind? I can call lost and found."

Aaron was ever the optimist, trying to shunt me off to another department. When would the young man realize that I was a special case? Even when I'd needed an electrician and a plumber it was for a different reason than most hotel guests had.

"I didn't exactly leave anything behind. See, my granddaughter and I left the hotel on Saturday morning for a while, then our other roommate, Rosie Norman, checked out of the room sometime later." I used my fingers to tick off the timeline. "Then, my granddaughter and I came back in the afternoon, and in between the room was cleaned."

"It was very neat when we got back," Maddie said. Was this what she'd meant by being "very quiet"? We'd have to talk.

"I need to speak to that person," I told Aaron.

"Was there a problem?" he asked.

Was that the only question Duns Scotus employees were taught? And Maddie had already answered it.

"Everything was fine, as my granddaughter said. I just need to see her." I leaned farther over the counter. Aaron stepped back slightly. "Actually, I have a present for her. She did such a good job. I was a little embarrassed to tell you, because I don't have something for everyone."

Fortunately, I'd picked up a couple of attractive chocolate gifts at the Ghirardelli shop, meaning to give them to Linda and Beverly for taking care of Maddie, but this use would be even better. I could make it up to my babysitters some other way.

I heard a small gasp from Maddie. I leaned down. "We'll still have the one you picked out for Taylor," I whispered.

"You can leave it here for your maid. I'll make sure she gets it," Aaron said.

I hated to do it, but it was time to bring out my schoolteacher voice. It seemed I'd used it more in the last few days than in all the intervening years since Rosie and her classmates graduated.

"Aaron, I need to see the housekeeper who cleaned room five sixty-eight last Saturday."

His Adam's apple made a complete trip up and down his windpipe. "Okay, let me call down. You can wait —"

I nodded, gave Aaron a big smile, and

352

Maddie and I headed for the couch.

I'd been avoiding looking at the tile bridge and the jungle it ran through. The setting, meant to be inviting, began a few yards from the front desk. I took a seat on the couch facing Maddie, with my back to the dark trees and bushes. Even so, the green paisley print of the U-shaped sectional took on the look of the jungle.

"That was a good idea, mentioning the evaluation card," I said to Maddie. "I hope he doesn't go looking for it."

Maddie gave me a quizzical look. "But I did fill it out," she said. "I wouldn't lie."

I patted her knee. "Of course you wouldn't, sweetheart. I meant it might be hard for him to trace it to our room."

"I wrote the room number on the card."

"I'm sorry, sweetheart. You know, I'm a little tense and not thinking straight."

She smiled, then returned the favor and patted my knee.

I wasn't lying about being tense, but the reason was the close call in leading Maddie to believe I would have approved of a lie.

I had a lot to learn before I could be proud of myself as a grandmother.

I'd put the talk with Maddie off long enough. Our cleaning person might show up any minute. We'd made an emergency trip to my car to pick up the Ghirardelli present when I realized I'd better produce it in case Aaron was keeping watch. The candy was allegedly my reason for wanting to meet our housekeeper.

We were now settled back on the waiting couch, as I thought of what to say.

"Maddie, do you know why I need to talk to the woman from housekeeping?" I asked.

"Not really. I just figured it must be about a clue."

She shuffled through a stack of leaflets she'd taken from the rack by the concierge's desk. Photographs and flashes of color passed in front of me: the green of the wine country a few miles north, the red of the double-decker tour bus that roamed downtown, the stark white of the majestic civic center buildings where the city hall was more ornate than the opera house.

"It's sort of about a clue. Remember Mrs. Norman's locker room scene?" Of course she did; I didn't need her nod. "Well, she mistakenly threw it in the trash and now we want it back."

One of these days I'd stop getting myself into situations where shading the truth, that is, lying, was a necessary part of my communication with my family.

"Oh," Maddie said. She hadn't stopped leafing through the brochures.

"Do you see any place you'd like to go?" I asked, happy to be rid of the touchy (for me, only, apparently) topic.

"Maybe this one."

Her grin told me I was in for a laugh. I took the leaflet and read. For only thirty-six dollars, twenty-six for children, we could take the Alcatraz day tour, which included a ferry ride to and from the former federal prison of movie fame and an award-winning audio guide.

I stuffed the leaflet in my purse. "Some other time," I said with a smile.

An attractive middle-aged woman in a brown housekeeper's uniform, came up to us. I couldn't recall ever seeing housekeepers in brown at other hotels — the Duns Scotus had gone out of its way to keep the monks' robes theme. I wouldn't have been surprised to see a hemp sash around her waist.

We rose from the couch as she extended her hand. "Marina," she said. "Like the neighborhood by the bay. But I don't live there, though."

"That's where the World Series earthquake hit," Maddie said.

I vaguely remembered the popular term for the 1989 quake along the San Andreas Fault. It was the worst in my memory and had been seen around the world because it occurred during a telecast of one of the baseball games in the series. The Marina District had suffered extensive damage, including several fatalities.

Marina addressed Maddie with affection. "You are too little. How do you remember the earthquake?"

"We learned about it in California History class. And I've seen videos of the cars that were crushed and the houses that just fell over."

It was strange to think that Maddie knew of the Loma Prieta earthquake, its official name, only as a fact of history, since it happened nearly ten years before she was born.

Marina seemed very nice and I felt ashamed that I hadn't left her a gift when I wasn't trying to bribe her. Too late now.

I handed over one of the Ghirardelli items — a small cable car, about seven inches long, filled with assorted chocolates. "This is for you," I said.

Her thank-you was so sincere, I hated to go on, but there was work to be done.

"Marina, do you remember seeing a little box with a scene in it? It was in the wastebasket in room five sixty-eight on Saturday morning."

Marina gave me a confused look and a slow shake of her head.

"There were miniature lockers all along one side of it," I explained, not willing to give up.

Another head shake. "No, I'm sorry, missus." Marina's accent sounded a lot like that of my GED student, Lourdes Pino, and I guessed she had the same Hispanic heritage.

"It was like a little dollhouse," Maddie said, using her hands to indicate the size.

"Ah, now I remember. Yes, yes. A tiny dollhouse with benches and cabinets."

That would be it. The child came through again, with a jargon-free description.

"Do you remember what you did with it?" I asked.

"Yes, yes. It was in the wastebasket by the door and it was broken, so I put it in my cart."

I pictured a large rolling cart (brown?) piled with soft vanilla towels and washcloths, sweet-smelling soap, tiny boxes containing shower caps and shoeshine cloths — and a trashed locker hallway scene with a hate message scrawled in bright red lipstick.

I held my breath. "Where did you take the

cart, Marina?"

"I take the cart every day to the basement and we sort out the laundry and replace the little bottles and the other things for the bathroom, and throw away the rubbish."

I didn't think I could take another dead end. "That's it?"

Marina nodded. "Yes, every day. But on Saturday a woman came by while I was outside that room on the fifth floor and she sees the little dollhouse."

"What did she look like?"

"Very small, with dark hair. And she had a patch over one eye." Marina covered her own right eye with her hand to illustrate.

A petite brunette with a patch on her eye. How many of those do you see in a day?

"What did the lady want?" I asked, nearly choking from holding my breath.

"She wanted to take the dollhouse. She said it was hers and she threw it away by mistake." Marina appeared to have a moment of realization. She gasped. "Oh, I'm sorry, missus, I let her take it. Was that a wrong thing to do? Was it yours?"

"Yes, but don't worry about it."

Marina seemed unduly upset. "You think I took the money, but I didn't take it, the money, I swear."

"She offered you money?"

"Yes, she had money for me, but I said no, it was hers in the first place. Now I see it wasn't hers. You won't tell my boss?"

"Of course not, Marina. You didn't do anything wrong. You've been a huge help to me. Can you answer just one more question?"

"Yes, I try."

"Do you remember what time it was on Saturday that the woman with the patch on her eye came by?"

Marina smiled and nodded. This one was going to be easy. "I come on for my shift at seven o'clock in the morning and I have my first break at quarter to ten. The lady came just before my break."

Maddie was taking no chances on my remembering the times. I watched her write them down on the edge of one of the San Francisco tour leaflets. I saw Sally Baxter, Girl Reporter, added to her résumé.

"Thank you so much, Marina." I reached into my tote. "I have another cable car. Maybe you have a child or a friend who might like it?"

I didn't have the heart to tell Marina not to leave town since she might be called to testify in a murder trial.

We stayed on the couch for a while after

Marina left. I called upon my usual hand-waving techniques to explain to Maddie what we'd just learned — that a woman in Rosie's high school class took the broken locker scene from the hotel room and put it where the man was who had passed away, so it would look like Rosie was guilty.

"A woman with an eye patch framed Mrs. Norman?"

"That's another way to say it, yes."

I reminded myself that I couldn't infer much more — that most likely it was Cheryl who planted the scene and then pointed the police in its direction to frame Rosie. It didn't mean it was she who had killed David. She was probably outside room five sixty-eight in the first place in order to plant something that would further incriminate Rosie. Seeing the locker room in Marina's cart must have been serendipity.

Her motivation didn't have to be to cover up her own guilt, but simply to carry out her vendetta against her competition. Why the beautiful, rich Cheryl Mellace would consider Rosie Norman a threat was beyond me.

I'd quickly worked out the time line in my head. The window for David's death was between four in the morning and seven thirty when his body was discovered. Cheryl could have done the deed on the early side and still had plenty of time to come back to the Duns Scotus to retrieve the locker room scene.

Now that I thought of it, I'd seen Cheryl coming into the Duns Scotus garage around eight that morning as Maddie and I were leaving. Why else would she have been reentering the hotel? In my mind, I heard her defense attorney ticking off the possible reasons.

Still, all in all, the whole exercise allowed me to keep Cheryl on my list of suspects.

CHAPTER 21

Neither of us wanted to leave San Francisco. On our way from downtown to the bay and back we'd seen a wide variety of architectural choices — Victorian houses, art deco office buildings, and a few modern structures. The international flavor was apparent in the different ethnic groups staying at the hotel, and the many languages we heard at Ghirardelli Square, rivaling what we might have heard on a world cruise.

Most of the time, I loved living in our small, Abraham Lincoln–obsessed town (every day-care child started out learning that he was the tallest president in history, and it took off from there), but once in a while I needed a break and our trips to San Francisco had served the purpose. It wasn't the city's fault that the reunion weekend had been marred by tragedy.

So, it was with some reluctance that Maddie and I decided to go home where we could spread out the printouts and talk in private. Using words like "fraud," "murder," and "payola" in a public place seemed unnecessarily awkward.

Maddie followed her recently established "hot day in Lincoln Point" routine: as soon as we got in the door, she pushed the button to retract the atrium skylight. She was so enamored of the technology, I feared I'd have to rein her in from opening my house to the cold and rain come the winter (such as it was in this part of the state).

Once we were both in lighter clothing, Maddie nibbled on one of the brownies we'd taken from Ghirardelli's, while I arranged the printouts on the dining room table.

"I can't believe you're hungry," I said.

"I didn't eat all my sundae."

"You mean you didn't lick the bowl?"

"Uh-huh."

Sheets of paper filled with charts and numbers were my least favorite thing to read, let alone study. My need to procrastinate was so great that I ate a snack of crackers and cheese myself.

Finally, we settled ourselves side by side at the table, Maddie perched on a stool so she could see the whole area. It had been a while since I'd had a glance at Skip's copy of the material. He'd highlighted areas of interest, which made it easier to focus. We were starting from scratch.

I started with the headings on the columns. At the top of each sheet was the designation *RFP Summary*, followed by the name of the project.

At the bottom of each page was a boiler-plate statement:

Reference numbers are to documents on file, specifying timeline for job completion. Proposals will be evaluated based on previous experience with similar projects, quality of previous work, time to completion, and cost. Scores will be assigned accordingly and the bidder with the highest score will be the awardee.

I also noted, in fine print, a statement advising vendors that they could appeal a decision within fifteen days of notification of rejection. I wondered if anyone had ever taken advantage of that right, especially Callahan and Savage.

Maddie and I each picked up a page for a closer look and read together, half out loud, half to ourselves. My first sheet was for an equipment upgrade on the heating and cooling system at the Duns Scotus in 2006. The *RFP Issue Date* was listed as February

6, 2006. The bids were submitted two months later.

RFP SUB.	COMPANY	REF. #	BID	SCORE
04/03/06	James & James	87654	389K	14
04/05/06	*Mellace	87655	420K	20
04/05/06	Thomas & Sons	87656	390K	16
04/07/06	Allgood Co.	87657	410K	14
04/07/06	Callahan & Savage	87658	370K	18

Maddie showed me a similar breakdown on her sheet, with an RFP going out on June 13, 2005, and bids coming in three months later. There were seven bidding companies, with Mellace's bid the second highest. Once again, Mellace had an asterisk next to its name.

"We've known this all along," I said to Maddie (and myself), dejected.

Skip had processed all this information already, and Barry had as much as confessed these irregularities. I'd been hoping that with a closer look, I'd be able to come up with more, something that tied David directly to fraud. Barry had mentioned an upcoming major remodeling project for the Duns Scotus, but either the RFP for that hadn't gone out or the printouts we had were simply outdated.

Reading these sheets, one could argue that Mellace Construction's high bid was worth it because of their years of experience or excellent customer references. Or that Callahan and Savage's low bid was balanced by poor qualifications of their staff or another criterion of which I had no clue. I had to resign myself to the fact that I'd come up with nothing new.

"Let's check the e-mails," Maddie said, sweeping the RFP summaries to the side.

We took our positions and focused.

The correspondence was much easier to read, being word-based instead of number-based. Almost all the e-mails were from David Bridges to Mellace Construction, a few to other companies that had won a contract.

"I guess it would look suspicious if Mellace got totally all the contracts," Maddie said, at the same time that I was thinking it.

The text of the e-mails was all the same, except for numbers filled in, for the amount of the contract and the agreed-to start and finish of the projects.

I'd lost track of the number of dead ends in this case, while my friend was virtually a prisoner of an elaborate frame.

"It's hopeless," I said.

"Let's not give up, Grandma. I'm not sure what we're looking for exactly, but we might still be able to find it."

I was sorry that I'd expressed my despondency out loud. To humor my granddaughter I put a positive face on and said, "Okay, let's try another approach. We could make up a time line, putting everything we have in chronological order, whether it's an RFP summary or an e-mail. Can you do that while I see about something for dinner? You must be starving."

I was only half joking, since Maddie had been in a heavy-eating phase all summer, not that you could tell from her skinny body.

"I'm starving for something good, like pizza."

"Ice cream sundae and brownies for lunch and pizza for dinner. I don't think so. Try again."

"Then can you make tuna casserole?"

Was Maddie the only contemporary eleven-year-old who even knew what tuna casserole was? "Tuna casserole it is."

"With no peas, and lots of potato chip crumbs on top."

"And you won't tell your mom?"

"Duh."

"Deal."

The best thing about tuna casserole was that I didn't need to look at a recipe. I had my own variation, adjusted to Maddie's taste at three years old right up to the present. No pimiento or almonds, and cream of celery instead of cream of mushroom soup. I did sneak in a better grade of cheese than the original recipe called for.

I assembled the masterpiece and put it in the oven. In thirty-five minutes, we'd be set to go.

"Something's funny here," Maddie called from one room away.

I walked into the dining room and peered over her shoulder. "Show me."

"Okay, see this line on the RPFs?" I saw no value in correcting her. "It tells you when the bids were asked for. So, look at this one, Project Number 20988, for fixing the air-conditioning units in the hotel. It has the date January 10, 2005." Maddie plucked an e-mail from the stack. "Then here's the e-mail letter to the Mellace company saying congratulations, because they got the contract for Project Number 20988. That's the same number. But the date is December 29, 2004. That's why I was confused. I was trying to put January after December. Get it?"

I certainly did get it. David Bridges informed Mellace of a winning bid and then sent out a request for bids ten days later.

Was there a time warp due to New Year's Eve 2004?

There was no Callahan and Savage bid on Project 20988, and it was a small Duns Scotus project, thus showing that David spread the fraud around, among different size bids.

"Are there any more pairs like this?" my voice carried an excitement that I know pleased Maddie.

"I don't know yet. Let's look."

We created a most interesting time line, with three more cases of an RFP going out after Mellace was notified of the winning bid. I hoped what we'd put together constituted the kind of proof Larry Esterman had talked about, the kind that could put someone in jail, the kind that someone might kill for.

Walter Mellace moved up a notch on my list of suspects. All the nice things Barry and Rosie had said and thought about David Bridges were taking their toll, and I envisioned David's deciding to play it straight, something Mellace would not be happy about. I was sure the LPPD would be eager to know my conclusions.

After I left a message at all of Skip's numbers, Maddie and I sat across from each other over a steaming tuna casserole.

Maddie was beside herself with agitation, trying to talk with large mouthfuls of noodles. "I can't wait to tell Uncle Skip," she said, though I know she had only the vaguest notion of the meaning of what she'd uncovered and understood only a fraction of the concept of fraud, as perpetrated by Mellace Construction and their coconspirators.

"I'll make sure Uncle Skip knows who the detective was this evening," I said.

Maddie shrugged. "We're a good team, right?"

I gave her my biggest smile. "The best."

A callback from Skip came about halfway through the second helping for each of us.

"I hope your news is better than mine," he said.

My first thought was that Rosie skipped town; my second, that there was more evidence against her. My second thought was correct.

"Let me talk to him, let me talk to him," Maddie said, nearly choking. She'd come to my side and was leaning in, trying to speak into the phone. I still had a height advantage, so I stood up and held the phone out of reach, almost knocking over my coffee mug. What was this? A spiraling back to an impatient toddler? Eleven was a tricky age.

"It's about something else," I told her.

"We got another call," Skip said.

"About that other call —" I wanted to rush in and tell him what I'd learned about the last anonymous tip he'd gotten — about the convenient location of Rosie's locker room box, right at the crime scene. There I was spiraling back from middle age to impatient youth.

Skip talked over me. "Someone who was staying across the hall on the eleventh floor of the Duns Scotus saw the whole scene that night."

"Friday night?"

"Yeah, he says he needed ice, but he checked the peephole first because he was trying to avoid someone. He'd heard the voices, and then when he looked he saw and heard the exchange on the threshold of Bridges's room. He said Rosie looked furious."

"He could tell what her expression was through a peephole?"

"That's what he says."

"And he called Rosie by name?"

"Not exactly. He said 'one of the two women outside Bridges's door' and I figured it wasn't you."

"What's this man's name?"

"I can't tell you that."

"Was he from the reunion class?" Silence, which I took for "yes." "Was he on the football team?" More silence, therefore, another "yes." "Well, can you at least check to see whether he's one of the gang who hung out with David and Barry?"

"I can do that."

"Does this new alleged tip mean that you're bringing Rosie back in?"

"None of this is anything but circumstantial. Unless we can put her in the woods at the time of the murder, we can't arrest her. Too bad those trees don't have cameras. I mean, to catch whoever did it."

"I know a lot of parents who would like that idea."

"I just remembered, you left me a message everywhere. What's up?"

"I have a couple of" — a poke from Maddie made me wince — "Maddie and I have some information for you. Can you stop by?"

"Not till a lot later. We have some visiting politicians coming in this week and they're making us rehearse a show-and-tell for them. You know, I'd rather ride my bike to your house."

"You hate to ride your bike."

"That's my point. If you come by here,

I'll squeeze you in."

It was already after nine o'clock, and a school night of sorts. I'd had a late night with Barry, and a long day, with stressful driving to and from San Francisco. I had to decide whether presenting the evidence we'd dug up was urgent. I thought not. The police already had Barry. Our little revelation was just icing on the cake, more a thrill for Maddie than something that would be a breakthrough in proving fraud, but nothing to clinch the murder case.

I felt another trick coming on, on Maddie, who, I knew, could be in the car and buckled up in a matter of seconds.

"That's too bad, Skip. We'll see you tomorrow," I said. Maddie was hanging on my every word, so I made a sad face for show.

"You don't want to give the little redhead a vote, do you?" Skip asked.

"Uh-huh, thanks. You have a good night, too."

Maddie had returned to the last of her tuna casserole. She drained her glass of milk and heaved a big sigh for a little girl. "We have to wait, huh?" It pained me to have deliberately kept her away from her big moment. "It's a good thing I have a lot of homework to keep me busy

373

tonight," she said.

In an unusual turn of events, Maddie told me she wanted to do some computer work early this evening. It seemed too much to hope that an interesting school project had balanced out the disappointment of a delayed meeting with the police.

"Are you late turning in an assignment?" I asked, though she'd never been one to cram at the last minute.

"No, I'm just excited about the programming and I'm almost finished."

"Can you tell me about it?"

We cleared off the last of the dinner dishes and loaded them into the dishwasher.

"It's nothing. You'd be bored."

"I might be able to learn."

"Okay, I need to fix some things on my avatar."

"Never mind."

"I'll show you later."

"Let me know when you're ready to say good night."

Maddie was at the door to her room. "Grandma?"

"Yes?"

"Knock, knock."

"Who's there?"

"Digital."

"You mean digital your mother you flunked math? Or digital your father you lost the game? Or —"

"Okay, okay." She entered her room and closed the door.

Tomorrow I'd confess that we were telling that one before she was born. Except we were referring to our fingers.

I'd already started Maddie's Christmas present and was glad to have a chance to work on it without prying eyes. My idea was to replicate her father's old bedroom, which was now essentially Maddie's room.

Maddie's things had been slowly crowding out Richard's, but she seemed reluctant to do this and often said she missed his baseball mitt, now stored in Richard's attic, or some other object that had been prominent in the room. I had enough photographs (and a good memory) of Richard's room the way he left it, and I thought it would be a nice surprise to give Maddie a miniature version. Then she'd be free to decorate the life-size room any way she wanted.

One of the hardest items to reproduce in miniature was Richard's baseball bedding. The ball and bat patterns on novelty fabric were usually large, with each graphic several inches in width or length — not suitable for a bed that was itself only six inches long.

Thanks to the younger members in my crafters group, who kept up with modern technology, I now had a solution to the problem. I was able to purchase a package of eight-and-a-half-by-eleven sheets that were a combination of plastic on one side and fabric on the other and would go through my printer. I'd simply have to scan a photo of Richard's comforter, size it as I wished, print it on the sheet, and remove the plastic backing. Voila, I'd have the exact fabric I wanted.

If I couldn't do it by myself (these things were never as easy as they sounded), I knew I could call on Karen or Susan in the group, so I wouldn't have to invoke Maddie's help.

Tonight's project, phase one, was to sift through photo albums to find the right view of the comforter. While I was at it, I'd select a photograph of Maddie and me, as she'd requested.

I sat in the cool atrium and turned page after page of history, starting with the books dedicated to Richard's preteen years. I found a few good candidates for photos to use, but I didn't stop. I kept going through later albums, caught up in the reverie until I'd gone through Madison Porter's birth announcement, infant years, and early birthday parties.

When she came out in her soccer pajamas and her eleven-year-old body, I was startled into the present.

She may have wondered why I hugged her tighter and longer than usual.

"I'm ready to sleep," she said.

"I'll be right in."

After I take a minute to ponder the passing of the years.

Maddie was in bed, ready for a brief recap of our favorite moments of the day and a good-night kiss. I brought her a snapshot I'd found from Richard's birthday party in the spring. Maddie and I were sharing a happy moment eating multilayer cake.

She looked closely at the photo. "This is perfect. Thanks, Grandma."

"I'll take it back for now, then, and put it in a frame."

"It's okay. It's better like this," she said, standing it against the base of her lamp.

I noticed she'd already turned her computer off.

"I thought you were going to show me your atavar."

She laughed. "It's avatar, Grandma. I forgot and shut down. And I'm ready to sleep, okay?"

"Of course."

"There were too many favorite things, today, anyway, Grandma," she said. "I could never pick. There was class and Ghirardelli and talking to Marina and tuna casserole and finding the date mix-up and . . ."

She trailed off, exhausted from the long list of wonderful things that had happened to her today.

I hoped life would always be that way for her.

CHAPTER 22

I started my work on the model of Richard's bedroom by cheating. I'd bought a tiny baseball glove from an online hobbies and miniatures supply store. Linda would be so ashamed of me. She, and many of the other crafters I knew, would have been manipulating pairs of tweezers, stitching tiny pieces of leather together, to make the glove. If I took that approach to my hobby, I'd get one thing done a month, if that. I was much too impatient.

At a miniature show in San Jose last fall, I'd met a woman who was displaying a four-inch-by-six-inch quilt made from 576 pieces. Each piece seemed no bigger than what fell from my nail clippers.

For me the joy of miniatures was in the originality and personalization of the scenes I made, not in the craft of making pieces more easily bought, like mahogany four-poster beds, or stuffed easy chairs with hand-stitched upholstery. Or like the rock-ing chairs Henry Baker turned out, I mused.

In my own defense, I did add two or three handmade pieces to each room box, and I had a few from-scratch specialties that I prided myself on.

One item I loved to make was the tiny pair of eyeglasses I put into my scenes. I made these with needle-nose pliers and fine-gauge wire of different colors. Any clear plastic, cut to size, served as a lens. When I was really ambitious, I added tiny beads to the rims and earpieces, for a Hollywood look. For sunglasses I dipped into my boxes of envelopes with photographs and negatives from the days before digital cameras. Small pieces cut from the edges of negatives made a convincing sunglass lens. I doubted the memory stick Maddie talked about, that was in her camera, would prove as useful in twenty years.

By ten thirty, I was ready to turn in. While working on a tiny trophy — cut out from foam board and painted bronze — for Rich-ard's bedroom, I'd thought over the facts of the David Bridges murder case. I'd been doing well, putting it in the back of my mind, until I took out a new container of tacky glue, and an image of David's lips came to me. Once Maddie and I talked to

Skip tomorrow about our interview with Marina, and our new evidence of fraud, I was finished. The only curious loose end was why Larry had stolen the bank record from my tote. And, of course who had killed David.

I packed up the work in progress and slipped the box on the floor under a crafts table where Maddie wouldn't find it. I looked forward to reading in bed, finishing my book club's selection, *The House of Mirth*. I'd have to brace myself for what I knew was a devastating ending. When it was my turn to choose a book in a couple of months I planned to offer several more upbeat titles. I had to admit, though, I was tempted to try decorating a room box with the costumes of the times portrayed in the book, perhaps a turn-of-the-century ladies' shop. It had been a while since I'd made a feathery hat or a parasol. I pictured a hat and accessories shop, with a row of pancake-shaped cha-peaux in different pastels and piles of necklaces (thin, broken chains from my jewelry box) on the counter.

On the way to my bedroom, at the back of the house, I hit the button to close the atrium skylight. In one of those comic moments, my finger hitting the button co-incided with a knock on the door. The tapping was barely audible over the sound of the motor that sent the skylight sliding over the fixed roof toward the front of the house.

Probably Skip, thoughtfully keeping his tap light at this hour. I remembered he said he'd be able to stop by later, though we hadn't confirmed it.

I left the skylight about one-quarter closed and walked to the door. I used the peephole just to be safe.

Staring back at me was Cheryl Mellace. I felt like my house was a waiting room for the police department. Was there an unmarked LPPD car out in front again? I shouldn't complain — my own private suspects were saving me a lot of legwork.

"What a nice surprise," I said, letting Cheryl in.

Like Barry, Cheryl had chosen to visit in casual clothes, befitting the weather. Her outfit, a matching shorts and tank top set in a yellow and black geometric pattern was much classier than his, however. Her eye patch was gone and any residual bruising was covered by her makeup.

Cheryl glanced up at my partly closed skylight cover. "We have one just like that in our sunroom," she said. "It's a godsend, especially in this god-awful weather, isn't it?"

I was too tired to play this game of chit-chat, but I was, after all, raised to be polite to guests. "Can I offer you a glass of ice tea?"

Cheryl put her designer-logo straw purse (I'd always thought the designers should pay the customers for advertising) on one of the atrium chairs and fanned herself with her short, slender fingers. "I'd love some."

"I'll be right back," I said, the same phrase I'd used with Barry last night.

A slight headache came on at that moment, as I tried to shake the feeling that I was caught in a loop, where every night I'd have a murder suspect in my atrium and would have to make them ice tea.

The more company I had in a given week, the more prepared I was and the more well stocked, except for my ginger cookies. I was back in a flash with tea and a plate that included the last four cookies. I hoped this meeting with Cheryl would result in some progress toward solving David Bridges's murder and getting me back to baking treats for my family and guests.

Cheryl had wandered to the edge of my crafts room, where a small table held newly purchased miniatures, not yet integrated into my crafts room supplies. I'd started to glue a stack of books together for placement in a cozy reading scene I was doing for a childhood friend in the Bronx.

"This is amazing," Cheryl said. "I don't know how you work with these little things, and it all looks so neat and finished. I was in charge of decorations at the hotel last weekend and I had an awful time."

"It showed" was on the tip of my tongue, but I didn't want to aggravate her.

I let Cheryl praise the minty tea and explain how she didn't eat sweets this late. Still very trim and muscular, she looked like she didn't eat them early in the day, either.

"I'm assuming you have something on your mind, Cheryl?" I folded my arms across my chest. I used this body language rarely in my classroom, but when I did, words came tumbling out of the student in front of me. And it was words that I needed now from Cheryl. Fortunately for me, tonight she looked more like Cheryl Carroll, my C-average ALHS student than Mrs. Walter Mellace, important society wife and charity fund-raiser.

We took seats across from each other in the atrium, ready for business.

"I know you're working with the police on David's case, and I think you have an idea that I was involved in his murder." Cheryl waved a finger at me and spoke in measured tones, as she might to her children.

I seemed to be locked in a power struggle, trying to be Cheryl's old teacher while she was trying to be my mother.

"What makes you think that?"

"I didn't do it," she declared.

"You flatter me by thinking you have to answer to me, or that I have any official status with the police."

She took a sip from her glass, leaving a large red lipstick mark on its rim, then looked at me sideways. "Come on, Gerry, everyone in town knows your, quote, status, unquote, with the Lincoln Point police."

One point for Cheryl, for reaching the "Gerry" stage. In his time with me, Barry hadn't gotten past "Mrs. Porter."

"While you're here, Cheryl, I do have a couple of questions for you."

"I'm sure you do, and I'll just tell you straight out that, yes, David and I had started seeing each other again. It wasn't the biggest secret in the world, though we hadn't exactly gone public with it yet."

I decided to ask the most important question. "Cheryl, why did you put the room box in the woods near the crime scene and then call the police?"

Cheryl blinked several times and took

another drink. I could tell I'd surprised her and I got the feeling she wished the drink were stronger than ice tea. She hung her head. I tried to remember if she'd been a member of the drama club.

"I'm ashamed of myself. I put it there because I didn't want the police looking at me. I knew I'd made a bit of a spectacle of myself Friday night. I'd had a little too much in the hospitality suite, you know?"

I recalled that another Mellace, her husband, excused his behavior in accosting me, by invoking the same reason.

"How did you know where to put it?"

"I have a friend in the dispatcher's office. He told me where David's . . . David was found. That clearing was a special place for us, you know." Cheryl's eyes seemed to drift up and off to the right. An onlooker might have thought she was stargazing through my open roof.

"The clearing is not as private as you think."

She dropped her gaze and seemed to freeze in time and space. "What? What do you mean?"

"Everyone knows, Cheryl." I couldn't believe I was the first to alert Cheryl that everyone past freshman year knew that the clearing in Joshua Speed Woods had been

386

the teenagers' haven for decades. I remembered the time a group of parents decided to drive to the parking lot where I'd been earlier today and camp out, hoping to head their children off at the edge of the woods.

"I have to go," Cheryl said. Looking at her expression — eyes glazed over, lips tightened into a thin line — I wondered if I should let her drive.

I opened the door, hoping to see the LPPD escort that Barry had received.

The street was clear except for Cheryl's own low-riding sports car, its top down. I watched wide-eyed as she climbed over the driver's side door to enter. It was as if she'd gone back thirty years and was trying out for the cheerleading squad. I couldn't imagine what had put her over the edge, literally and figuratively.

I mentally took out my grade book from the days of yore. As of this interview, my verdict for Barry Cannon was "not guilty," for Walter Mellace, "guilty," and Cheryl Mellace, "deadlocked." It crossed my mind that Walter was suffering from not having knocked on my door for a late-night drink.

In spite of the hour, I was wired from Cheryl's visit and wished Skip would come by. I felt it would be disloyal to Maddie if I called him myself, but I'd be blameless if he showed up and asked me to share.

Until I could unload all the little findings of the past day, I'd have trouble sleeping, I knew. Sometimes writing things down helped me let go, so I made a list of what I needed to tell Skip.

I wrote my cryptic notes: *room box journey from hotel to woods; e-mail chronology off; Larry? Cheryl?*

I surprised myself by putting Larry Esterman on my list. Rosie's father, a murderer? I doubted it, but as more and more people told me how angry he was at the students who perpetrated the terrible humiliation on his daughter, I found it hard not to entertain the possibility. Carrying a grudge for thirty years could make anyone snap.

The last, *Cheryl?* referred to a nagging bit, a possible clue I'd thought of while Cheryl was here. It might not even have had to do with her, but something that came to me by my looping, associative mind.

I took the notes with me and put them on my night table.

There. Now I could sleep and let some other force do its part.

CHAPTER 23

Maddie was torn between two good options on Wednesday morning.

She swung her cereal spoon to her left. "I really want to go to class today because I have big things going on with my project." She swung the spoon to her right. "But I don't want to miss anything." She aimed the spoon at me. "Do you promise not to go to Uncle Skip's office before I'm out of school?"

"I do."

She paused a minute. "Do you promise not to invite him here?"

"I do."

More thinking. "Do you promise —"

"Sweetheart, I promise to wait before I talk to Uncle Skip about what you and I, mostly you, figured out, until you are by my side." That ought to cover it. It took fewer words for many legal procedures.

"Okay," she said. "I won't crab anymore."

She kept her promise through breakfast and even on the short ride to the Rutledge Center.

I was grateful for a cooler day in the forecast as I headed for the library. I much preferred to have all the windows open in my car to using the noisy, windy air conditioner. Maddie, on the other hand, wanted the air conditioner all year long, it seemed. You might have thought she grew up in the Bronx as I did, and hadn't been cold since leaving the Grand Concourse.

My morning would be taken up with a tutoring session at the library with Lourdes Pino. Otherwise, I'd have bitten my nails to the core waiting for permission from my granddaughter to contact my nephew.

It never took me long to refocus when I met Lourdes Pino. Her enthusiasm and energy for studying was contagious. If she'd been in any of my high school English classes at ALHS, she might have inspired some of the duller students whom I was unable to reach.

Although Lourdes had earned her GED last spring and was ready to start her first year of community college, she asked if we could continue our weekly sessions in the Lincoln Point Library.

"I want a leg up," she said, grinning. "Is

that the right saying?"

"You could have said, 'I'm eager to pursue a course of study that will give me a competitive advantage over less zealous students.' "

It was always good to start a session with a laugh.

Lourdes showed me the catalog description of one of her classes, an English class that "integrates reading, critical thinking, and writing assignments." It sounded good to me and we drafted a plan for me to work with her through the semester, helping her with homework as needed.

Today Lourdes and I met in the new wing of the library, where small meeting rooms were perfect for tutoring sessions. We were glad for the sorely needed upgrade to the facility. Week after week, Lourdes and I had met in a tiny room that had also served as the mailroom and the office supply closet. It was now possible to have comfortable space available outside of regular library hours, for community meetings and educational programs such as Literacy for All, which had brought Lourdes and me together several years ago.

The new room was nicely appointed, with poster-size photographs or drawings of literary giants on the walls. Shakespeare, T. S.

Eliot, and Virginia Woolf, among others, looked down at us.

The wall directly beside us was devoted to a children's project. A set of posters titled California Authors caught my eye. The young students had compiled a collage of photographs of famous west coast writers: William Saroyan, Robinson Jeffers, Jessica Mitford, Gertrude Stein, Eugene O'Neill, and many others, whom, I was sure, the children would appreciate only later in life.

The photograph of Wallace Stegner seemed to have loosened from its backing. I looked closely and saw that many of the photos and clippings were coming undone. Another case of poor craftsmanship, like the posters at the thirty-year reunion, managed by Cheryl Mellace.

A bell went off in my head, loud as the sound of the beginning of class. I raised my eyebrows in a silent aha moment. I knew what had been nagging at me.

Lourdes picked up on my change of mood. "What's wrong, Mrs. Porter? A spelling mistake on the poster?"

I smiled. "Something like that. I hope you don't mind, but I have to leave a little early, Lourdes." I stood and packed my notes and books. "I'll type up our schedule and drop it by Willie's later today. Is that all right with you?"

"Yes, yes, Mrs. Porter. You have something very important to do, I can tell." Lourdes shot me an exaggerated wink. "For the police, yes?"

I wished I weren't so transparent.

The Lincoln Point Library is only one building away from the police department. If it weren't for my need to follow up on my flash of awareness, it would have taken all my willpower not to take a detour to the LPPD building and see if Skip was around. I'd been disappointed that he hadn't called. I had to balance that with how pleased Maddie would be when we traveled together to talk to her uncle.

With the promise of a breakthrough at the front of my mind, I headed home.

For once my lack of organizational skills paid off — I hadn't cleaned out my tote bag since the reunion weekend. I rummaged around in it now and hoped I still had the program.

I breathed a long sigh when I found it between a package of glue gun sticks and a bag of M&M's. More good luck: the program listed the decorations committee:

Cheryl Mellace, chairperson, and, under her, Allison Parker.

Allison, who still lived in town, was a customer of Rosie's. I'd run into her several times in the bookshop, making it easy to approach her for a favor. I rushed to the bedroom to find the updated yearbook Rosie had produced, found Allison's phone number, and called her.

Another stroke of luck, when Allison picked up the call. "Hi, Mrs. Porter. I was sorry I didn't get a chance to talk to you at the reunion. It was just crazy wild, and then that awful thing with David, it was so upsetting, I almost didn't go to the banquet on Saturday night, because my husband was sick besides, but I figured David wouldn't want everyone just to stay at home and not get together, which he was so looking forward to."

Now I remembered. Allison was a lot like Linda, with record-breaking run-on sentences and nonstop rambling. When Allison took a breath, I offered my few words, commiserating about the loss of David Bridges. It bothered me that I never seemed to take very long to grieve before wanting to get back to the investigation of his murder. I hoped that could be counted as respect for the dead.

"I don't remember seeing you at the groundbreaking," I said. As if I'd been keeping track.

"No, we didn't make it. My husband and I were at San Francisco General Hospital from Friday night to Saturday morning. By the time we got out, it was already close to noon and we knew we couldn't make it, but we stayed around anyway and waited for the banquet. Andy was sick right after the cocktail party, losing everything, you know, and we didn't want to take a chance, being away from home and all, so we went to the ER and they said it was probably food poisoning. We thought of the shrimp immediately. I don't know if you had a problem with it. I didn't, but Andy has a sensitive digestive system. Anyway, they gave him something to calm his stomach down and he was okay, but by then it was too late to go back to Lincoln Point for the groundbreaking."

I thought it must have been my personal best at not interrupting a story I didn't care about. Except, I did care in the sense that it gave Allison Parker an unsolicited alibi for the time of David's death. In case anyone asked.

During the story, I'd held the phone in the crook of my neck while I poured myself a glass of ice tea. "Allison, I wonder if you could do me a favor? Do you still have the posters that were on display in the hotel ballroom? The ones you helped Cheryl with?"

"Yes, and I'm not sure what to do with them, to tell you the truth. I guess I've become the official archivist for my class, although —"

"Do you mind if I take a look at them again?"

"Sure, no problem."

One of my pet peeves reared its head. "Sure" meant she did mind, when I knew the opposite was true. I hadn't been in charge of Allison's grammar lessons for many years, however, and I passed on the need to correct her.

Though she didn't ask, I felt I should explain, or rather, create a fictional explanation for why I wanted to see the posters.

"I remember that some of the photographs showed students in the background whom I've been trying to reconnect with, and I'd like a closer look. Also, I thought you might be able to help me locate them."

"Oh, you're so good, Mrs. Porter, keeping up with your students from so long ago like that. I always liked you."

I never forgot where my students fell on

the grading curve. "That's because you were such a good student, Allison."

"Thank you, Mrs. Porter. Sometimes I wish I were back in high school when life was so simple."

Not for everyone, I thought. Not for Rosie. "Are you free now, by any chance? I wouldn't need to see all the posters. The ones I'm interested in are the medium-size, about fifteen by twenty-four." No sense in having the poor girl lug all that heavy cardboard for my sham research. "Can we meet downtown somewhere?"

"Oh, gosh. I'm just leaving to pick up my grandson because his mother is tied up with a client. She's in real estate. Is this evening okay? I could even swing by your house. You're in the Eichler neighborhood on the upper west side, right?" Allison made our humble residential area sound like the real Upper West Side of Manhattan. I felt a pang of longing for my former, big city life, where I'd never been involved in a murder case.

"This evening is fine, Allison. I have my crafts group, but I'll certainly be able to take a break with you."

I gave Allison directions to my house and rejoiced in my luck. If Allison came through, my crafts group were exactly the people I'd need to consult with tonight.

Nothing to do now but listen to my messages.

There were three from the crafters, about this evening's meeting. Linda wanted to know if she could use some pages of my large stack book instead of lugging hers to my house. Mabel needed a ride to my house since Jim was not feeling well. Susan alerted me to the fact that she would be bringing a sweet potato pie from her grandmother's recipe, so I didn't need to bake.

The fourth message was from Rosie. "Gerry, I tried your cell but can't reach you." Uh-oh. I realized I'd turned the phone off while I was in the library with Lourdes, and hadn't turned it back on. "Now they have my father, Gerry. He went over to Barry Cannon's house and a fight started, and the police have him in custody. Can you come to the police station? Call me. Please. This is Rosie."

I wondered if Larry Esterman had been caught with a bank record clutched in his fist.

I left quick messages to say "yes" to Linda and "thanks" to Susan and asked Susan to pick up Mabel, in case I was busy till the last minute. Instead of calling Rosie, I grabbed my keys and rushed to my car.

I had no choice. I had to go to the LPPD,

Maddie or no Maddie.

This time Rosie was in the waiting area, and her father was inside the confines of the LPPD.

Rosie sat in an uncomfortable police department chair, her hands in her lap, her eyes staring straight ahead. Anyone who didn't know better would think she was relaxed. But it seemed a long time since I'd seen Rosie at ease or in good humor — behind the counter of her shop, bent over a new box of books, or scanning a bookshelf for a title. Now she was as tight as the bolts that held her bookcases to the wall for earthquake safety.

I looked around the large room. Drew Blackstone was on duty. Did the man never get a day off, or did he show up just to accommodate me? I resolved to bring him a tin of cookies soon. For the first time in a while, I hoped I wouldn't run into Skip.

Rosie stood up when she saw me. "Gerry, where have you been?"

When this was all over I was going to have to sit Rosie and Linda down and explain that I wasn't required to be on call twenty-four/seven. They should have known that most of the time when they couldn't get hold of me this past week, I was investigating a murder case, trying to clear Rosie, and that I had a life. Maybe not that last one.

"Do you know what this is all about?" I asked Rosie.

"As I told you in my message, the police are holding him for assault."

"On Barry Cannon? Barry must be thirty years younger. What was your dad thinking?"

"He, uh, took a weapon with him."

I was stunned. Mild-mannered Larry Esterman with what? A gun? A knife? Another trophy?

"A gun," Rosie said, before I asked. "I didn't even know he had one, but I guess he got it when his business was robbed a couple of times years ago. Some kids broke into his warehouse and took a lot of inventory. I'm sure he'd never use it. He just wanted to scare him."

I couldn't tell whether Rosie was talking about the kids of long ago or the kid Barry Cannon, of the present. Probably both.

As Rosie and I took seats, Drew and I exchanged waves and smiles across the wide room. I figured he was wondering when I was going to saunter over and ask for a favor.

"Have you heard anything about what's going on in there?" I asked Rosie, pointing past Drew to the innards of the police station.

Rosie shook her head and sniffed. "No one's come out to talk to me."

"Where did they pick him up?"

"At my house. He didn't do anything to Barry except wave the gun and yell at him. Then he came to my house. Barry must have called the police after he left. My dad's gun is registered, Gerry."

"I'm sure they'll take that into account."

Why was I saying something I didn't believe in? Did we want everyone in town with a registered gun waving it in our faces when they wanted to settle a feud or make a point?

The bigger question was, why hadn't I been a better friend to Rosie? If I'd been stronger and not so afraid of alienating her, I might have helped her to be more realistic about the reunion in the first place. Then David wouldn't have had the chance to rebuff her and Larry wouldn't have been forced to relive a thirty-year-old humiliation. For all I knew, David would still be alive, though that connection wasn't as clear to me.

"Just before they took him away . . ." Rosie broke down, reacting as if she'd never see her father again. She pulled a wrinkled, folded piece of paper from her purse. "He handed this to me. He said you gave it to him?"

I could tell immediately that it was the bank record he'd taken from my folder. I started to clarify for Rosie the manner by which Larry Esterman had acquired the page, but she didn't need any more grief. (There it was again, that fear of bringing displeasure to anyone I cared about.)

I unfolded the sheet. Larry had written all over it, in bold, possibly angry strokes. He'd circled a row of numbers on the top right of the page and written *off-shore;* he'd drawn a box around an alphanumeric code on the top left and written *Cannon.* A yellow highlighter marked large dollar amounts in the middle column.

Apparently, Larry had done some research and had determined that not only David but Barry Cannon was also profiting from the fraudulent scheme.

He could have just asked me, instead of stealing my property. Then he might not be in police custody.

It must have galled Larry that the ring-leaders of the terrible stunt his daughter had suffered from were raking in money, profiting from an illegal scheme that also caused his own employer to lose contracts.

If David Bridges had been shot instead of bludgeoned to death, Larry would probably have been arrested instead of simply brought in for questioning.

Rosie had been watching me as I perused the sheet of paper and speculated on its meaning.

"Does it mean anything to you?" she asked me.

"Not really," I said.

I'd given some thought in the past couple of days to the folder that had landed on the seat of my car. I was convinced that Ben Dobson, the ambitious Duns Scotus supervisor who worked for the late David Bridges, had put it there. I figured that even though his boss was dead by then, Ben had wanted to bring down everyone connected to the scheme, without having to get involved directly. I wondered who his Maddie-like hacker was. I wished I could contact him to tell him his work was likely the last straw of evidence needed to bring the perpetrators to justice.

And to ask him what he was doing in the Joshua Speed Woods after David's memorial service. Maybe he was looking for more evidence of the fraud. Or maybe he hadn't lied to me after all, about answering nature's call.

CHAPTER 24

My cell phone rang, showing Skip's caller ID. I didn't think Rosie needed to hear even my side of the conversation, so I stepped outside to answer.

A majestic set of steps led from the sidewalk to the plaza level of the police department building. From this vantage point, I could see the entire main shopping district of our town, and as far as Rutledge Center where I could picture Maddie working furiously on her project and looking forward to being where I was now.

Fortunately, according to the oversize digital display in front of the civic center buildings, the temperature had dropped to a mere eighty-two degrees and I wasn't too uncomfortable.

"How come you're being patient there in the waiting area and not beating down my door?" Skip asked.

"How come you know where I am?" Or at

least, where I'd been when he rang.

"Duh," he said, echoing Maddie. I needed to break down and adopt that handy syllable (I couldn't call it a word) myself.

"What can you tell me about Larry Esterman?" I asked.

"He's on his way downstairs now, but he's wearing an ankle bracelet while we figure it all out."

"You think he's a flight risk? I doubt the man has been out of town for decades."

"He did attempt to assault a man."

"Uh-huh. And with a deadly weapon, right?"

"Not if it wasn't loaded."

"What?"

"Esterman claims the gun wasn't loaded, that he doesn't even own any bullets. In fact, we searched both his and Rosie's houses and found no ammunition, or even a record that he'd ever bought any."

"He owned a gun but never loaded it?"

"It appears that way. As I said, we're sorting things out."

"So, you don't think he killed David?" I whispered, though there was no one within earshot. The only people in the vicinity were three smokers who stood on the lower steps of the building in a tiny spot of shade that spilled over from a tree on the sidewalk.

"You said you have a couple of things to share with me?" Skip said, leaving me hanging as to whether Larry was considered a suspect by the LPPD.

Larry had dropped off my own private list. What killer marches over to confront another potential victim with an unloaded gun? Strangely, even before I knew the gun wasn't loaded, I'd lost interest in Larry as a suspect — he seemed more like a desperate old man with the means and the motive, but not the will to do anything as horrible as commit murder.

I imagined Larry devising a con, much like the one perpetrated on his daughter thirty years ago — let Barry think he was about to be shot, then say something like, "April Fool," and walk away. Too bad Barry didn't appreciate the turnabout.

Now I was faced with a decision about talking to Skip without Maddie.

He'd called me; he'd asked me to share. I ran through my defense to my granddaughter, who'd be getting out of class in a half hour.

"I'll be right up," I said.

I reentered the building by the side door on the east end of the plaza, to avoid Rosie and/or her father. I expected to hear repercussions later.

On the way to Skip's office, I called Beverly and asked if she could pick up Maddie at the Rutledge Center and bring her to the police station.

"Absolutely," she said, with more gusto than usual. I knew she'd been feeling bad that she'd let me down by not showing up for late night atrium visits. I hadn't had a chance to tell her that for two nights in a row she'd been replaced by murder suspects.

Skip was waiting for me at the head of the interior stairs and escorted me back to his cubicle.

"No cookies, I suppose," he said. I shot him a "naughty boy" look. "We need to get this case over with so you can get back on schedule." I knew he was aware that his grin would soften me.

"Your mom will be bringing Maddie by in about a half hour," I said. "Your cousin once removed has some things she wants to tell you herself."

"No problem. And I have a big surprise for her. Lavana is going to give her a special tour of the building. How's that?"

"She'll love it."

"So, just tell me everything and I'll act surprised later, okay?"

How could I do that to my granddaughter? Easily, it turned out.

After Skip made a very brief trip to the cold-drink machine for both of us, I started my report on the interview with our Duns Scotus housekeeper, Marina. Maddie hadn't been too involved in that aspect of my snooping, except to translate my overblown language into ordinary English.

"You just happened to stop by a hotel in San Francisco two days after you'd checked out?"

"We missed it. But, the point is, isn't Cheryl's story revealing?"

"It is."

"And you'll file it under 'things that tend to clear Rosie Norman'?"

"I will. What else?"

I felt underappreciated. I'd uncovered the mystery of the anonymous caller who directed the police to the location of Rosie's trashed scene. I expected more. But I wasn't eleven years old, so I moved on.

"There's the matter of the RFP material and contract awards." I told Skip what Maddie had uncovered, how David had been granting Mellace an award on one day, and asking for competitive bids the day after. "You may not even need all this if

Barry has spelled it all out for you."

"Not true. We need something solid like this. Barry clammed up. My guess is that he thinks he can contain what he told you."

I didn't mention Cheryl's visit to my house. I did produce the folded sheet Larry Esterman had marked up, however, and wished him luck putting the whole case together.

Not that we were any closer to determining who killed David Bridges. For that, I was hoping this evening with my crafters would settle the matter and we could put everything to rest by morning.

Maddie bounded into Skip's cubicle, nearly knocking over the partition. Behind her was Beverly, and behind her their escort, Officer Lavana Rollins, taller even than Beverly.

Maddie gave me a suspicious look. "How long have you been here?"

Skip spared me and took over. "Your grandmother has done nothing but go on and on about the cool work you did on this case," he said, waiting for the beaming smile that followed. "She wanted to wait but I browbeat her" — he held his fists up, boxer style — "until she cracked." He threw punches into the air and did surprisingly fancy footwork in the cramped quarters.

"Bam, bam. Bam, bam."

Maddie laughed when the last "bam" landed on her nose. I doubted I'd have been able to smooth things over as easily.

More kudos to Maddie as Skip spelled out how because of her work, a judge might now allow them to dig even deeper into all the finances of the bad guys. "If you hadn't noticed that your grandmother Googled Callahan and Savage" — he threw up his hands — "I don't know where we'd be."

Skip let Maddie explain how she kept digging into Callahan and Savage and then went on to a state business site and finally put everything together in order to construct the time line. She elaborated on how she quickly noticed the dates were off. Maddie's story was somewhat embellished and quite creative in parts, but no one critiqued it out loud.

Her summary was brilliant: "I'm sure I could do even better next time if I knew a little more about how a police department works."

"Let me think about it," Skip said. He rose from the chair and snapped his fingers. "I've made my decision. Officer Rollins, would you be so kind as to take Ms. Porter on an insider's tour of the building?"

Beverly and I stood by. I knew she was

marveling as I was, at the performance of the two best negotiators in the family.

Officer Rollins saluted, for probably the first time since her induction.

"The jail, too," Maddie said.

"The jail, too, Ms. Porter," Lavana Rollins said, scaring me. "Of course, it's illegal for anyone under eighteen to be within the confines of the jail, but you're eighteen, right?"

Maddie screwed up her nose. "Not today," she said.

I didn't care whether Lavana was stretching the truth, or outright lying, for that matter, as long as Maddie saw nothing that might give her nightmares.

Back home, Maddie couldn't stop talking about her tour. She told me about the fax machines, the meeting rooms, the records storage area, and the copiers. (ALHS had all of these, also, but I doubted she'd have been as impressed to see them in a school setting.)

Not available at ALHS were many other highlights, however. "Officer Lavana has the coolest job, Grandma. She works with judges and lawyers and dogs," she said.

Officer Lavana had showed her the dispatch center with its enormous map of the city, the booking area, and the two kinds of interview rooms, one for suspects and one for witnesses.

I took it all in, nodding pleasantly and uttering words and syllables of interest — uh-huh, hmmm, oh — having resolved not to pass judgment. The last thing I wanted was for Maddie to choose a career just because it wasn't what her grandmother had in mind for her.

"They took my picture," she said, producing mug shots of her adorable face.

She showed me the set: one in profile and one face front, a placard around her neck. I doubted any criminal who'd been photographed by the LPPD had such a wide smile for the camera. The sign around her neck had LINCOLN POINT POLICE DEPARTMENT in caps, today's date, and a long string of numbers, not unlike that of a Swiss bank account. I hoped the number on the card was a made-up one and wouldn't be entered into the system by mistake.

Maddie placed the two mug-shot views on the table in the atrium where everyone who came into the house would see them. I tried to remember if she'd been this excited when she'd had her photograph taken with all the animals at Disneyland.

I thought not.

■ ■ ■ ■

We had time for a crafts fix before dinner. I'd been eager to try something recommended by a woman I met at a dollhouse show last month. She'd taken seeds from a green bell pepper and dried them, simply by leaving them on a paper towel for a few days. She'd piled the seeds into a tiny wooden bowl, available in quantity at any crafts store, and, lo and behold, she had a bowl of potato chips. I'd put some seeds out a couple of days ago and Maddie and I finished the project this evening.

"Do you think Mrs. Reed will like this, or would she want us to carve the chips out of real potatoes?"

"Good one," I said.

My granddaughter had told a miniature joke, of sorts, giving me my thrill of the day.

"That reminds me, we need to have a lunch or something with Taylor and her grandfather, so we can finish the witch joke. Remember: why does a witch need a computer?"

"We'll try to get together soon," I said.

"Tomorrow?"

"We'll see. Don't you have some homework to get done before the crafts group gets here?"

"Yeah, I do. I have to fix my avatar. It has a wobbly head."

"I hope it doesn't leave a scar."

"If you take a laptop computer for a run, you could jog your memory."

"I give up," I said, ceding the stand-up stage to my granddaughter.

The crafts group, with Susan bearing the promised sweet potato pie, arrived around seven. Rosie was understandably missing. I hadn't talked to her since she and her father left the police station with his newly acquired ankle jewelry. I predicted an eventual full recovery for both of them and hoped I'd be able to help make it shorter than thirty years.

Karen had knit a yellow afghan for her nursery, big enough to fold in quarters and still be a substantial size (about two inches on a side). My afghans tended to be much smaller and not as perfectly bound as Karen's. She'd be able to fold hers and drape it over the back of the miniature glide rocker in the nursery, meant for mother and child bonding.

Mabel was eager to show us her nearly completed ship's cabin, a replica of one she hoped to share with Jim on their cruise. We admired the highly polished walls and the tiny bathroom she'd constructed, much like that on an airplane.

Linda, who'd missed last week, brought a new room box with a Halloween theme. (Another plus for our hobby: miniaturists celebrated all holidays all year.) I hoped the scene wouldn't remind Maddie again of the witch joke. To my relief, her response to Linda's scene was, "Do you want to see some potato chips to go with your candy?"

I worked halfheartedly on my Christmas scene. Unless I had a brilliant flash of inspiration, there wasn't much more I could do with it.

I had one ear on the group chatter and one on the door, waiting for Allison to drop by with the posters. I was proud of my friends for not exchanging "I told you so's" about Rosie's misadventure, especially since she wasn't present. The only references to Rosie and the ill-fated reunion weekend were in private, to me.

Susan had made a second sweet potato pie for Rosie. She gave it to me in the kitchen. "You're bound to see Rosie before I do," she said. "Tell her I hope this sweetens her day."

Karen approached me soon after, with a small set of books she'd made for Rosie, who kept an ongoing project of a miniature bookshop in her own life-size one.

I was glad to see that Susan and Karen, who'd been hardest on Rosie from the beginning, had both come through for her in the end.

I hoped I could do so as well.

When the doorbell rang, I was deep into embroidering Richard's name on a Christmas stocking for my room box. I jumped, though it was the sound I'd been waiting for all evening. I'd already told the group that I was expecting company who would take a few minutes of my time. I excused myself now and left to open the door.

"Hi, Mrs. Porter," Allison said, juggling three posters that kept sliding against one another. "I came as soon as I could. I hope I'm not too late. My youngest needed to go to a parent-teacher conference and I forgot I said I'd babysit, but she's back now."

"Perfect timing," I said and ushered Allison through the atrium, open to the sky, to the dining room table.

Allison had kept her schoolgirl figure, which was on the large, curvy side, not fit for jumping from the shoulders of classmates in uniform, as Cheryl Mellace's could. In knee-length denim shorts and a white polo shirt, she was mercifully brief in her answers to my obligatory inquiries about her family. The logo on the shirt, it turned out, was a cardinal, the mascot of her middle grandson's elementary school in nearby Cupertino. I hoped Allison wasn't planning on getting even with me for my pop quizzes by springing one on me, covering all the trivia she doled out.

We spread out the posters. "If the people you want aren't on these, don't worry. I stuck the rest in the trunk of my car, just in case."

How obliging. I felt worse and worse about this ruse to gather evidence for a murder case. It was the same old means-and-ends issue that I'd wrestled with daily over the past week.

We looked at the posters, one by one. I played along with the "find the student" game, while really checking out the glue job on the project.

I put my finger on a photograph that was particularly badly glued to the backing. "Isn't this Marsha Lowe?" I asked, touching a figure in the background of a candid from the senior ski trip. "She seems to have dropped out of sight and I just learned we have a mutual friend and I wanted to get in touch with her."

I had to admit there was something to run-on sentences. They conveyed an excitement in and of themselves.

"Yes, that's Marsha. You're right. She met someone on a ski trip to Switzerland and married him and stayed there, but she's back now, in San Jose."

For the sake of credibility, I fingered two more students in the photographs. Allison knew them both and was excited to be able to give me information that I already knew. I decided to make her a batch of ginger cookies, soon, to distribute among all her above-average children and grandchildren.

I owed food all over town, it seemed.

"This is just what I wanted, Allison. Would you mind if I kept these photos? I'll be very careful with them and I'll be sure to return them." If they don't end up as a prosecutor's exhibits in a trial.

Allison waved her hand and clicked her tongue. "Of course, Mrs. Porter. Who's going to miss them, huh?"

I lifted the photographs from the poster, being careful to take the dried glue along with them.

"Hmm. Some of these pictures weren't glued down very well. What kind of adhesive did you use?" I asked.

"Oh, Cheryl picked some up at one of

those everything's-a-dollar stores at the last minute. I guess it wasn't a very good brand."

That was more good news for me. Cheryl may have had designer taste in clothes and cars, but not in adhesives.

"Do you have the glue?" I asked. Allison gave me a curious look. "I like to compare different brands of glue for my crafts classes," I added.

That seemed to satisfy her. "Cheryl took all the unused supplies — the extra poster board, tape, and all. I could ask her exactly where she bought the glue, if you want."

"No, no. Thanks, Allison, but don't bother." I slipped the photos into an envelope. "You've already been a great help."

Allison didn't stay long, since, as she explained, her cousin from Reno was driving in early tomorrow to attend a birthday party for a friend. More pop-quiz material.

I couldn't wait to look more closely at the back of the photos I'd stuffed in the envelope. A quick glance while Allison and I were at the dining room table confirmed what she had implied, that the glue was an inexpensive generic mucilage, not the kind sold in the better crafts stores.

And not the kind a miniaturist would use for anything, not for gluing tiny pieces in place, and not for gluing together the lips of a murder victim.

I didn't think it would work, but I made an attempt to bypass my guest crafters and inspect the photographs under my large magnifier lamp in the corner of the crafts room. I had all of fifteen seconds before everyone crowded around me.

"What's that you're doing?" Karen asked.

I placed the photograph, upside down, directly under the light.

"Give me a minute," I said. "Then I'd like you all to take a look at this."

I looked through the magnifier at the top of the light and prodded the glue with toothpicks. The glue had congealed into hard brownish clumps. I pictured the source, with an orange rubber tip on the bottle and a slit for the syrupy glue to come out. I hadn't seen the brand in years but I remembered it as a staple in the crafts rooms of my childhood.

One by one, I had my crafter friends check out the glue, with and without the magnifying lens, with toothpicks, fingers, and noses all brought to bear.

"Is that a glue Rosie would use?" I asked.

"Not hardly," said Mabel.

"Nuh-uh, y'all," said Susan.

"No way, Jose," said Karen.
"Why does it matter?" Maddie asked.
"I think I know," Linda said.

Chapter 25

I worked out the scenario in my head, over and over, after the group had left and Maddie was fast asleep.

Skip had as much as admitted that the test for matching the glue on David's dead lips to the glue on Rosie's locker room box had been hurried and inconclusive. It had been done by a rookie, he'd said. Preliminary, he'd said.

I was convinced that with this sample from Cheryl's glue and a credible test, we'd have incontrovertible evidence that Cheryl had murdered David and then done everything she could to direct the police to Rosie. She'd even glued his lips together to indicate that a crafter had been at work. Her desire to humiliate Rosie, and even destroy her life, seemed to have no bounds.

It had been a long day, starting with my meeting with Lourdes and ending with Allison (truthfully, ending with sweet potato pie), with a lot of stress at the LPPD in between.

Tomorrow morning, first thing, I'd take the sample photographs to Skip. Then maybe I'd see about arranging a date to finish the witch joke with Henry and Taylor. I'd probably have to promise Henry that I'd never bother him again afterward.

For now, I needed to sleep.

My head couldn't have been on the pillow more than a minute before a loud thumping noise startled me. It came from the direction of the atrium. June Chinn, next door, had been having problems with raccoons on her roof on a regular basis. Most of the Eichlers in our neighborhood were flat-roofed and easy for an animal to reach. Had the raccoons finally found my roof?

I couldn't remember whether I'd fully closed the skylight before coming to bed. What a nightmare it would be if an animal had climbed up and then jumped onto my atrium floor and was now trapped inside.

A quick contingency plan formed in my mind, to call animal control if there was a raccoon or other creature in my home. The atrium was closed in, mostly by glass doors that led to the other parts of the house, which surrounded it. To let anyone into my house, I'd have to either enter the atrium and cross it, to the front door, or exit by the patio door from my bedroom and walk all around the side and use my key to let in an animal handler.

I got up and trudged across my bedroom to the small hallway between the living room and the atrium. As soon as I rounded the corner I could tell that I'd left the roof open. The skylight cover was not transparent, but cast diffuse light into the area, with colorful patterns, due, I supposed, to the texture of the acrylic material. Tonight I could tell my house was open to the stars. And to other elements of nature.

I looked through the heavy glass doors to the atrium, scanning carefully for unwelcome signs of life. All seemed quiet. I'd been lucky, but I needed to go out there and close the roof. No sense in tempting nature.

I unlocked and pushed open the glass door. I tiptoed down one step onto the atrium floor. Maddie hadn't been awakened by the original noise; I didn't want to disturb her now.

I headed for the button to slide the roof into the closed position.

Wham!

I was knocked to the floor, facedown. I

felt my nose crack and I knew I'd broken it. The idea that I'd tripped on a loose piece of slate was short-lived.

"You couldn't let it go, could you, Gerry?"

The feel of a heavy boot in the small of my back conflicted with the sound of a woman's voice.

Cheryl Mellace had jumped into my house.

In spite of the pain as my face ground into the floor, I had to gather my wits.

"The police know you killed David, Cheryl. It won't do any good to hurt me." I could barely understand my own words, coming as they were from lips scrunched together and twisted to the side, and a bloody nose that was throbbing painfully.

"I was ready to give up my life for him." Cheryl's breath came in short spurts.

I knew I was taller and heavier than Cheryl, but I had no idea whether she had a gun. I didn't dare move. All I could do was look at my beautiful ferns, bamboo, and blooming begonias from a different angle than usual.

I felt I could easily throw off Cheryl's foot and tackle her, but what if she had a weapon? On the one hand — why would such a petite woman enter my home without one if her plan was to do me harm? On the other — she'd done a good job on David using only a weapon of convenience.

"Cheryl —"

"You're not in front of the class, Gerry. This is my story. You're like David. You think you're the only one who calls the shots."

At this moment I didn't want to be thought of as "like David." I wondered what kind of magnetism he possessed that was lost on me — two women, at least one of them quite intelligent, were willing to throw themselves at him, one humiliating herself in the process, the other killing him.

I shifted under Cheryl's boot and tried to make out from her weak shadow whether she was holding anything. She pressed down harder on my back. My nose, already beating pulses of pain, took another hit.

"Stay down," she said. I smelled alcohol on her breath. I couldn't decide whether that was good news or bad for me. Could she be more easily thrown off balance? I hoped so. I needed something to make up for the age difference between my attacker and me.

Her voice was loud and my greatest fear was that Maddie would wake up. I tried to recall whether Cheryl had ever met Maddie, whether she knew Maddie was in the house. Cheryl might have seen Maddie at the groundbreaking ceremony or at the reunion banquet on Saturday night, but she'd have no way of knowing that she was staying with me. Maddie had been asleep when Cheryl came by last night. I could only hope that my granddaughter's presence in the house tonight would never enter Cheryl's mind.

"Let me explain —"

Another slam of her boot. If only I could get a word in, I'd let Cheryl know that my whole crafters group had seen the kind of glue she'd used on the posters, and Linda knew more — thanks to her EMT friend, Linda knew about the glue that sealed David's lips.

"After all we'd been through, David cared more about my husband's money than I did," Cheryl continued. "He'd rather give me up than get cut out of his little scam with Walter. We were supposed to be reliving our senior year at dawn in the woods on that Sunday, the day after David won his trophy."

Something was off. David had been killed at dawn on Saturday, not Sunday. I realized Cheryl had intertwined the events of thirty years ago with those of four days ago. A common occurrence among her classmates.

Maybe I could take advantage of Cheryl's confused state to best her.

Physical combat was not in my skill set, but I had to do something or I'd bleed to death through my nose. I wriggled, but only slightly, not to upset Cheryl, to determine on which side I had more freedom of movement. I was glad for my lightweight summer pajamas, which were less likely to get tangled than one of my oversize winter nightgowns.

My left side, toward the patio doors to the hallway, seemed my best shot. Mustering all my strength, leveraging my arms, I made a sudden turn, rolling to my left.

Crash!

One of my clay planters shattered on the floor next to me, where my head had been. Cheryl had missed, but recovered quickly, picking up another planter, this one with blooming mums. Again she hurled and missed.

I stood up, finally, perspiration running down my back. My attention shifted to a shadow behind Cheryl, in the glass doorway to the hallway outside Maddie's room. The crashing pot must have wakened Maddie.

I panicked.

Though I averted my eyes so Cheryl wouldn't follow my gaze, I caught a flash of neon green. Maddie's pajamas. I was sure she'd fled to summon help; I wasn't sure I could last as long as it took for help to arrive.

On my feet, I had the advantage now, unless Cheryl had an ace up the black sleeve of what looked like a Catwoman outfit.

She did.

She reached back and pulled a tire iron from my planter bed. Her tool, not mine. She came at me as if she were gathering momentum to jump on my shoulders. She held the tire iron like a baton.

Cheryl slipped a little while she swung the iron. More and more I had the sense that the effects of alcohol were working in my favor.

We grappled with it for what seemed like ages, switching positions of advantage. Finally the iron flew across the slate floor, sending scraping sounds up into the night sky.

The front of my pajama top was covered in blood pouring from my nose. Cheryl must have had some of it on her rappelling suit also. It was little comfort, but at least I knew a DNA match was possible should it come to that when Cheryl was tried for my murder.

I took a needed but dangerous breath and

saw Cheryl headed for me. She'd retrieved the tire iron and had gained amazing speed, given that she had less than twenty feet of runway. I waited until she was almost on top of me, then swung my body down and away from the attack.

Cheryl hit the glass doors to my family room head-on. She lay crumpled, writhing in pain.

I guessed she was used to having a formation stand in place while she jumped on them.

The sound of sirens and the flashing of red-and-blue lights filled the open space in my atrium roof. I ran down the entryway and let in what seemed like a squadron of uniformed officers.

Then I ran back and into Maddie's bedroom. I held her shaking body and rocked her until Officer Lavana Rollins found us and joined us for a three-way hug.

CHAPTER 26

It took a couple of days for Maddie to leave my side. She was as concerned about me as I was about her. All there had been between Maddie and Cheryl was a locked glass door, which seemed entirely too flimsy to me. I hoped this was the closest she'd ever be again to the kind of ugliness that had taken place in my atrium. I finally got her to class the Monday after her dramatic rescue call. I worried that she wouldn't finish her project, but she assured me she was way ahead and would be ready on Labor Day. One week from now, she'd demonstrate her master-piece to the throngs who were due at my house for the annual barbecue.

Many of the calls and visits I received during my brief recuperation period included apologies. Allison Parker's was first.

"I can't believe what happened, Mrs. Porter. I feel so guilty. I called Cheryl when

I got home and told her you were interested in where she got the glue and what brand it was. I thought I was helping you because you said you liked to collect that kind of information for your crafts classes."

For Allison, it was a short apology. I assured her that I in no way blamed her for my bruised face, raccoon-like black-and-blue-rimmed eyes, sore back, and broken nose. Not to mention my destroyed atrium.

Skip and June took immediate charge of restoring my planter beds and adding a new, magnificent fern to change the look of the atrium.

June felt she should apologize, too. "I didn't see or hear anything, Gerry. Someone was on your roof and I slept through it all. What kind of neighbor am I?"

"You're a wonderful neighbor," I said. "I'm sure Cheryl was visible only for a minute or so."

"It was quite an impressive performance for a woman her age," Skip said.

"Do you mean Cheryl or Gerry's?" June asked. A nice gesture that caused Skip to stammer, "Both, I guess."

"It's a piece of cake to get to a roof in this neighborhood," June said. "The roofs are low and flat and scaling the wall is not that big of a deal. I could do it."

"I'd like to be here when you do," Skip said.

June gave him a playful poke. "You wish. What I don't get is how Cheryl knew Gerry would go to bed and leave the skylight open?"

Skip's explanation brought me no comfort. "It didn't have to be open. Cheryl has a retractable system just like Aunt Gerry's, so she was aware that it could be pried open relatively easily even without the electrical power."

Nice to know.

Rosie and Larry stopped by one evening with candy and flowers. "These really are from Dad and me, Gerry. It's not a trick." Her smile seemed relaxed and her good humor restored. She told me she needed just one more thing before she could start over.

"I'm hoping for your forgiveness, Gerry. I can't even count the things I should apologize to you for."

"Don't bother, Rosie. Just get back to work and get busy with that list of books I gave you last week."

She gave me a hug, then produced the order for the books. "Done," she said. "And they're on the house."

"For the rest of your life," her father added.

Every year that I taught I gave an end-of-year prize to the student who'd made the most progress. Today the prize would go to Rosie.

To add to my store of candy, Beverly brought her own homemade divinity, which I loved.

"Gerry," she started, then teared up. "I'm so sorry —"

I cut her off by stuffing a piece of her own delicious candy into her mouth.

There was no note of apology from Barry for stealing my purse. He'd convinced Skip he had no idea that Cheryl killed David. I believed him and almost felt sorry that he'd essentially lost two of his closest friends. I had a note from Ben Dobson, no return address, saying, *Nice work, lady. Sorry if I scared you. I knew I could count on you,* which I took to be his admission to leaving the incriminating bank record in my car.

Ben didn't know that he should have directed his praise to Larry Esterman, who had taken control of that piece of evidence.

One afternoon, Henry and Taylor paid a

visit to my specially arranged lounge chair in my atrium. My face had turned a sickly yellow hue. My back was on the mend, but my family decided I needed to lounge a little while longer.

Maddie and Taylor spent most of the time in the kitchen, preparing a special lunch that I wasn't supposed to have anything to do with. Maddie had cajoled June into taking her grocery shopping, so I had no idea what the menu would be.

"Frozen pizza," I guessed, when Maddie came by with plates for the atrium table.

"Nope," Maddie said.

"Hot dogs," Henry said.

"Nope," Maddie said.

I thought Taylor might be an easier mark, but when she came in with the napkins, she was humming a song — "America the Beautiful," I thought.

"Taylor?" Henry said. "What's up?"

"Maddie told me you'd try to pump me for information, so I decided to sing. '. . . For amber waves of grain . . .'"

With the girls so busy, Henry and I had time to talk. He was an easy person to be with, as was anyone willing to discuss the best way to install lighting in a dollhouse. He seemed delighted to hear that I might need his help — my crafters group had pitched in and bought me a complete, up-to-date lighting kit for my largest dollhouse.

In the spirit of all the apologies floating around my house, I felt that Henry was due one from me.

"I was focused on only one thing, and that was doing whatever it took to exonerate Rosie. Otherwise, I'd have been hanging around your workshop full time." I cleared my throat. "I mean —"

"You can't imagine how glad I am to hear that," he said.

"Lunch is served," said in unison by Madison and Taylor, saved us from an awkward moment.

What a treat. The girls marched in with a small-scale version of our brunch at the Duns Scotus. They crowded the small atrium table with platters of shrimp, salads, cold cuts, rolls, and fruit. The biggest tray, which needed its own side table, held desserts — brownies, cookies, and enormous éclairs, the likes of which we hadn't seen outside of a five-star hotel.

I couldn't imagine what the spread had done to Maddie's funds. She must have known I'd have that reaction — Maddie leaned over and whispered to me. "Don't worry, lots of people chipped in to pay for this."

The girls stood together, hands folded in front of them, cleared their throats, and began an obviously rehearsed performance. "Why did the witch need a computer?" Maddie asked.

Silence, except from Taylor. "She needed a spell check."

The suspense was over.

The laughter and applause all around filled the atrium as we dug into the best meal of the summer.

I was always glad for the approach of fall, when it was time to return to school, whether I was the student or the teacher. I loved the smell of newly cleaned classrooms and a just-opened box of chalk and the feel of new books and polished furniture.

I no longer taught in a regular school, but once unbearably hot weather and summer vacations were over, my crafts classes at the Mary Todd Home and my weekly tutoring went into full swing. In a week, I'd meet a new GED student to replace Lourdes. I knew she'd need me less and less.

And who didn't long for the rash of holidays just around the corner, ripe for festive miniature scenes, with witches, turkeys, and Santas galore.

Ken used to say that, like most East

Coasters who relocated to California, I missed the idea of seasons, not the seasons themselves. But he'd been thinking of endless chores like raking leaves and shoveling snow. (I managed to romanticize even scraping ice from windshields.)

This Labor Day brought the usual gathering to my home for a traditional barbecue, with the welcome additions of Nick, Henry, and Taylor. Richard and Mary Lou would be driving home from Tahoe and stop here first. The downside was that they'd take Maddie home to Palo Alto at the end of the day.

The highlight of the afternoon was to be the unveiling of Maddie's technology camp project.

Maddie was beside herself with excitement, spending a great deal of energy for days before, polishing her work and preparing her presentation. She wanted us to gather around the computer in her room to watch the game she'd designed.

At ten in the morning, Maddie made an announcement to me.

"I'm going to clean my room," she said.

I liked the game already.

"Can I help? I could vacuum for you," I offered.

She shook her head. "I'm afraid you'll find

my DVD and play the game without me."

"You have no respect," I said, going for the tickle area.

Maddie came out several times in the next hour, with requests I'd never heard cross her lips: "Do you have any dust cloths?" "Can I serve refreshments in my room?" "Do you have a bigger sponge?" and, finally, "I need a big trash bag, Grandma."

"Do I get a preview of the game?" I asked. "Everyone will be here pretty soon."

"No previews. I want you to be surprised, too."

Frankly, I thought I'd had enough surprises lately.

With everyone milling around my house, the most recent crime scene in town, there was bound to be some talk of Cheryl, who was awaiting trial for the murder of David Bridges.

Linda had been following every word in the press, with its daily revelations about the marriage of society couple, Walter and Cheryl Mellace, and the business dealings of Mellace Construction. She summed it up for us. "Cheryl expected a moment of romantic exhilaration in Joshua Speed Woods, where she would give herself to David again after all those years." She released her hands from their position in front of her bosom and opened her arms. "But David couldn't give up the sweet deal he had going with Walter, who had company on the side himself. If only Cheryl hadn't wanted more than a marriage held together by their status in the community and their children! Poor David" — now Linda raised her hands over her head, as if they held a trophy — "that was the end of David. It's the stuff of Hollywood."

I thought I heard a few groans and an "Amen."

After lunch, we all crammed into Maddie's bedroom, as clean and sweet smelling as it was when I'd prepared it for her a month ago, but hadn't been since. I couldn't figure out where she'd put all her worldly goods. Her desk had only the computer on it; her two night tables held pitchers of Linda's ice tea and lemonade mix and plates of cookies I recognized as Beverly's chocolate chip.

Maddie dimmed the lights and a hush fell over us. She clicked on an icon on the desktop of her computer.

We heard the music first. The theme from *The Pink Panther.* Soon, a title sequence appeared on the screen, in rainbow colors. *A Good Team,* it read, while small graphical images floated by. I saw a piece of rope, a silver candlestick, a small revolver, a knife, a wrench, and a section of lead pipe.

"I get it," Linda said. "The weapons from *Clue*."

"Shhh" came from many sources in the room, especially Richard and Mary Lou.

Next up was a room that looked familiar. My atrium? Not a photograph but a pieced-together room, almost like a comic book, but more realistic, with all the elements of my atrium — planter beds, ferns, blooming plants. Was that even the same chair-and-table set? It certainly was the identical floor plan of walls, glass doors, and a patchwork slate floor.

On the screen, a man entered from one of the patio doors. A whoop erupted when we saw that the head of the man was Skip's, from a photograph. The head and body were only loosely connected, but there was a large, unmistakable LPPD detective shield in the center of the man's chest, and a magnifying glass in his cartoonlike hand.

The rest was no surprise.

Out I came from the left patio doors, and out came Maddie from the right, both also holding magnifying glasses.

The three of us walked around the patio, inspecting leaves, grass, and furniture, bending now and then to get a closer look. After a while, the Maddie character found a piece of paper in the bushes and held it up. The screen went blank except for the image of a treasure map, followed by another dark screen with the word *Aha!* How fitting, I thought, an updated version of silent movie placards.

After another minute or so of action in the atrium, with more "evidence" being turned up, we heard the voice of the real Maddie coming from the Maddie on the screen. I could see that I needed a whole new vocabulary if I was to participate fully in the twenty-first century.

"I used an object-oriented program to create my video game," the screen Maddie said. "Choosing predefined motions, I was able to model the actions of avatars of three detectives — a man, a woman, and a teenager."

"A teenager?" Mary Lou interrupted.

"It's fiction," Maddie, the preteen, said.

"What's with the detective work? Is there something going on that I should know about?" Richard asked.

"Shhh," Skip said, but the narration was over anyway.

The presentation ended with a bow from all of the players, and a roll of credits: written and produced by Madison Porter. *The Pink Panther* had played throughout the game, at various levels of volume.

In the dim light I looked over at Richard and Mary Lou. I didn't even try to hide my tears. Maddie's production had taken less than ten minutes to watch, but we couldn't have been prouder if it were an Oscar-winning feature film.

Maddie switched the lights on and smiled at her audience. "If anyone has any questions, I'd be happy to answer them to the best of my ability."

In fact, there were questions from the more technically literate of the group, and there were more viewings of the video. I'd have to wait to watch it again when my vision cleared.

I moved one room closer to Maddie, as Richard and Mary Lou took my bedroom for the night. They'd decided they'd done enough driving for one day. Fine by me.

I went in to say good night to the family star.

"I'm so proud of you," I said, in case she hadn't heard me the first few dozen times.

She looked at me with sleepy eyes. "We do make a good team, don't we, Grandma?"

"The best."

"Remember the coin I threw in the Ghirardelli fountain?" she asked me.

"Of course."

"I wished you and Mr. Baker could be BFF."

I smiled. "You'll be the first to know."

Before I turned in, I went to the crafts table that held my Christmas scene. I took two Christmas stockings and sketched out names that I would embroider on them later. One would say *Taylor,* and the other, *Henry.*

It was a tiny addition, but held the promise of something big.

BATHROOM PLUNGER

Make a bathroom plunger of any size for your dollhouse or room box.

Materials:

1. Suction cups of the scale you're working in. These are available in hardware or office supply stores, and often in the household section of a grocery store. Usually they're made of vinyl or rubber and often are attached to a hook or another storage or hanging mechanism.
2. A rod or pole of the appropriate scale. This can be of wood, such as a barbecue skewer or a long toothpick, or plastic, such as a straw or other stick-shaped part. Remember it doesn't really have to be strong, the way a real plunger does!

3. Acrylic paint of your choice.

Directions:

1. Remove extraneous wire or hooks from the suction cup.
2. Make a hole in the top of the cup, big enough to hold the rod (handle) you've chosen.
3. Paint the cup inside and out. Black or deep pink are the most likely to give a realistic effect. Let dry.
4. Insert the rod into the hole at the top of the cup.
5. Place the assembly in a convenient place in your miniature bathroom, and never have to call a plumber again!

CRACKER CRUMBS

Add realism to your dollhouse or room box kitchen with crumbs from crackers, bread, or cookies, a sure sign that someone lives there!

Materials:

Soft clay or crafter's dough or clay
Fine grater or crafts knife
Needle

Steps for cracker crumbs:

1. Fashion crackers from the appropriate color dough, either white or yellowish. Or paint the dough the color you desire. Make small, flat circle shapes, or small square shapes, or a variety for your counter. Use a needle to make holes or lines before the dough sets, depending on the kind of cracker you've chosen. *Hint:* choose a color for the crackers that will show up on the counter you'll be placing them on.

2. After the dough/crackers are completely hardened (the method will depend on the kind of clay you've chosen), use your finest (real-life) grater to shave the edge of one cracker until it is completely in "crumbs." If the crumbs are too big, cut with a crafts knife. *Hint:* wear gloves to protect your fingers while grating the tiny crackers.

3. Arrange several crackers, plus the crumbs from the one cracker you used to make them, on a counter in a haphazard manner, to look as though someone didn't clean up after himself!

You can also do this for breadcrumbs or cookie crumbs, just by changing the colors and shapes of the dough.

ACCESSORIES FOR A BOY'S ROOM

A teen's room is full of odds and ends that can be replicated simply. Here are some ideas for things you might find in a boy's room.

1. Make a winter cap by cutting the tip from a finger on an old pair of woolen gloves. Turn up the brim and toss on the floor!
2. While a baseball mitt is hard to make, a bat is not. Fashion one from modeling clay of an appropriate color and lean against the closet door.
3. Make a jigsaw puzzle: glue a picture to a piece of thin cardboard. Cut the picture into puzzle shaped pieces and place in a small box, or lay the pieces haphazardly on a slightly larger piece of cardboard. If you have a second copy of the picture, glue it to the cover of the box.
4. For a small boy, make a kite using balsa wood for the frame and colorful tissue paper for the covering.

5. Look for party favors such as small wagons or gumball machines and place in the room. Check for toys also in the cake-decorating department.

6. Make a dartboard for the door using cork scraps and a Magic Marker. You can also use cork scraps to make a bulletin board for the wall. Add tiny notes, photos, and ticket stubs.

7. Don't forget to add food snuck into the room late at night! Cut tiny candy wrappers or potato chip bags from ads in the newspaper and glue onto foam board or wrap around wads of tissue.

ABOUT THE AUTHOR

Margaret Grace is the pen name of Camille Minichino. She is a lifelong miniaturist and is currently at work on the next Miniature Mystery. As Camille Minichino, she is the author of several other mystery novels as well as short stories and articles. She lives in northern California and can be reached at www.minichino.com and www.dollhousemysteries.com.